D1577956

DAYS COME & GO

DAYS COME & GO

HEMLEY BOUM

Translated from French by
NCHANJI NJAMNSI

TWO LINES
PRESS

Originally published in French as: *Les jours viennent et passent*
Copyright © 2019 by Hemley Boum
Published by arrangement with Agence littéraire Astier-Pécher
All Rights Reserved

English translation copyright © 2022 by Nchanji Njamnsi

Two Lines Press
582 Market Street, Suite 700, San Francisco, CA 94104
www.twolinespress.com

ISBN: 978-1-949641-35-6
Ebook ISBN: 978-1-949641-36-3

Cover design by Gabriele Wilson
Design/typesetting by Jessica Sevey

Cover art by Lorna Simpson: *Up in the air...*, 2013
Collage and ink on paper, Unique
29 1/2 x 21 5/8 in (74.9 x 54.9 cm)
Framed: 31 x 24 x 1 5/8 in (78.6 x 61.1 x 4.1 cm)
Copyright © Lorna Simpson
Courtesy of the artist and Hauser & Wirth

Library of Congress Cataloging-in-Publication Data:
Names: Boum, Hemley, 1973– author. | Njamnsi, Nchanji, translator.
Title: Days come and go / Hemley Boum; translated by Nchanji Njamnsi.
Other titles: Jours viennent et passent. English Description: San Francisco,
CA: Two Lines Press, [2022] | Originally published as Les jours viennent
et passent. | Summary: "Chronicles the beauty and turmoil of a rapidly
changing Cameroon through the story of three generations of women"
--Provided by publisher. Identifiers: LCCN 2022002132 (print) |
LCCN 2022002133 (ebook) | ISBN 9781949641356 (hardcover) |
ISBN 9781949641363 (ebook). Subjects: LCGFT: Novels. Classification:
LCC PQ3989.3.B686 J6813 2022 (print) | LCC PQ3989.3.B686 (ebook) |
DDC 843/.92--dc23/eng/20220131
LC record available at https://lccn.loc.gov/2022002132
LC ebook record available at https://lccn.loc.gov/2022002133

Printed in the United States of America
1 3 5 7 9 10 8 6 4 2

This project is supported in part by an award from the
National Endowment for the Arts.

I

Abi had been driving around the neighborhood for the past fifteen minutes when a car in front of the hospital drove away, freeing up a parking spot. *Maybe there's a god after all*, she thought to herself, slotting her car into the spot.

Her mother, Anna, was asleep and snoring noisily. The early morning wash, the few steps down the stairs, the four mouthfuls of yogurt—painfully swallowed—and lastly the half-hour ride in Paris's mid-morning traffic jam had gotten the best of her. Ordinarily, she enjoyed the ride across the city. She would observe, saying something about all the details Abi now overlooked. The Haussmannian buildings, she'd say, were built at an ideal angle to reflect light, their shadows standing out like cathedrals on the asphalt.

"Stop, we can spare two minutes, right?" she asked.

Although weakened by sickness, she was still adamant. Anna had woken up and spotted a small street flanked by blooming cherries.

"Pull over so we can stroll for a bit, would you?"

Abi obliged without protest. Her mother pulled herself out of the car laboriously and inhaled the cold air. Then she took Abi's arm by the elbow, always in the same way, and slowly they walked, seeking out the sidewalks lit up by the early spring sun.

Anna greeted passers-by, stopped to chat with garbage collectors, gave change to beggars—quite unlike the average Parisian. When her pace slowed as she ran out of breath, Abi picked a café where they could sit on the terrace. The old lady always ordered the sticky treacle Parisian cafés call hot chocolate. Some days, more frequently now, her pain ruined her appetite, robbing her of the taste of food. She would then content herself with raising the huge mug to her nose and taking long inhales of its aroma.

"This is good," she said, smiling.

Abi smiled back. She had to submit an article to the culture magazine she worked for, about a performance by a white South African artist portraying Black people in cages and reenacting the human zoos of the early twentieth century. Art morphed into obscene voyeurism, insult and, dressed up like that, was on open display all over the world. She also had to create content for her blog, meet the manager of the nursery about her little Jenny, do some shopping, and think about that evening's dinner. Her time was precious, fleeting; some mornings, the young woman woke up to the feeling that she was already two hours behind schedule. None of that mattered. Every minute, every hour was pegged to her mother's hand holding her by the elbow, to the sick old lady's erratic step, her emaciated features, her short breath... *My mother is dying, oh mother...*

They had reached the terminal phase of the illness. Abi barely slept. She woke up frightened by the silence if her mother wasn't making any sound. Or when even the least suspicious sound seeped from the next room. One night, she ended up coming out when she heard her mother in the corridor. Abi switched on the ceiling light and, just in time, held her mother back as she was about to take the stairs.

"Mother, where are you off to?" Anna, blinded by the light, had stopped in her tracks.

"Oh, Abi, did I wake you? I'm sorry, go back to bed. I am going to the bathroom. Everything's fine."

No, everything was not fine. Her mother, confused in the darkness, would have fallen down the stairs had Abi not stepped in. She was forced to exercise a calm she did not feel, not even remotely. Her hands trembled and, in her stomach, and down her spine, she felt an unsettling tickle like an electric shock: irrepressible fear, a certainty that things would only grow worse and that there wasn't much she could do about it. Abi had led her mother to the toilet:

"Wait outside, please. I can still wipe myself, you know." The old lady had smiled.

Abi hadn't responded. Her mother could no longer take care of her basic personal hygiene, she who was always such a clean freak. The young woman would return to the bathroom later to clean the floor if necessary. It did not bother her, not anymore.

The first time Anna had unconsciously soiled herself and then the bathroom floor, the shock had rattled Abi so violently that it left her paralyzed. She stared at the feces as if they themselves would realize the strangeness of the situation and disappear out of shame. Then she had scrubbed and mopped the floor, then cleaned her mother. If she didn't do it, no one else would. That night, Abi had brought her mother back to her own bed.

"You should consider hiring a home care nurse," the doctor had advised after her last hospitalization. "Your mother wants to stop chemotherapy. Her state will worsen quite rapidly. We can reduce the pain, but not by much. She no longer has the strength to take care of herself."

She is sick, not deaf. She is still very much in her right mind. She is conscious of what is happening to her. Speak to her like a human being, Abi protested under her breath. She did not want to antagonize the doctor, the nurses, anyone who could ease her mother's pain. With gritted teeth, she endured their coldness, the raw, technical, definitive words they dished out with professionalism and indifference. The untreated breast cancer had metastasized. It had spread to her pancreas and liver. Chemotherapy would enable her to live six months, a year at most. This time would decrease drastically if she continued refusing treatment. And Anna continued refusing. The aftermath of her first chemotherapy session had convinced her to stop her treatment.

"Well, if the poison they are pumping into my body can't save me, I would rather stop," she had objected to an exasperated Abi.

Treat her kindly. I know you see helpless, terminally ill beings every day. I understand the need to keep their suffering at a safe distance, but you must understand: to me, this woman is much more than just a failing body, Abi pleaded silently. *She is a loved one, a precious life ebbing away in silence.*

Abi did not reach out to any nurses. She was horrified by the mere thought of a stranger touching her mother's enfeebled body. Some mornings, the old lady examined herself in the mirror. Her hair and eyebrows, now lost. Her muscles, shrunken under flappy skin. She felt like an empty envelope. She even had a glazed look in her eyes now.

"Do you remember how beautiful my hair used to be?" she murmured, caressing her hairless skull.

Yes, Abi could remember. What nurse could boast of such a special skill?

"You're my mother now," Anna told her. "I never knew mine; it has taken me getting old and falling sick to taste a mother's love."

Yet, the illness spread at such speed that Abi's sacrifice was rendered useless. The cancer was literally eating away at her mother from within. Abi imagined it as rats gnawing on her liver, stomach, pancreas…stopping only when they'd devoured every single inch of her body. In the beginning, she'd hoped every moment of happiness would keep the old lady alive, the same way one uses all manner of tricks to hold back guests at the end of a dinner. "You can't leave now. Have some more dessert. Do you care for tea? Come on, take one for the road!"

Walks in Paris, hot chocolate, butter croissants on café terraces, little Jenny's laughter, visits from her son, Maxime... Indeed, in the beginning, all of this had meaning, but not anymore. Pain clogged the present, permeating every moment of joy. Smiles turned to grimaces.

I do not know how to help you anymore, mother. I do not dare touch you anymore. I'm scared I would hurt you without meaning to. I'm scared I would do something clumsy and make you more uncomfortable while trying to ease your pain. I'm sorry, mother, so sorry. I don't know how to help you anymore. Abi cried on their way to the palliative care unit.

Her mother sat snoring in the car. The desolation and torment of the past few days had been terrifying; nothing brought her any relief. Initially, Anna had forced herself to maintain an ounce of normalcy, but her weak body no longer obeyed her. Any physical effort exhausted her. Her every gesture grew slow, labored. She stopped getting up from her bed in the morning or feeding herself. The least sip of water triggered groans of pain. "Mother please, just one sip, try again," Abi kept insisting.

Deep within Abi, a harsher, more urgent voice echoed: *I'm not ready. I do not want to lose you now. I'm not ready...*

Even deeper within her echoed an awareness of the imminent end and the futility of her prayers.

"Look, mother, it's spring. The plane trees are green, cherries are in bloom, potted flowers on windowsills are blossoming in the sun, garages are draped with colors, girls are baring their tanned legs. Paris is looking at herself in the mirror of light and smiling back at her reflection, look mother…"

Palliative care centers offer all the care you cannot find in a hospital. Doctors look you in the eye. Nurses do not hesitate to touch you when they talk to you. A psychologist asks you about your journey so far. They all encourage you to unpack your pain. Here, there is no need to lie to yourself anymore; anyone who comes in here won't ever leave the same. For both patients and their caregivers, the end of the road is near.

"Tell her family to come see her now," doctors tell you.

"How much more time do we have?" you enquire amid your mix of worry, hope, and despair.

You want to know the exact date, precise hour—just like any important appointment—not to miss a thing, not to take any risk.

"Tell them to hurry."

Watch and pray, the Scriptures say. Keep your lamps burning for when the Bridegroom returns.

ANNA

Dying is such a long journey. I have come to the end of my road. My daughter's anguish hinders me, holds me back. I linger despite the pain and despite my desire to get it over with. I stay because of Abi.

I have always harbored a secret place within. A place where I could retreat no matter what. I call it my stronghold. In this room, because I see it as a room, the walls protect my heart on days of anguish, and happiness is let in as abundant showers of light. It is where I cry out in my pain. It is where I put words to my fears, and also where I sing at the top of my voice. I speak loud. I debate, always brilliantly, finding words that free and unshackle me. I stand at the window when I need to observe the world, then close the shutters when I feel like stepping away from it. This place exists only in my mind, but it's as real to me as the air I breathe—it's where I paint the world with my soul's rainbow. Nobody who has passed through my life, whether family, friend, lover, or husband, has ever entered this room. None except Abi. Barely had she been born when, for the first time, I heard a voice other than my own in this shelter of mine. It was the babble of a child that I recognized right away. I knew then that I was whole at last.

I never knew my mother. She died bringing me into this world. Just like her mother and her mother's mother before her. Three generations of girls orphaned at birth. Lives starting amid loss and grief. Abi came along to break the curse.

From the few stories I was told, my great-grandmother was not from our village. She was tall, with a tapered waistline, wide hips, dark skin, delicate features, lush hair. Everyone called her "Samgali"... This uncommon name was the starting point for Abi's research. She thought that my ancestors may have been Fulani and "Samgali" was the result of a mispronunciation of "Senegalese" in the local language. I laughed at my daughter's rich imagination but, on thinking about it more, it was not far-fetched.

Islam came to Cameroon through the Sudano-Sahelian route. First came Shuwa Arabs, as early as the seventeenth century, followed by the Fulani or Fulbe in the eighteenth century. The religious conquest only started in the nineteenth century, when Usman Dan Fodio stretched his Upper-Niger empire to the Adamawa and authorized Modibo Adama to create lamidates in Ngaoundere, Garoua, and Maroua. The new conquerors either enticed or forced natives to convert, but were stopped by the immense equatorial forests in the South—to which they were unaccustomed—and by Christianity, which was already deeply entrenched. They settled in the northern part of the country and made it a habit to cross our land during their seasonal livestock drive. Abi explained all this to me. My daughter is a passionate scholar.

Where did Samgali come from? What violence forced her to flee? What strange migration had dropped her off at our doorstep like an offering? If anyone knew the answers, no one ever told me. As contradictory as it seems, our societies are built on both bonds and silence. Our joys are loud and our grief demonstrative. Our voices are strong and our laughter thunderous. But rarely do we say a word about our private lives. We don't have as many taboos as people claim, but esoteric interpretations blur the messages.

Abi is in tune with her era. My grandson, Max, even more so. They demand answers, all sorts of explanations. They ascribe all sorts of virtue to transparency, which they label truth, and have no patience for pretense. Where do they get this strength from, this confidence that I envy, this arrogance? We are so much more than the sum of our parts. Our gray areas would not stand the light. What world could survive the systematic exposure of everyone's secrets? This is blasphemy in Abi and Max's eyes. I understand what they're saying. I always thought that there were instances where silence buttressed the bond better than baneful truths, but I am not so sure anymore.

I grew up in the care of Awaya; she was an old village woman, widowed several times over. She had raised my

mother before me and had known Samgali. She was
our bond: the link between the dead women and their
daughters.

Awaya was a tough, hard-working woman. She'd
married young to a polygamous man and been bequeathed to his brother; most of her children were grown
and had already left home when I was born. Only the
two of us lived in her house. She was the first person to
tell me about Samgali. They had been married to brothers
and shared a great friendship, the kind that sometimes
unites two souls that just click instantly.

Samgali died while giving birth. Awaya took in her
young daughter, fed the baby her own breast milk, and
raised her like her own child until misfortune struck again
with even more brutality. One of Awaya's sons became so
madly enamored with Trissia, my grandmother, that he
lost his mind. They had been raised by the same woman,
in the same house: as far as everyone in our community
was concerned, they were siblings. For them to be in love
was therefore forbidden, incestuous. But the young man
did not listen to reason. He was doomed by his yearning
for Trissia. He decided to force destiny's hand by getting
her pregnant. History bears no account of little Trissia,
the object of this impure affection. If I reckon correctly,
she was no older than twelve then. She died giving birth
to my mother. Poor child, a young offshoot torched pre-
maturely, gone up in smoke. The young man fled the village when he learned that his beloved had died. This is
how Awaya lost her two children.

My mother's fate was even worse; she married a man

famous for his fits of madness and violence. He beat her furiously one time too many while she was full term.

This is the tragic story of my mothers, the cursed daughters of Samgali.

Awaya took me in just like she had done with those before me, pitting her sense of duty against the cruelty of fate, steadfastly believing in life's eventual triumph against fatalism. From the day I was born, she called me "Bouissi," sunrise. Defying the anathema, she decreed that the Stranger's curse ended with me; we were worthy of the light of a new day. And she made a resolution that would change the course of my existence, but would also pull me away from my family and cause me to betray this woman who had done so much for me, for us. Awaya decided that I would be an educated woman and enrolled me in the mission school.

Every Sunday, my elderly guardian went to church, where she prayed to the Lord fervently. This did not stop her from living out her traditional spirituality with just as much passion, though. When I was born, even before my mother's funeral, she took me into the forest and marked me for protection. "Enough is enough, Samgali. Enough is enough, my sister. This must stop," she murmured, cutting my newborn skin with a blade and rubbing a concoction of her own making into the wounds.

Both of my wrists, my ankles, the small of my back, my upper chest, and my forehead still bear the thin, finely drawn scars. They are quite hard to see, but the cuts must have been deep, since the scars have stood the test of time.

Throughout the time I spent in her home, Awaya

always blessed me before I left in the morning. She warmed leaves by the fire and then pressed them against my chest and stomach, summoning protection over me from all the forces in her power—God, the Virgin Mary, our ancestors. She'd close with an appeal to Samgali every time: "Here goes our sunrise, my Samgali. Watch over her every step, my sister. Be my eyes and my ears around her. Bouissi is heading out."

On my first day of school, the white nun, my schoolteacher, called me "Anna." I did not respond. I hadn't understood that she was talking to me; nobody had ever called me by my Christian name before. Everyone in the village called me Bouissi, just like Awaya. I immediately loved this Anna I was meeting for the first time and decided that at the first opportunity, I would drop Bouissi to become Anna. I'd study, read, become a learned, confident, remarkable woman and elude the fatality of ordained grief. I would no longer be that defenseless baby that was taken into a forest in the dead of night and entrusted to spirits, or a little girl under the protection of a deceased woman who had been unable to watch over her own self. Someday I would become Anna, as the white lady had called me.

And I did study, read, and work hard because, for people marked by fate like myself, school—Western education—was the only possible path to progress. I mimicked my way into a passionate yet calculated love affair with Catholicism, because this foreign man-child-God of a redeemer promised me a form of spirituality that required severing ties with one's past, turning away from one's own family to be born again, delivered. A form of spirituality in which the first would be the last and vice versa. All I had to do was sail with these clergy, stay the course, speak like them, carry myself like them, jettison the obscurantism of my people. This belief was tailor-made for someone like me. I slipped into it seamlessly, the way one finally returns home.

I passed my school certificate examination with flying colors and stood out from my classmates through hard work and my desire to learn more, the reverend sister told Awaya. Her order had decided to encourage me by paying for my tuition from then on. The Ursuline community had opened a new girls' college in Bafia and were ready to pay the tuition for a limited number of girls who, in primary school, had been outstanding in both academics and behavior. I had shown the devotion, discipline, and intellect worthy of this scholarship. The reverend sister told us how proud she was that a pupil from her small school had been awarded such an honor. I had just one guardian, which was an advantage; in our community, everyone in the family had a say in a child's education. As such, both close and distant family members could, with endless consultations, dictate your future. Awaya had pulled off the feat of being the sole custodian of my life. She accepted the reverend sister's proposal without hesitation, although she disliked the sister with a passion; an enmity that was, once again, the result of me.

At eight, I had a tooth that grew sideways underneath my fully formed incisor. The adult tooth, instead of the

ectopic one, fell out. This anomaly made me uncomfortable smiling. I picked up the habit of putting my hand over
my mouth to avoid being mocked by my friends. Awaya
was not bothered by it. "Those are baby teeth," she said.
"They will fall off. Your smile is as pretty as your mother's."
The words were kind, but they did not cheer me up in the
least—who would want a dead woman's smile?

One day, the reverend sister asked me to meet her in
the presbytery after school. I was shown into the kitchen
where there were things that I was seeing for the first
time in my life. An oven, a refrigerator, huge chests of
drawers made from raw wood. The shutters were open
and the immaculate white voile curtains flapped gently in
the wind. A table stood in the middle of the room, covered with a polished canvas and surrounded by six chairs.
I have forgotten many things in my life—encounters
and important events swept from my memory—but this
shining kitchen, this impression of order, the cleanliness,
the beauty, the smell of freshly baked chocolate cake…
all of it remains forever engraved in my mind. That room
was my dream of comfort and safety, although I would
have been unable to name half the objects in it.

The reverend sister cut a slice of cake for me. "Sit,
Anna, and eat," she ordered, setting a small plate, knife,
and fork before me. Did I have to use these objects? *Could
I not just pick up the slice of cake with my fingers instead?* I
asked myself, a little scared. She then served herself and
sat across from me. I picked up the cutlery and, watching
her attentively, mimicked her every gesture; what a smart
and obedient little monkey!

"Pick up your fork in your left hand and stick it into the part you will put in your mouth. Then, using your knife, cut away the part you have pricked. No, Anna. Do not pull. Cut as gently as possible, my dear. Make your wrist more flexible. Like this, see? That's a table knife, not a machete. There you go. Good job, Anna. Bravo! You really need to learn to use cutlery. Well-educated people do not eat with their hands."

It took me endless minutes to relish a slice of cake that I would have gobbled down in an instant if I'd had my way. I was very proud of myself nevertheless. Endeavoring to follow the rules made this delicious feast taste even better, if that was possible. I was right where I'd dreamed of being. Afterward, the reverend sister served me, in a glass—a real glass made of glass if I may say so, not one of the stained plastic cups I was accustomed to—a red liquid that she then diluted with water: grenadine! My God, it tasted so good, so sweet. Never before in my life had I drunk anything like it. Oh, how I loved this woman. How I loved her food. How I loved this life, how I yearned for it!

When I finished eating, there were still cake crumbs on my plate.

"Reverend Sister, may I tongue the plate?" I asked my benefactor, my plate already in hand, my tongue ready for release.

"No, no. Don't 'tongue' plates," she spluttered, seizing it from my hands. "Do not 'tongue' anything, ever. And the word is not 'tongue,' but 'lick.' Plates are not to be licked after eating."

Really? Why not? At home, grown-ups and children alike tong...I mean, lick the plate until it is as clean as if it has just been washed, and no one sees anything wrong with it.

I would soon realize that the reverend sister had not had me over to give me cake and enlighten me on the unwritten rules around table manners among the civilized. In fact, she had a far less pleasant plan in mind.

"Wait for me here," she said, disappearing into an adjoining room. I leaned over in my chair, trying to catch a glimpse of her; what great gift did she have in store for me? I stamped my feet with impatience. She returned with a tin box bearing a red cross. "Are you a brave little girl, Anna?" she enquired, taking gauze pads, Mercurochrome, a bottle containing a blue liquid that I could not name, and a good-sized pair of pliers out of the box. "You will have to be brave, my little Anna. This is going to hurt, but you will thank me when you grow up." She wrapped a towel around my neck. "Sit down and relax. Are you comfortable? Show me your teeth. Do you trust me, Anna? Do you? Then open your mouth wide and close your eyes. You'll be less afraid if you close your eyes."

I complied, obviously; her gentle voice sounded like a purr, as pleasant as the chocolate cake and grenadine. Of course I trusted her!

I felt the cold touch of the pliers pressed against my gums, in the gap left by the incisor. I felt it clamp down on my ectopic tooth and a splash of pain ripped through my head. The reverend sister pulled, zealously. She kept me seated, pushing down against my shoulder with all her weight. Blood flooded my mouth. The chocolate cake and grenadine traveled back up my throat. I yelled while she pulled, wiggled, and ultimately uprooted my tooth. I cannot say how long my ordeal lasted. All I know is, it was so long that dark spots shrouded my sight and my bladder caved in.

"There you go, pretty little thing. It's done," she finally murmured, breathless. "Look. Here is that nasty tooth. Come with me."

She led me into the bathroom. I was in no state to marvel at the porcelain toilet, the stockpile of fresh towels, and the dizzying brightness of this room that was never anything but sticky, smelly, and fly-ridden back home. She filled up a big glass with water. "Rinse out your mouth until the bleeding stops." Then she poured a huge quantity of the blue liquid that I had noticed earlier into the glass. "Use this to rinse your mouth one more time!" The bleeding stopped eventually. She told me to undress: "Step into the shower. I will give you a bath. It will do you some good." She turned a tap and a soothing stream cooled my skin instantly. *A shower...so this is the name of the miracle rain gushing from the wall...* She scrubbed me with a bar of soap, working up a lather on my body that smelled like flowers. I felt the urge to open my mouth beneath the shower like I did when my friends and I went dancing outside in the slightest rain, but I did not dare it. "Tonguing" plates was forbidden, so I imagined the ban applied here as well. "Dry yourself off while I try to find some clothes your size," the reverend sister said, offering me a towel. For fear of rambling, I won't comment on the unique softness of that piece of cloth. Besides, the pain I had forgotten in the shower came rushing back into my mind and tears welled in my eyes.

The reverend sister regularly received tons of clothes from her country, and gave them to children in the village. She returned with a clean dress and underwear. I cried, ashamed of my weakness. I did not want her to think me ungrateful; I accepted the pain she had caused and still trusted her. The pain had left me teary-eyed in spite of myself, but my heart was awash with gratitude. I feared that, thinking I was a bad girl, she would repudiate me. Above anything else, I wanted her to love me, to keep me in her world. So I tried to hide my tears.

"Are you crying? You're obviously in pain. Wait here. Put on your clothes. I'll be back." She brought me some tablets. "Take these. They will make you feel better."

I swallowed the medicine, but I did not feel better right away. *If it's that useful, why not apply it directly to the wound?* I wondered. *Why swallow it?* I did not have a stomachache. Whenever I felt pain, Awaya always gave me some herbs, a mixture she'd concoct herself, to apply directly to the location of the pain. I did not understand the logic of the tablets. But I contented myself with doing what she asked of me.

After all these years, I now remember that, aside from bellowing like an animal being slaughtered when my tooth was uprooted, I did not utter a single word, except to ask whether I could lick the plate. The reverend sister asked the questions and answered them herself. I had been given a bath, been draped in new clothes, relieved of my recalcitrant tooth. She looked me over from every angle; I am convinced we were both experiencing a feeling of pride over a job well done. "You were very brave, my little Anna. I am proud of you."

She put some more tablets in a sachet, and told me to take them before going to bed, and the following morning too, if I still felt pain then. Finally, she exempted me from homework before sending me back home.

The pain had subsided considerably by the time I got home, but I did not make any direct link to the medication. Never again in my life would I eat chocolate cake or drink grenadine; their smell alone would suffice to rekindle the memory of the pain throbbing where my missing tooth had once stood.

It was evening when I returned to Awaya's hut, passing by the huts where some of my classmates lived. I wanted each one of them to see my pretty dress, notice how good I smelled, and, possibly, choke on it out of spite.

My story did not make life easy. Here, as everywhere, children are mean. Our daily lives were a violent cocktail of insults, mockery, and fights; bully today, victim tomorrow, I did my part. Living in such close quarters made privacy an illusion and nothing remained a secret for long. Insults hit where it hurt the most. The fights I got in—and there were many—often ended with a reference to the witches I had for mothers. This was my revenge: my classmates would see how well the white mother Jesus had sent me—were the reverend sisters not Christ's brides?—took care of me. I wanted them to see what a beauty she had turned me into.

When I finally got home, Awaya had been back

from the farm for a long time and had single-handedly done the chores we normally did together. The food she'd brought back had been put away, the yard swept, water for the next morning fetched, and dinner cooked. Our whole compound was draped in darkness, except for the kitchen where Awaya waited for me, which was lit up by a wood fire.

"*Bouissi bamè*—my Bouissi—is everything okay? I was told the reverend sister kept you after school."

Awaya never yelled at me, whereas mothers were fond of yelling at their children. She spoke to me calmly, even when I went too far. Mothers in the village thought they were responsible for the upbringing of all children— their own and others'. This is why I received my fair share of slaps, scoldings and, sometimes, even more; but never from Awaya. She did not come to my defense necessarily, did not stop anyone from "raising" me the hard way, did not console me when this happened, but she did not make it any worse either.

"*Nyedi*—mother—look at my pretty dress," I interrupted her, all smiles. The toothache was nothing more than a bad memory; I was healed and happy.

"So, that woman kept you until nightfall only to give you old, oversized clothes? She could at least have brought you back home. I wonder what she uses the car rusting away in her yard for!"

Awaya gleefully indulged in her mockery and irony. That was her way of letting me know she disapproved.

"What do you have in your mouth? Did you hurt yourself?" she continued, suddenly looking worried.

I explained what the reverend sister had done, how she had relieved me of my bad tooth. Awaya sprang to her feet:

"Open your mouth and show me," she ordered. "This white woman pulled out your tooth like that? Without numbing the pain? No woman who had carried a child in her womb would do this to another woman's child. How can a human being do this to a child, huh? Is this woman crazy? Is this barren witch serious? Who gave her the right to lay a finger on my child, eh? Who?"

Awaya bellowed her outrage, her high-pitched voice stretching far into the silence of the night. It was such an uncommon occurrence that neighbors rushed into our kitchen, summoned by the outbursts. Without waiting to be asked, Awaya explained, gesturing, holding my mouth open.

"Look what this woman has done to my child! The little girl's mouth is swollen as an orange. She pulled out her tooth, a firmly rooted tooth that wasn't even loose. Even an adult would have a hard time enduring such pain. Who wakes up in the morning to do such a thing to a child? Is this woman crazy? Is this not witchcraft? Her coven asks her to offer a child, so she chooses mine? Did she leave her heart in her mother's womb when she was born?"

I was distraught! My white mother, Christ's bride, so gentle, so neat, so civilized, labeled a witch, heartless, accused of practicing witchcraft, of devouring children's souls…and everyone was having their say:

"No way! Open your mouth, Bouissi. Let me see.

Show me what she did to you. Look at this gaping hole! How did your tooth offend her, eh? Unleashing such pain on a child… Only a witch would do that!"

Raised to obey adults, I kept my mouth open despite feeling like these women would not stop sticking their filthy hands into my mouth and blasting bad breath on my face, until they had each, without exception, scrambled in my mouth.

"By the way, where is the tooth?" one of them asked out of the blue.

A blanket of silence fell on the mob of harpies. *Come to think of it, where is my tooth?* I asked myself. Everyone knows that witches need something that belongs to you to cast their evil spells. Ideally, they need a piece of you; a strand of hair, nail clipping, a tooth…a tooth? I broke into tears. The pain had returned. I felt it in my head. I felt it all over, but I was no longer the center of attention. I could have closed my mouth then if I hadn't been busy bawling my heart out.

A distinctly angry neighbor decided to march to the reverend sister's house to demand an explanation and, most especially, to recover my tooth. As the thought of these villagers storming my benefactor's beautiful abode in the middle of the night hit home, I doubled down on my moans. Awaya immediately rushed to my side.

"It'll all be okay, Bouissi, my little girl. Everything will be fine," she promised.

Then she turned to the other villagers.

"Thank you, my sisters, but nothing good is accomplished in the night. Go get some sleep. Tomorrow, I will pay that woman a visit to collect Bouissi's tooth."

Taking the medication the reverend sister had given me was now out of the question; in any case, I wasn't convinced that it was effective. I quietly accepted the painkiller made from sweet potato leaves and a plant my friends and I called "touch-me-not." Awaya pounded the leaves together and mixed the paste with hot water. I was supposed to use it as a mouthwash for a few days. With the rest of the mixture she made a paste that she had me apply on the painful part of my gum. The pain subsided instantly, and I fell asleep under the weight of the day's emotions.

In the morning, after breakfast and the usual blessings, Awaya dressed up like she was heading to church, instead of the shabby attire she wore every morning to go farming. She forced me to drink some of her medicine again and took me with her to the school, my mouth closed over my tongue and my teeth turned green by the mashed plants.

It was quite a strange walk; every mother in our village seemed to have decided to see their children off to school. The church, the presbytery, and the school all stood on the same piece of land, about one kilometer from our home. Ordinarily, we walked along the path playing around, laughing or arguing like children all over the world would. Not this time. Our mothers passionately discussed the reverend sister's revolting behavior, trading assurances of the righteousness of their rescue mission. Not a word was uttered by the children. We kept silent, scared by this expedition, by the determination our mothers displayed. Determination to…what precisely? I feared the worst.

The reverend sister was delighted when she saw all of us arrive.

"Oh, Awaya," she said smiling widely, "you came to thank me? You didn't have to. It was natural for me to help Anna. We couldn't afford to allow such a vile smile ruin her pretty face, could we?" she said.

She said "pretty face" while cupping her hands around my head. Forgetting my greenish teeth, I smiled instantly. *I love her so much*, I told myself again. Awaya and the other women clearly hadn't expected such a welcome. It left them quiet for a while, and the reverend sister, puzzled, did not know how to continue the conversation.

"Reverend Sister, I have come for Bouissi's tooth," Awaya finally said in her flawed French.

Bouissi? Who here goes by the name Bouissi? I wondered angrily. Didn't she hear the reverend sister call me Anna? Was it so difficult to simply say "Anna"?

The white lady was still smiling, rather mischievously.

"The thing is, I no longer have it—the tooth," she said.

Then, she turned her focus to me.

"The tooth fairy came around, my dear. She took away your tooth and, in return, she left you a gift."

She handed me a parcel wrapped in an immaculate white linen towel that I would keep for a long time. I unwrapped the gift. It was a white dish, a knife, a fork, a big and a small spoon, a toothbrush, toothpaste, and a bar of Bébé Cadum soap. I felt like happiness and gratitude would crush me on the spot. Awaya watched me keenly. I, however, only had eyes for my benefactor, my guardian angel, my white mother. I didn't notice the cloud of sadness casting a shadow over Awaya's face.

She took the parcel from my hands.

"Let me take your treasures back to the house, Bouissi bamè," she said to me in our native tongue. "I can't wait to watch you eat your okra soup this evening using these things."

The sarcasm was easily lost on me.

The reverend sister had a habit of calling me her sweetheart, her little darling, and other even more endearing names. In class, she encouraged me at the slightest progress and called me a role model to motivate the other students to work harder. I sat in the front row and made it a duty not to disappoint her. She became both my dream mother and my model.

The school year ended, and I was admitted with flying colors into the fifth year of elementary school. The reverend sister showered me with praise and gifts. She gave me a series of books chronicling the adventures of a little girl named Martine. *Martine à la plage, Martine à la ferme, Martine au cirque…* I read every one of them until their pages tore out, until I knew every word by heart. I was fascinated by this little girl, her home, her parents, and all her adventures. In those moments, I was Martine and I too went to the beach, the farm, or the circus.

I held on to my old copies for a long time. Maybe they are still in the house in Douala. Abi has teased me about them for years now.

"So you dreamed of becoming this overly silly little white girl?"

I have never been able to explain to my daughter, who had grown up in the privileged world of little "Martines," that I was drawn more by the comfort and carefreeness that marked her childhood than by the color of her skin. What she ate, how she ate it, her home, her bed, her bicycle... Touched by her beauty, the world's fairy godmothers seemed to have all agreed to give her a perfect childhood. My Abi wouldn't have understood, I don't think—or maybe she did. Maybe I was the one having a hard time acknowledging the fragile thing I was then.

In my mind, the memory of these children's books is connected to my daughter. I was born in the maternity ward at the same moment Abi came into this world. That is no metaphor as far as I am concerned. Awaya had made that unexpected encounter with my child possible by changing the course of a destiny that, for several generations, had deprived the girls in my family of their mothers.

The untamable love my child triggered in me scared me way more than it made me happy. Oh Abi! She fulfilled me, completed me, made me whole. That wasn't the issue: I distressed over the *how*. How else could I be the mother to this extraordinary being if not by equipping her to face life confidently and boldly? And where would *I* get the means to bequeath to Abi the legacy I owed her?

In my bid to be a good mother who provides safety, in my merciless fight to give her the comfort of a safe childhood, I overlooked tenderness and intimacy.

Abi distanced herself from me as soon as she could, and drew close to people who did not look like me. As an adult, she showered me with attention, but still from a safe distance.

I had to wait until I was at the twilight of my life, sick and vulnerable, when the walls built to shield me from adversity crumbled like a house of cards, when the roles we played in each other's lives were reversed—Abi as the mother and I, the faltering child—yes, I had to wait until those final moments for my beloved daughter, my dearly beloved, to wrap me in the warmth of her unfailing affection as she walked me through the long, painful journey to my final resting place.

I underestimated how Awaya felt in the wake of the tooth incident. Her anger was so deep that it did not subside over time. We were all going to witness the tenacity with which she could hold a grudge.

The reverend sister and the white priest living in our village would go on holiday in August. The school, the presbytery, and the church would therefore be closed and the traveling parish priest would go from village to village to say mass. That year was no different.

The humid and rainy month of August waved good-bye to the harvest season as the new planting season started. Come rain or shine, the entire village—men, women, children, students on break—was busy with farm work. We spent long, exhausting days farming, while all I dreamed about was reading, curled up in bed, my feeling of coziness heightened by the storm thundering away outside. Time seemed to go by so slowly that I started counting the days left until school resumed.

In September, the reverend sister returned to brighten up my days. We heard her tiny Renault 4 from a distance. A swarm of kids were running after the car shouting happily, rejoicing in advance at the prospect of the sweets that she shared generously and the small gifts that she brought back from her trips.

Awaya and I were in the kitchen. I was giving her a hand shelling pumpkin seeds when I heard the sound of the car. I sprang to my feet.

"Where are you off to?" she inquired. "Did someone call for you? Did someone call your name? Don't move an inch; we are not done yet," she told me.

I complied, grudgingly.

Much to my surprise, the reverend sister stopped in front of our hut. She alighted from her car with a big backpack. She had brought some clothes and books for me, she said. She wanted to give them to me right away. The package was so beautiful it was a present in itself. Awaya took the parcel and thanked her immensely. "Come say thank you, Bouissi," she garbled in broken French. The joy of seeing the reverend sister was so overwhelming that I felt like jumping into her arms, dancing, laughing, and crying, all at the same time. Her plump body swathed in her white dress, her spotless headscarf, the strange blue color of her eyes—every inch of her shone in a halo of light. But Awaya's big smile and the cold stare she gave me smothered any desire to display warmth.

"Thank you, Reverend Sister," I muttered under my breath.

"Err," she hesitated, taken aback by my shyness. "So, see you in school, tomorrow?" she asked.

Our school would not resume the following day. The start would be postponed by a week.

Someone had broken into the reverend sister's room while she was away and left a huge dead rat on her bed. The animal had spent the whole month broiling in the moisture of the closed room, drawing other, equally unpleasant, creatures. The reverend sister and the priest, hit in the nostrils by the stench, hurried back outside, overpowered by nausea. The mattress and sheets were burned, the entire house disinfected and cleaned from top to bottom, and then ventilated for weeks to rid it of the putrid odor.

"But why? Why? I thought they liked me," the poor woman wondered sadly. "Am I not kind enough to them? Who could have done this? I can't believe one of our very kind, pious, and cheerful villagers could nurture such bad intentions."

"The culprit must be a sibling of the fairy to whom she gave your tooth," Awaya smirked. "What do you expect? Vile creatures attract other vile creatures."

I knew right then it was her!

Back then Awaya was roughly seventy, maybe older. I could not imagine her walking across the village, past the small garden along the edge of the presbytery, climbing over the wall close to the house, breaking through the door, and illegally entering the sister's room while holding a giant rat in her hand every step of the way. She couldn't have carried out this act by herself. However, I was certain that she was the brains behind it. This was exactly the kind of devious idea she would come up with. My guardian was a calm and affable person, if not as charismatic or self-confident as the other village women. But Awaya readily responded to every attack with an attack of her own—a highly respected trait in our village.

I remember one Sunday morning we were on our way back from Church. The priest had delivered a sermon about the law of retaliation; an eye for an eye, a tooth for a tooth. He preached that Christ had abrogated this commandment from Moses and that Christ, being love, wanted us to turn the other cheek and forgive those who hurt us. On our way home, Awaya would always comment on the sermons, interpreting them in her own way. She would talk to me, since we walked home together, but she might as well have been speaking to herself, which she often did by the way—a privilege that comes with age. She was not pleased with the parish priest's sermon. "Turn the other cheek…these people really say nonsense sometimes. I wonder how many times he has turned his own other pink cheek, all plump from the good food he eats. Eye for eye, tooth for tooth works for me just fine. This means that if somebody pokes your eye out, you can't, out of vengeance, burn down his house, rape his wife, or sell his children into slavery before killing him. But it also means that such a person should not expect any mercy from you. You poke out their eye too and you two are even. That is justice. Their ancestors had so much more common sense."

Christian forgiveness was not her favorite virtue. Awaya had carefully planned her revenge, recruited accomplices, waited for an opportunity, and executed it. She was now savoring her victory. In her eyes, the sister had hurt me. Worse, the sister had disrespected her. If the reverend sister had flogged me because I had not learned my lessons, or because I had behaved poorly, she wouldn't have uttered a word. This was part of the authority she had transferred to the sister when she enrolled me in school. However, the brutal treatment she had inflicted on me had shocked Awaya. The sister's condescending tone and self-righteous attitude the following morning had only worsened things. The reverend sister had presumed that she came first and Awaya second in matters that concerned me, and that she knew better than my grandmother what I needed. Whether I shared her opinion or not was beside the point; the sister had offended her inadvertently but Awaya would not forgive her cavalier attitude. Her revenge was proportionate to the offense she believed she had suffered.

Even an unsophisticated or illiterate woman can study a more privileged woman and figure out exactly how to go about crushing her. I was not the only one who had taken due note of the meticulous care the sister devoted to her clothes and the upkeep of her home. Awaya had hit right where she was sure of hurting the sister.

The reverend sister changed after this incident. She lost her enthusiasm and her naïveté, I guess. Her more experienced colleagues had to remind her of just how important it was to keep a safe distance with primitive people. She grew stricter with all of us and smiled less. She kept pushing me down the path of academic success, but the little kind words disappeared from her vocabulary. Were these events solely to blame? Whatever the case, life at the presbytery was reorganized. Two new sisters, both old and bad tempered, were brought in. They took turns teaching at the school and the place was never left unoccupied again.

How did this make me feel? I was disgusted; I had caught a glimpse of the future I aspired to in that house—comfort, cleanliness, the hope of rising above my current status and fleeing my conditions. I had fallen in love with the floor tiles, the lights that came on at the flick of a switch, the water that gushed from a wall, the perfumed soap, the sparkling white kitchen free of a thick layer of filth left behind by smoke, the delicious meals, the cutlery, the soft clean towels… Awaya might as well have slipped a dead rat into my gleaming dream!

I considered going to see the reverend sister to tell her that I had no part in her misfortune, that I wasn't like the rest, that I was worthy of her. I would have loved to give her the names of the culprits as proof of my good faith. On several occasions, my steps led me to her door, with words waiting on my tongue, determined to restore the truth and my innocence, but I never made it past the threshold. I contented myself with working even harder, striving to eat with silverware like she had taught me, and brushing my teeth every morning—until I ran out of toothpaste and all the bristles fell out of my toothbrush and I did not dare ask for a new one. I soaped myself at every bath, until the soap melted away entirely despite my using it with scrupulous frugality. By the grace of God, Awaya didn't make any disparaging comments.

My two lives came to a standoff of sorts, until I completed my final year of primary school and the reverend sister came to suggest to Awaya that she should send me to secondary school. But I wouldn't have guessed how Awaya reacted.

The college was in Bafia, twenty kilometers from our village. "Who will look after her? Where will she stay?" was all my grandmother asked. I was taken aback by her concern. Bafia was the closest town to our village and we had family there. Children attending secondary school were looked after by uncles, aunts, and other members of the community. That wasn't even an issue. What Awaya was trying to tell the reverend sister was that no one wanted me; she, Awaya, was all I had in this world. The underlying question she was asking was whether this woman could step into her shoes. Did the reverend sister understand the question? I couldn't say for sure. If no extended family could host me, she would talk to the mother superior of her order, she replied. In exchange for performing household chores, I could live with them. She was making an impersonal commitment, entrusting me to her order, a system she had complete trust in. The sisters there lived on the school's grounds too. I would come home for holidays and Awaya could visit whenever she felt like it, she assured us.

"These women are offering you knowledge that I do not possess, Bouissi bamè. They will give you something different. I can see how you are drawn to them. They claim you work hard in school. I cannot say whether that is true or false, but I will not always be around, and there's no security for girls like you. No one is thinking about you or waiting for you anywhere. Your ambitions are yours alone. In some respect, this will make life easier for you. You'll see. When your course through life is yours to chart, all options are on the table. Your future rests firmly on your shoulders," she concluded.

I barely paid any attention to her speech. I was leaving, going to live with the reverend sisters, in their beautiful residence... I was going to study and become someone important... I was leaving...

My disappointment equaled all the hope I had placed in this adventure. Although the interior of their dormitory was tidy, some of these women were, nevertheless, slobs. They expected me to clean up after them, even in their private quarters. I had never had to wash underwear or sheets stained with menstrual blood that was not mine before. I had to overcome the disgust I felt. My hands became ridden with blisters due to excessive contact with bleach. I came to understand in a visceral manner the actual cost of those beautiful, thoroughly starched white gowns.

They gave me an alcove at the end of a corridor. That is where I slept and lived. No one ever invited me to eat with them or bothered with whether I used cutlery.

The convent was home to fifteen sisters—teachers or nurses working in the dispensary attached to the college—a priest, and two young boys who aspired to the priesthood. One was tasked with managing the library while the other taught catechism classes to groups of children. My job was to keep their rooms and laundry clean. I had to scrub the floors and common rooms.

I wasn't pampered. At Awaya's, chores were a daily reality and some were often tedious. I was a hard worker, a real girl from the village. But the tasks I was given at the convent left me feeling humiliated because nobody really cared about me. No one spoke to me, except to bark orders or scold me when I failed to perform a chore to their satisfaction. They weren't evil people, just indifferent. Having been the center of Awaya's world, feeling so unseen and so unimportant in the eyes of these clergy was unsettling.

So, I lived in their midst, but always on the fringes, insignificant, and they spoke freely in my presence.

I saw how little regard they had for us, how they held us in such low esteem. They didn't know us and were not really interested in knowing us either. By virtue of their faith, their mission, and their biases, they did not have to—they knew better than us, both what we needed and how we should live.

I cannot discount the unparalleled work they did in education and healthcare. I would not have had a formal education had it not been part of their plan. The free dispensary was always full, rolling back childhood diseases in the region. I saw them clean the most putrid wounds with a straight face. Yet, their mission required the locals to forfeit their ancestral practices, including our native tongues, which we were forbidden from using in their presence. The essence of our being in the world, its core tenet, ingrained in us across generations, was being violently questioned. Their work demanded allegiance, utter surrender, from us. I did not realize this then, but these demands threw us off balance, divided us, made us doubt ourselves, and weakened us. They birthed a cruel conflict in us, putting our loyalty to the test. We were inhabited by a childish and conflicting desire to please and resist them all at the same time.

Our people claimed neither detachment from the world nor dominion over it. We didn't put the universe and its mysteries—meant to be conquered and subjugated—on one side, and humankind, the mighty owner of it all, on the other. We were the world, and the world was us: water, wind, sand, the past, the future, the living, the dead...we were all woven into the fabric of the world. They, however, had appropriated it, simplified it to make it intelligible and malleable. They had invented words and concepts that dismissed our more complex and comprehensive intuitive understanding of reality. There is no denying that, seen through their eyes, conceptualized in their words, the world was unmistakably coherent, logical. For those of us who embraced the mysteries of the world, the encounter was a matter of course, and a tragedy. I doubt we will ever fully grasp the exact extent of our distress.

Today, I believe Western knowledge is both simple and despotic. There is only one God and he is present in churches. Education is found only in textbooks. Art is separate from spirituality, confined to specific spaces.

The law applies equally to everyone and all values have a price. The sole measure of success is material. Our paths in life are already charted, marked out, and you can choose to follow...only the path assigned to you. A promise of comfort, a ready-made life so enticing it warrants universalization; a dream every human should have. Masters, gurus travel the world to guide lost peoples toward this path to salvation, readily resorting to violence to crush any resistance, driven by the firm conviction that their philosophy is *the* philosophy and their religion *the* religion.

Perhaps it spread so far and wide due to the active proselytism inherent to the Western vision of the world, or maybe it was so easy to replicate because it was the most simplistic doctrine ever developed by humans; it did the best job of dismissing our diversity and disregarding our complexity. Our material reality would be more comfortable, that was the promise. That nature would be devastated, and our souls left shuddering with anxiety from this was secondary.

Back then, I suffered from a deep malaise induced by my exposure to the world of these clergy, but knew not how to name it.

The first term was difficult. I was always scrubbing. My fingers rotted from constant immersion in bleach. It started with blisters, then my nails fell off. I didn't like the food, not as much as I had anticipated. I was not eating well and was quickly losing weight. There was no one to encourage me in my studies, so I struggled a great deal during that first year of secondary school.

Life at the school wasn't made any easier as I became aware that I was poor. Back in my village, class differences were less obvious. The new girls' school in Bafia had a good reputation. Excluding a few students on scholarship like myself, the other young girls were the offspring of the new elite of the now independent Cameroon that lived nearby. Teachers were either more or less kind, depending on the social standing of the student's parents. For my part, I worked as a little maid to earn the right to attend this school that was meant to host the cream of the society's future women. I wore nothing but secondhand clothes from foreign donors. Given my skinny frame, they never fit. I didn't get to wear a dress that fit until I was sixteen. I learned to be discreet, humble, and grateful—as I was expected to be.

The Christmas holidays were quite a relief. Awaya did not comment on my appearance. We only discussed my time at the college once, and that was at the very beginning of my visit.

"How is everything over there?" she asked.

We were in the kitchen. I was heartily eating the white mushroom stew and pounded plantains she had cooked to celebrate my return while she busied herself with the countless tasks that always needed her attention in this room.

"It's a little difficult," I replied without looking up from my plate.

I knew the subtleties of my grandmother's body language. Had she wanted a more elaborate answer, she would have asked her question differently; she had no need for it. We had been away from each other for three months now. My worn-out look and gargantuan hunger were self-evident.

"Everything is going to be all right," she said with the same casual tone.

This was Awaya's way of showing me the limits of her protection and her unvoiced faith in my ability to carve out a place for myself in that new environment. All she did was forbid any chores. "Have you seen your hands?" she pointed out as I insisted on pounding cassava leaves for our supper. She handed me a small calabash containing a mixture of palm oil and antiseptic plants, advising that I rub it on my hands several times a day while prohibiting any activity that required me to dip my hands in water.

I went to the farm with the women in the morning and sat down out of the way, delighted with the unexpected break, and the opportunity to discuss the latest village rumors without having to sweat over yam or co-coyam beds.

Some of my former classmates had stopped after primary school. While I was laboring with the reverend sisters, they had acquired their own plots of land and were about to sell the crops they had farmed. Discussions were underway for them to marry young men from the village. I felt like I had been buried alive. In a few months, they had grown, evolved. They were about to enter adulthood while I was still marking time.

I had avoided the reverend sister from the primary school since my return. I was too ashamed of my poor performance during my first term in secondary school. In my village, I had always been in the top of my class. My position was undisputed. I was the teacher's favorite. The secondary school, though, was a concentration of dozens of smart students from all over the region. Those who did not stand out through their academics did so in other manners completely unfamiliar to me, and I envied them for it. Here, I was either Bouissi or Anna, in a quite tangible way. I had substance. There, I struggled, lagging behind in everything, feeling like I was betraying the hopes that had spurred me on until then.

The reverend sister ended up intercepting me after Sunday mass.

"Oh Anna, why have you not come to see me since your return? How are you coping with secondary school? The head sister told me your behavior is exemplary but that you are falling behind in your studies. Don't worry. You know, it is never easy to leave home and go live among strangers in a strange place. Besides, year one of secondary school is nothing like primary school, with all the new subjects, and different teachers for each. No surprise the beginning has been difficult. The changes are just too many for a little girl, even one as smart as you are. But don't worry, you're going to make it. I have faith in you, you know? I would not have sent you if I didn't. Be strong. Work harder and you will see the results, okay? You promise?" she asked insistently.

"Yes, Reverend Sister," I answered.

True to herself, the reverend sister answered each question she asked, sparing me the trouble of having to say a word. In her own way, she was sending me a message similar to Awaya's: "The ball is now in your court."

These two women shared more in common and complemented each other more than they could have imagined.

In retrospect, I realize that, deep down, my personality was shaped by fear, shame, guilt, and envy.

I crumbled under the weight of the faith my former teacher and Awaya placed in me because I felt so incapable. I burned with the desperate desire to please the reverend sisters at the secondary school while despising them at the same time. I loathed my illiterate former classmates back in the village, yet I helplessly envied their newfound freedom.

Everyone else seemed to have a sense of direction—they came from somewhere and were expected somewhere. Meanwhile, I was stuck in one place, conflicted, a burden on myself, so lonely.

I had to return to school once the holidays came to an end. Awaya prepared some medication for me to take along for my hands. "Can you take some food with you?" she asked. I secretly wanted the *egusi* pudding and *bobolo* she was referring to, but shook my head to say no. Where would I keep the food? In the fridge? In the beautiful chests of drawers polished with beeswax, next to the rice, noodles, and canned food families sent for end-of-year celebrations? Under my bed?

I felt a knot in my stomach when I thought about what awaited me. I wanted to plead with my grandmother to let me stay with her. I wanted to tell them how wrong they were to think me worthy of such sacrifice.

"You have to go back," she said, as if reading my thoughts. "Your life can no longer be here. Go show all those white witches that Samgali's descendant is no mere mortal."

Awaya said nothing more, but she had transferred to me the strength so deeply rooted within her that I had never paid any attention to it until now. It was a sort of fierce impassibility that commanded rebellion against the diktat of fatality, that enjoined you to dream with as much persistence as needed to outmatch the power of adverse winds.

That day, I was ready to give up. But that was the last time the idea ever crossed my mind.

Élise Morin was finishing up washing the old, emaciated lady. Anna thanked her kindly. She had grown fond of the young woman. Here, the medical staff never barked at her. They quietly administered the painkillers she needed every time the pain became unbearable. The goal now was no longer healing. This is how healthcare was regaining its earlier reputation.

"I would like to go while my mind is still intact," she pleaded. "Don't let my body outlive my sanity."

She recalled a conversation she had had with Abi about this:

"My entire life is wrapped up in my spirit, my thoughts. I'm not as bothered by physical degeneration and death as I am about the idea of not being able to grasp the world around me. I can't imagine looking at you without recognizing you, or waking up in the morning not knowing who I am, do you understand? My greatest fear is that everything I have experienced, all those I have loved, my precious memories, everything that makes *me* will disappear into thin air while my body lingers, as incongruous as persistent smoke from a fire that has long gone out."

"If that should happen, you wouldn't know it, mother. You would be too far gone to suffer."

This rather plausible idea scared her even more.

She had started telling her life's story in response to an idle remark from her nurse's aide.

Through the window, Anna contemplated the purplish-mauve flowering of a paulownia tree blooming with the return of spring.

"How strange, these seasons that come and go, turning nature upside down. You know, where I'm from, the changes are more nuanced, less blatant. Time goes by stealthily, slipping through your fingers if you are not careful."

"In your state, I guess being away from home must be difficult," the young woman replied with that rather calm voice they all had here; it was neither inquisitive nor laced with excessive pathos.

Anna wanted to tell her that having her daughter close by during this final journey was far more important than the comforts of home. Instead, she found herself untangling the long and complex story of her life. Then Élise Morin's shift ended and she had to leave, but Anna did not stop talking. Even if she had wanted to stop, some secret urge compelled her to continue. And she did not want to stop talking. She soliloquized, and the sound of her voice, her own words, the memories she evoked, reduced the pain, fear, and anguish of disappearing that threatened the fragile balance of her spirit. Anna had found a way to face her death.

"Don't be too long, my little Élise. Time is against us."

Élise Morin stumbled upon Abi in the corridor.

"How did she sleep?" Abi asked, anxious.

"She is as fine as she can be given the circumstances," Élise replied, striking a reassuring tone.

This was the undiluted truth. The old lady had fallen while trying to get to the bathroom because she didn't want to bother the nurses on duty that night. Early in the morning, Élise found her lying on the floor, shaken, a deep bruise etched into her fragile skin. She came to the old lady's aid, and then cleaned her up. She saw that Anna's situation was getting worse. Despite all her experience with patients, the nurse's aide was always taken aback by how the state of terminally ill patients evolved. A disease that had developed over years and even decades suddenly spread swiftly. In mere hours, the wounds worsened. The entire body declined at an appalling rate, like a horse galloping faster upon catching the smell of the stable.

Her patient had set out to tell her story. A casual discussion that had resulted in a monologue, Élise merely serving as the pretext. Anna continued speaking even when there was no one to listen, her shrunken face reflecting the intimate and secret emotions wrapped in her words. She laughed or cried while wringing her hands; she got angry or melted with tenderness every time she went down memory lane. One would have thought that those past years, buried, and those absent people, dead, were coming back for one final performance before they parted ways, or before they met again.

Élise disappeared down the corridor before backtracking to talk to Abi.

"Your mother talks endlessly, whether she's awake or asleep. She is telling her story, I think, revisiting her life. I thought…" She hesitated. Her job was to assist her patients based on *their* needs, not on desires that struck a chord with her. Yet, her instinct was telling her that the old lady's final words would be distinctly important to her family.

Abi looked at her, attentively, anxiously.

"Yes?" she spurred the aide on.

Élise noticed the elaborate makeup, the manicured nails, the groomed hair, the meticulous outfit, but also the dark patches under Abi's bloodshot eyes, the cold sore on the corner of her mouth, and the fingers clutching the strap of her handbag. The nurse's aide had dealt with terminally ill patients and their distraught relatives for so long that she wasn't fooled by smoke screens. She could recognize bare sorrow, which became blatant with repeated exposure. It was as easy to perceive as the perfume of defeat, through clumsy gestures, impending tears, frozen smiles, the attitude toward the medical staff— trapped between submission and contained fury, as if the staff was both the promise of a miracle and the cause of the disease.

This woman is on the verge of a breakdown, she noted. *She grooms herself because she likes to, needs to, or out of habit. However, no foundation cream and no alluring fragrance can conceal the panicked hopelessness of the inner child soon to become an orphan. The adult knows death is near, inescapable, but the child rejects what is apparent. She is here every morning; no absurd world would continue to exist without a mother. The child has never known any, and the very thought of it oppresses her spirit.*

Abi calmly waited for Élise Morin to start talking again.

"...Perhaps you would like to record her last words," she proposed.

Abi shuddered. She had heard only the last part of the sentence and asked once again about how much time was left.

"How much more time do you think..."

The words died on her lips. She didn't have the strength to express her thoughts more clearly. But the aide had understood her quite clearly.

"I don't know. Just make the best of these moments. They can sometimes become fond memories."

Abi stared for a moment as the woman walked away before gently knocking on the door to her mother's room and going right in.

Anna was mumbling with her eyes closed, lost in a world now removed from the present. She did not hear Abi enter. Abi placed her things on a chair and sank softly onto the side of the bed. "Mother?" The young woman rubbed her mother's arm. Her ultra-thin skin felt silk-paper smooth. She ran her fingers up across her mother's chest. In the hollow beneath the bony protrusion of her overstretched collarbones, her unstable pulse beat. Anna smiled with her eyes closed. "Is that you, my daughter?" Abi took off her shoes and cautiously laid down in the small single bed. She nestled her head against her mother's neck, sifting through the smell of disease and the recent bath in search of the warm almond fragrance that would take her down the path to memories of her childhood. "Were you expecting someone else?" she asked smiling. Anna kissed the crown of her head and took her by the hand. "You're cold. You smell good, like the outdoors." Abi closed her eyes. The feeling of her skin against her mother's was enough to quell the fear of losing her. She had no childhood memories of hugging Anna. Her father tickled her, took her up in his arms, but her mother was there for the hard knocks of everyday life. Their tactile closeness had started with the illness, like a symptom.

Anna wandered off into her ramblings once again, leaving Abi alone with her thoughts.

The old woman had been hospitalized for two days now. When they arrived, Abi had filled out the administrative forms, and spoke with the doctor and psychologist at length. She had also met the blonde, roundish aide with the radiant smile whom she was angry to learn would be the one to take care of Anna. Abi believed her mother would be more comfortable if she was cared for by a Black person. She thought of taking this up with the doctor, pleading her far-off origins, requesting this as a favor for a terminally ill old lady who was losing touch both with political correctness and her inhibitions. But Anna grew fond of Élise Morin. Barely had they settled

in than she was asking her name, about her family and
her origins. Her daughter decided to let things be.

Anna's first night in the hospital was both calm and difficult for Abi. She was relieved that others, more compe-
tent than she was, would be caring for the old lady. But
it also meant that her mother, the one she had known
and whom she had hoped would remain the same until
the end, would not walk out of this place where people
came to die.

Entrusting her daughter, little Jenny, to anyone was
difficult for Abi. Dropping her off at the day-care center every morning before heading to work was in itself
a heart-wrenching experience. She was apprehensive
about leaving the baby with a strange babysitter all night
long. Her son offered to come stay at her place to watch
over the little one. Max had witnessed so many deaths
and separations recently that Abi feared that his grandmother's illness would be one fateful blow too many.
However, Max was handling the situation quite maturely.
She was proud of the adult her son was turning out to be.

Anna tossed and turned through the night, murmuring
in her sleep.

Abi eventually left her side and settled into her
own cot, given to her by the hospital. Dark thoughts
came back to haunt her as soon as she broke physical
contact. Anxiety creeped through her body like some
bodily impairment, a fever. She decided to take a bath
to cool down. Wading through the tiny room in the

dark to avoid disturbing Anna, she hit her pinky toe so hard against the bed that the pain kept her rooted to the spot. The pain, which she anticipated for long seconds before finally feeling it, was sharp. It was as ruthless as she had imagined it. She limped the rest of the way to the bathroom, closed the door behind her, then groped for the light switch before slumping on the bidet. The pain continued spreading, traveling up her leg in successive waves. Abi directed the showerhead to her aching foot and let the cool water ease the pain. She had been on edge since learning that there was no hope for her mother. The doctors had warned them right away that the only outcome was death. Abi had cried ceaselessly since then. Sometimes over trivial things, minor daily headaches that suddenly seemed insurmountable to her. She was almost grateful for the physical pain she felt; it gave her a good reason to shed tears.

She finally turned off the tap and took off her clothes in front of the mirror. She spent a moment examining her body under the unflattering light. Hers was the body of a forty-year-old woman. She passed a hesitant hand over her hefty chest, her stomach—crumpled since the birth of her son—and her thighs that already bore traces of cellulite. While Anna had always been slim and muscular, her daughter had inherited a propensity for portliness from her father's side of the family. Throughout her life, she had been scared that her flesh would spill over, and the small love handles around her hips would fill up with fat if she did not watch her weight, so she wore herself out in gyms.

Her fingers lingered on her breasts. She thought of her ex-husband, Julien, who adored her voluptuous figure. Their divorce was now final and even if, thanks to Max, they were gradually rebuilding a cordial relationship, the wounds were still quite fresh. She would have wanted him by her side now, nevertheless. He knew Anna and had really loved her when they were married. "I now realize, by discovering the original, that I fell in love with a poor copy," he had joked, mesmerized by the charm of his mother-in-law. He knew how complex the relationship between Abi and her parents was—all those things that no longer needed explaining after years of living together.

She recalled a memory from her childhood, a conversation between Anna and her mother's friend, Ma'Moudio. The two were talking in front of her without taking any precautions.

Anna was telling her friend an anecdote about her husband's mother. The two women were not huge fans of one another; Anna was often caustic and mocking when talking about her mother-in-law.

Her father-in-law, well into his seventies, had brought his mistress—a much younger woman—into the marital home. His wife reported her misfortune to the family. Their grown-up children were summoned to a meeting to try and make the old man change his decision. They were furious, uncomfortable about being dragged into the private lives of their old parents, whom they thought now lived sexless lives.

The matter had been dragging on for months. The

mother-in-law had carried her sorrow to the homes of each of their children in turn, forcing them to unwillingly take due note of her desolation, and thus act to rescue her from the shame her husband was inflicting on her. The father-in-law did not say a word. His silence was another insult, because he would retire to his new partner's bedroom every night and their laughter, their giggles, their shameless lovemaking kept the poor woman awake. Furthermore, the man was now primping. He, who would usually spend the whole day in a faded pair of trousers and a questionably clean vest with his shaggy gray body hair spilling from the seams, now wore clean shirts, shaved, and bought plant powders and God knows what else from the hawkers, supposedly to restore the vigor of his youth. He now walked with a spring in his step. He was ten years younger.

"Cheating wasn't the problem," Anna pointed out. "Nobody around here really cares when a man breaches the marriage contract or brings home his bird. What really bothered my mother-in-law was the fact that her man was suddenly in excellent shape. You age, your husband does too. Your children all grow up, get married, and then you can finally take a break, thinking that the hardest part is behind you. Then, all of a sudden, your man, like a long-distance runner, seems to get a new lease on life. He picks up his pace and you can't keep up. That, is betrayal."

The mother-in-law threatened to leave the house and move in with one of them if her children did not make their father see reason. Horrified by this prospect,

her daughters-in law compelled their husbands to intervene, which they did half-heartedly. The father insisted
that his new partner should attend the meeting. The
mother accepted, convinced that in the presence of her
children, her loyal supporters, the dispute would play out
in her favor.

The four sons traveled from Douala and Yaounde,
where they lived with their respective wives and children,
to spend a weekend in the family home in Dschang.

Hostilities started almost immediately as they got
out of the car. Their father, dressed to go out, refused to
partake of the meal cooked for the occasion.

"Let's get straight to the point, I have a reunion to
attend in a few hours," he announced right away.

"Is she an old student of yours too? Is that why you
are taking her along?" the mother replied, pointing a
finger at her husband's young mistress, who was freshly
changed and made up.

Their father's new wife shocked his children. She had
been rumored to be young, and the age gap was wide
indeed—she had to be around thirty-five. She was light-
skinned, slightly stout—which they all thought suited
her well—and her curvaceous shape was carefully high-
lighted. They, too, found her sexually attractive. The father
noticed the look on his sons' faces and silently puffed up.

They had barely settled in when the mother began
unrolling her long list of grievances: the money being
spent to please the newcomer, the outfits, jewelry, a new
television set, and even a house that he had set out to
build for her in the village. The father, whose pension

couldn't sustain his lavish lifestyle, had sold off a plot of land and was planning to sell off more assets. Everything basically revolved around this squandering of family property. "Listen, you don't want her to live here. So, she will have her own house and you will have yours," he argued. "What about our inheritance?" the children asked, upset. The old man took offense. "The money I worked for all my life? I am not free to spend it how I choose? I raised all of you. I gave you the means to earn a living for yourselves. Don't expect anything when I die. I got nothing from my father, but I still did my best."

He put his hand on his belle's thigh and the entire family froze. For as long as they could remember, they had never seen their parents touch or even brush up against one another. The young woman placed her hand over the old man's. "Rightly so, you old fool. She's only after your money. What else do you expect?" the mother cried out hysterically after this umpteenth provocation. The old man sat quiet. The mother ranted and raved a little longer. And then, as if consumed by the absence of a reaction from her husband, her voice finally died out. He sighed, and then said, "Listen, I have already asked you to let this matter be. If someone is taking care of me, why does that offend you? Let us admit that nobody would love me for me and that it must be for the money. How is that your problem? You have children and respect. I have left you in the house. Why does it bother you if someone takes a part of me you have long had no use for?" The woman screamed that this lecherous old man was only interested in the immoral, perverse things he did with this insolent little prostitute. That she had stumbled upon him kissing her on the lips. Yes. Him, with his rotten teeth. As if he were suddenly an actor in one of those degenerate movies broadcast on television all day long. Never on earth would she accept such things in her house.

"You should have seen the looks on the children's faces..." Anna told her friend. Both women roared with laughter. "Suddenly, we were dragged into the bedroom of these old people. Into private things that we, under no circumstance, wanted to know about."

Ribald-eyed, the father turned to his child and asked, "Do you know what a BJ is? Yeah, I guess. Well, I have only just discovered it. A long life and I am only discovering it now..."

At this stage of the story, Anna and her friend were shedding tears of laughter. They gasped, unable to stop. With truncated, disjointed words, and a tiny scrap of voice choked by outbursts of laughter deep down in her throat, Anna relayed that his sons had sprung to their feet, like one man. "Come on, Father. Come on. You too!?" they chimed in unison. Alarmed, the mother inquired, "What is he saying? A what? What is he talking about? But what is he really talking about?"

To which the old man responded with a loud voice, over the tumult, "What I am trying to say, woman, is quite simple: If you are done quenching your thirst, don't muddy the spring from which others might drink... As for you," he said to his children, "this is the last time you poke your nose into things that are way beyond you."

Every child hurriedly gathered up his family and

they all, frowning, returned to their respective homes, leaving their mother distraught by the turn the meeting had taken.

Back then, Abi did not really grasp the seriousness of what was happening. She remembered her mother chuckling in the car. "A BJ. Oh my God! Simply imagining it made me want to throw up my breakfast. What had become of the decency of the elderly?" she wondered. Abi's father, eyes firmly set on the road, strongly scolded her, "Anna, that's enough! We're talking about my parents. My poor mother is unhappy. He disrespects her in her own house." Anna turned and leaned her head on the window, trying unsuccessfully to hold back her amusement. "A BJ… For the love of Heaven!"

Abi knew very well what PJs were. Her grandparents each owned a pair so she did not understand why it was so unsettling. Her mother was laughing hysterically while her father, clenching his teeth, focused on driving. The atmosphere in the car was tense. "Can we play some music?" the little girl dared ask. "No," both her parents replied in unison. When scolding her, everyone always saw eye to eye, her irritated ten-year-old self thought.

Even when she heard her mother telling the story to her friend, Abi did not understand everything right away. All she saw was her grandmother—ever more emaciated, bitter, dressed in her old faded *kaba*—who was creating chaos in the homes of her children, and her grandfather—dashing, dressed in a freshly ironed and starched matching *abacost*—ever so kind with her. She would learn her lesson much later, when she got divorced from her

husband. The metaphor of the long-distance runner getting a second wind would finally make sense, as well as
the tragedy that had played out before her eyes as a child.
However, it hadn't been her husband who had cheated.
He was not the one who suddenly found fulfillment in
another person. She was the one.

Love, desire, sex. That story is as old as the world and
yet it is still just as destructive.

Julien had guessed she was having an affair.

As she left the hotel room after spending a few hours
with her lover, she found him sitting in the lobby right
across from the elevator.

Abi saw herself through his eyes. She had just taken
a bath and her skin was a little wet. Her eyes shining like
a woman who had had fun. Were her lips swollen from
all the kissing? Between her thighs, she could still feel the
heat of her lovemaking. She felt as if her husband saw all
of this in her. Her flushing face, her fervor, her lips whit-
ened by all the pressure made her turn cold with dread.
"He's going to kill me," she thought to herself as her legs
collapsed under her.

She and her lover were discreet. He wasn't single either. He had come down from the hotel room before her
and had seen Julien in the lobby. He had tried to warn her.
Her phone did not ring. Maybe she had already been in
the lift. The message tone only rang when Abi was face-
to-face with her husband, unable to think. She took her
phone from her handbag and read the message: *Danger!
Don't come down now.* Julien took long strides and pried

the phone out of her hands. "Too late, you bloody fool!" he screamed at the phone before throwing it against the wall where it broke into pieces. The other people in the foyer stopped their conversations. Everyone was staring at them. Julien screamed insanities. Given the situation, she wouldn't have expected him to keep calm, but she was taken back by the violence with which he reacted. Julien was not a man to make a spectacle of himself or embarrass himself in public. He said such vulgar, insulting things that he left Abi paralyzed, ashamed for both of them. Nobody in this hotel lobby could ignore the unfolding scene. Reception employees gestured for security, and two muscular men came toward them. "Madame, Sir, kindly leave the premises," they ordered.

Julien lost it. "My wife gets laid in this rotten pigsty, in this brothel you call a hotel, and you're throwing *me* out… Goddamn it, go screw yourselves. Don't touch me. Let go of me!"

The security guard grabbed him brutally. "Sir, kindly leave," the security guard insisted. Abi put her hand on the man's arm in an attempt to calm things down. "Please, we're leaving! Let go of him, please," she pleaded. He gave her such a spiteful look that she quickly removed her hand as if she'd been burned. "Leave!" he barked at her. *Let's leave*, Abi thought, incredulous. *I have become a Jezebel. Men would come together to stone me if they could.*

The hotel's security unceremoniously threw them out. Julien was still angry. Across the street, Abi saw her lover waiting. She could not believe his temerity. Why didn't he just leave? Was he driven by an overflow of chivalry, hoping to come to her rescue? Challenge Julien to a duel? Handle it like men? A murder was the only thing left to mark this detestable moment. She could already see the headlines in the tabloids: *Jealous Husband Murders Sculptor X*, and the mouthwatering interviews with hotel customers. She drew her husband toward the car parked nearby. "Come on. Let's leave, please. We'll talk at home," she said. He roughly pulled away the arm that she had caught and quickly got into the car. Abi got in after him, never daring to look at the sidewalk opposite.

Julien did not utter a word on the trip home.

Abi's mind drifted toward practical details. Max would return from school. She would have to make dinner. Make sure their teenager was okay. She analyzed her counterattack, or her defense. It all depended. She immediately decided to end her affair.

Unanswered questions, one more alarming than the last, made the rounds in her head. How had he known about the hotel? How much information did he know about her affair? Abi knew that she would never have the courage to ask him, but Julien was an engineer and quite well versed in new technologies. She suspected that he had installed a tracking app on her smartphone. Had he gone further? Had he accessed her private messages? Had he seen the lascivious, daring pictures she sent to her lover? Had he read their sexts? The idea made her stomach churn. What had come over her not to delete everything?

Max was there when they got home. Julien went up to the bedroom without saying a word, while Abi went about her chores in the kitchen, replying absentmindedly to her son's noise. *We will talk. Everything is going to be fine*, she thought, weak. *This is a major crisis, but we have faced others.* She recalled her husband's affair. Despite the terrible pain she'd felt then, the keen feeling of betrayal that she thought she'd never recover from, she hadn't thought for one second of leaving Julien. She had, on the contrary, decided to give him a greater margin of freedom. She wanted to focus on the family. Build a beautiful, harmonious life. Julien had claimed that the affair was a onetime thing. She decided to believe him because she needed to believe that they were still both committed to what mattered—their partnership and Max's happiness. Abi decided not to let herself get distracted: *If you believe your enemies are possessed by the Devil, do not run after them*, her mother had said. She made concessions instead of digging her heels in.

Julien was not a womanizer. Far from it. They had met at college and fallen in love.

"A white man?" her family had asked, worried. "A Black woman?" Julien's distressed family had asked. The young couple had laughed at their families' apprehensions. For Christmas, Abi had given her mother-in-law—a bourgeois Catholic from the country—a CD featuring the stand-up show of French comedian Muriel Robin titled *Le Noir*. She had not found the gift funny. "We aren't racist, you know that, Julien. You know the Traorés, that Ivorian family that attends our church? Well, I find them charming, but marriage is completely different. Are you sure? Is it that Abi needs papers? Is she an illegal immigrant? We all agree she is pretty, but ultimately we are so different from those people…" she'd concluded. Ordinarily open-minded, Anna also cringed. "But why must you two marry right away? Live together for a while and see if it works for you. Is your white guy at least circumcised? And your children, how are they going to be raised? They will forget our customs. Those people are not like us," her mother argued. Her mother, so resolutely modern, was suddenly worried that her grandchildren would forget the traditions she herself had not handed down to Abi.

The men were much more welcoming. Or maybe they just expressed their concerns less. "If he makes you happy, my daughter, I have nothing else to say," was the only thing Abi's father said. She did not expect anything else from the person who had always supported her choices without reservation.

It was agreed that the civil ceremony would take place in the town hall of Cherbourg, the groom's hometown, while the church ceremony would take place in Dschang. That was the only condition Abi's father gave. He wanted to host the wedding of his only daughter in his stronghold and wouldn't change his mind. Julien's mother protested. They were quite active church members, she'd argued. Her son had received all his sacraments in their church. And the engaged couple lived in Paris after all. Their friends lived in Paris. It was only normal for them to marry there. "And Abi's family is in Cameroon," the Tchoualé parents countered. "A man gets his wife from her family. These are our traditions." They also insisted on funding the entire wedding party. Anna gathered from God knows where such a huge sum of money that the tides changed. "I have been saving for this particular occasion for years now," she announced without further ado. The stinginess of Julien's father put the matter to rest: "Well then, in these circumstances, we'd be delighted to visit your beautiful country, right Charlotte?" Charlotte was not the type of woman who went against her husband's will. She muted her disapproval and agreed with everyone.

Max was born five years later. They had taken their time.

Julien, a young engineer, was recruited by a leading phone company. Abi interned with several dailies before she was recruited by a reputable magazine where she managed the culture desk. They loved one another. Shared the same values. Were environmentalists. Members of the anti-capitalist movement. Christians more as a result of upbringing than conviction. They had some regard for morality all the same. Before Max was born, they traveled the world on less touristed routes, and visited several unexpected places. Their friends came from diverse backgrounds. They vaguely discussed having a second child but never went through with this plan. Julien's brother had died in a motorcycle accident before they met. Abi was an only child. They really did not want to have a big family. The couple built itself happily around Max. Julien had light blond, almost ginger, hair. Their son inherited a unique mix of features. His sienna brown skin made him look Indian, providing a striking contrast with his fawn-colored eyes and his lush curly hair that was somewhere between light and ginger brown. Max was so handsome. From the day he was born and almost every day of his childhood, adults swooned before this unique child. Showered him with compliments. Were in awe of his beauty without the attention seeming to sour his character. He was intelligent, easygoing, and loving. Max was Abi and Julien's ultimate pride. In fact, he was the centerpiece of the family they built. When he was born, they moved out of their one room and kitchen house in the trendy Marais neighborhood and into a beautiful house with a garden in a rich suburb nearby, which was more appropriate for raising a child. Comfortable holidays in all-inclusive clubs replaced their previous life as carefree travelers. The world they built, which centered on Max's welfare, shrank right under their noses.

Abi had discovered Julien's affair unexpectedly, while calculating household bills. She saw that he had used his debit card to pay for an afternoon in a Paris hotel. Curious but far from imagining he was with another woman, she had asked him about it without thinking twice. Julien had fallen apart. He stammered before ultimately confessing his infidelity to the mesmerized Abi. "Midday on a workday? You asked for time off to go screw your tart incognito, but you paid with your debit card? Is it possible to be any more stupid?" Abi screamed angrily.

They went through the standard phases. Stormy arguments. Venom-tipped questions asked by the person who felt betrayed, certain in their right to do so. Sure of their position as a victim. The confused responses of the traitor. Contrite. Worried about redemption. Ready to make any compromise. The tears. The insults. The mounting desire under pressure. The threats. The begging... And Max, who they miraculously shielded from the crisis. The very act of protecting their son convinced them that they had not yet reached a point of no return, and wouldn't reach it as long as they didn't drag their precious child into their emotional vagrancy. Julien promised over and over again, and he was never, it must be said, found wanting again. Abi forgave but she never forgot; she adjusted her feelings, consciously or otherwise, accordingly.

It was now Abi's turn to be grilled. To be the person who shamefully toes the line and apologizes for breathing. She loathed Julien's anger, and was disturbed by the skewed image he would now have of her. And, most importantly, she regretted all the pain she was causing him. His crimson face and his accusing, murderous look in the lobby of that hotel would haunt her for ages. However, at no point did Abi imagine that it would put an end to their relationship. She braced for difficult weeks, months ahead, marked of course by flare-ups after they had thought the storm already weathered, but they would survive it. They would rally like they had in the past. They would overcome all of it, and their relationship would come out of this stronger, their feelings reinforced. They... She was so caught up in her thoughts that she barely overheard her son wish her goodnight, as she was in a crazed frenzy cleaning the house. She only came back to reality when she saw Julien coming down the stairs, luggage in hand. Abi ran toward him.

"Where are you off to? What do think you're doing?" she asked.

She stood in his way. Tried to wrestle the bag out of his hand.

"Julien, where are you going? Please, let's talk. Stay. Julien, listen to me," she begged.

Without looking at her, he strongly brushed her aside. Abi held on.

"Julien, we've been through this before. Don't you remember? We'll overcome it again," she said.

Julien froze in his tracks.

"What are you trying to say? What are you talking about?" he asked.

Abi stared at him in disbelief. Could he have forgotten his own act of betrayal? Could it be that he hadn't established any link between the two affairs?

"But what..." Julien blurted. Then, as if a light bulb had turned on in his mind, he said, "Are you kidding me? Are you comparing your numerous sexcapades with a fling I had years ago and which you made me pay for dearly? How are they related? You're an idiot, my poor girl. This doesn't compare. Not a bit. But how..."

He was getting angrier. He raised his voice.

"Where will it end? You...you disgust me. You're revolting. What a bloody hypocrite," he concluded.

He was screaming. Stunned, Abi dared interject to say, "I'm begging, Julien, our son..."

"He deserves to know his mother is a slut, too," he declared.

Abi was still holding on to the luggage. He violently pushed her away and didn't look back when she lost her balance and fell down. Julien left, slamming the door behind him.

She spent the evening and the rest of the night hoping obstinately.

He will return. Of course, he will return. Anyway, where could he go: to his mother's in Normandy? A hotel? Even more than she, Julien was attached to the comforts of their life. The nice house in the suburbs, slippers in the doorway, the slightly lopsided sofa, books and newspapers lying around, home-cooked meals, the dining table around which they each had a specific seat. Simply put, a comfortable and safe routine that contrasted with the chaos of her family.

Abi made herself tea and settled in front of the window. A stream of cold air filled the room. She grabbed her mug and drank slowly.

There was nothing exciting about the suburb where they lived. New buildings, begonia planters on apartment windows, houses surrounded by tiny well-tended gardens, a neighborhood of upper mid-level executives, most of whom worked in neighboring business districts or freelanced. Any slight commotion you heard at night was just people returning home, and if the teenage son of the Durands, who did not really care about the neighbors' sleep, did not coordinate some impromptu drinking spree with his friends in the middle of the night, time went by uneventfully. A quiet stream uninterrupted by any whirls. Abi wondered about the tragedies playing out behind closed doors. About the silhouettes through the blinds. About the shadows cast by the cleverly laid out lamps. They had lived in the neighborhood for over ten years now. She had heard some gossip about each couple. Had witnessed births, divorces more or less well handled, like avoiding or not avoiding veering off the road in a sharp turn. Abi was surprised that nothing more seeped through on this cold January night.

The air streaming in through the open window was dry, cold, and unpleasant. It was a winter night in the suburbs. The suburbs are a fine place to live but there are no lights. No beautiful monuments. No narrow carriage streets. They lack the charm of Paris. They lack the rustic, rural beauty of a countryside town. A winter night without charm. Flat-out cold. Unpleasant. Nothing could have changed that dullness—not even the muted, bitter passions, unbridled ambitions, and the joys or miseries veiled by the lowered shutters. No human emotion trickled from those thick fortresses. For the first time ever, Abi wondered what this charmless place said about those who chose to live here. Julien had his affair just a few months after they'd bought the house. Maybe he'd already understood what she was realizing only now. Maybe it was a form of unconscious resistance. They were early career professionals and did not have the means to buy a house in Paris. They were heavily indebted, having rejected financial assistance from their parents. This comfortable, safe place aligned in every respect with their idea of a home. Julien was still attached to it much more than

she was. She had to be convinced of it then and still had
to be now. Her vague act of defiance—or whatever explanation could retroactively be found for her sole instance
of misconduct—did not change the situation. He would
come back. For sure. Julien had nowhere to go. She and
Max were his family. His home.

Abi served herself some more tea. Her thoughts were
all over the place. She had no control over the string of
dangerous ideas that bolted through her mind. Her inco-
herent and illogical thoughts occupied her solely to feed
the hope that kept her seated in the cold night air.

She dozed off despite her efforts not to.

*Max was seven. Seven, not six, eight, or even seven and
a half. Only seven. They had just celebrated his birthday the
day before. He had received a baby's scooter as his gift and was
tearing down the slope across from their home. "Be careful,
sweetheart. Stop at the sidewalk." Busy texting her lover, Abi
paid only vague attention to her son. The alley opened into
a rather quiet one-way street, and she wasn't particularly
worried. "Mama, look. I am as fast as the wind," screamed
Max, delighted. "Great job, my dear," replied Abi mechan-
ically while typing on her phone. Then, prompted by a dark
premonition, she raised her eyes in time to see a white truck
swinging around the street corner. She screamed her son's
name and ran after him. The scooter was going down the slope
at top speed as Max laughed… The driver couldn't have seen
him. The lane was perpendicular to the sidewalk. Apparently,
the driver was familiar with the street and knew there were
rarely people, and he didn't slow down. Abi ran, calling out to
her son, realizing that she was not making enough progress.*

She wasn't fast enough. The scooter was going so fast. She would not catch up with him. Never. The child and the truck both hit the sidewalk at the same time. Abi heard tires screech. Saw the driver desperately trying to slow down and swerve at the same time. She heard the sound made when her son's little body hit the car's hood. She screamed his name.

"All right. No need to shout like that. I heard you," he said.

Abi woke up startled. Max was standing on the staircase. His pajamas were buttoned wrong. Quite disheveled.

"What time is it?" the teenager asked, seeking out the kitchen clock with his gaze. "Six in the morning, mother. I still have at least an hour and a half of sleep to go! Why are you screaming like that? Are you crazy? I am going back up to sleep," he said.

Without paying any more attention to his mother, and with the cavalier attitude of kids his age, he went back up the stairs yawning and disappeared into his room.

Abi stayed, stuck there. Her pulse raced. Her skin was soaked in a cold sweat.

She knew that nightmare all too well. The scene had indeed taken place the day after Max's seventh birthday. But it had been way less dramatic. Back then, she hadn't met her lover yet. Her son was trying out his new scooter on the steep lane and had braked perfectly at the edge of the road like she had taught him to, giving way to a white van that was moving at a normal speed along the small street. An ordinary scene. Danger-free for Max. The meaning of which her spirit had, for reasons unbeknownst to her, transformed into a terrifyingly real hallucination.

Every time Abi felt powerless, crushed, defeated, every time the will of steel she used to keep her life on the track she had chosen was tested, part of her, naked and defenseless, represented by her seven-year-old son, created this senseless dream.

She stood up and shut the window, shivering. The room was icy. *It's time to go take a bath and get ready for the day*, she ordered her aching body.

"Where's Dad?" Max asked when she came back downstairs, finding him sitting in front of his cereal.

"He left early," she answered.

"Well, it makes sense, if you scream at dawn, nobody would want to stick around," he declared.

He grabbed his schoolbag and, with his mouth still full, headed for the door.

"Remind him there's volleyball practice this evening. You know, to prepare for the father-son tournament next week. It's at six in the gym. He better be on time," he warned.

On a normal day, she would ask him whether...

"Aren't you going to ask me whether I brushed my teeth? Whether I have my canteen card with me? No 'zip up your jacket. It's cold this morning'?" asked Max jokingly as he backtracked. "Mom, you sure are strange this morning. Are you sure you're all right?" he asked.

He put his hand against her forehead, pretending to take her temperature.

"Nothing. No fever. Just half-asleep, poor thing. Well, I'm out. See you tonight," he announced.

Abi smiled as she watched her grown boy leave.

What had happened between the little bundle he'd been at birth and the fourteen-year-old handsome, funny, intelligent, lazy, and troublesome guy he'd become? Where had time gone? What had they done with it? It felt like yesterday that she was teaching him to count. "Twenty-eight, twenty-nine…twenty…ten?" She could still see his confused, worried face. His look yearning for approval from his family. A mother's mementos. She alone would always remember that particular Max. Those fleeting moments. The happiness laced with pain swept away by the current of life.

She wanted to call Julien, then remembered she no longer had a mobile phone and used the landline in the house. She was redirected to voicemail and tried again several times before hanging up. He hadn't picked up, but she felt better. The scene with Max, then the reminder about their evening practice had lifted her spirits. Julien would come back. No doubt about it! He wouldn't miss the volleyball practice for any reason. He would not abandon their son without any word.

First thing: get a new phone, she thought while starting her car. The weather was clear and icy. Abi turned on the radio and with a lighter heart, plunged into the traffic.

Julien missed the volleyball practice and didn't respond to her numerous phone calls. This went on for weeks. Abi reached out to their friends, but nobody had heard from him. Everyone said the same thing in turn. She heard the embarrassment, reticence in their voice. "No, sorry,

Abi, Julien did not tell us anything. We don't know where he is." The thing was, nobody asked why she was calling about him. None of them questioned her reason for calling. The news, she was sure, had reached everyone and was the cause of countless speculation in their homes.

Abi was a woman without female friends. She didn't have close friends besides their joint friends. They had known each other since they were quite young. They did things together, and gradually their circle of friends had shrunk, leaving behind only those with whom they shared the same interests. What had become of that one friend of Julien's: the forever-young teenager who insisted on writing poems that nobody cared to read? And his friend Denise: the independent and unapologetic man-eater? They now hung out only with couples their own age, with children the same ages as theirs, in the same social class, sharing the same boring ideas. Where had this plain, self-absorbed, narrow-minded couple come from? She had never felt the need for a girls' night out, or for sharing juicy secrets. She thought she had healthy, friendly relationships with people. And she even thought she shared a bond with her colleagues. They led a satisfactory social life, and Abi was now surprised that she had nobody to talk to. "Where is everyone?" she wondered, flipping through her phone book.

Julien was still nowhere to be found and Max's attitude had gotten worse. He had always been a bright, kind, self-confident kid. In only a few weeks, her son changed. His grades dropped. He rebelled. Became undisciplined. At home, he was intolerably rude. He got into the habit of shoving her. If they were standing in front of a door, he would cut through first, knocking into her in the process. If she was in the kitchen and he wanted to take a glass, he would stretch right over her, forcing her to bend over, to stoop to give him space. If she was sitting, he would cut in front of her and step on her toes. As for the rest of it—the uncalled-for statements, the anger, slammed doors—she tolerated them. But these confrontations scared her, this physical encroachment. It unsettled her. Her adorable boy, who had grown too big overnight it seemed, was morphing into a caveman, fierce and aggressive.

Anna called her daughter. The young woman had been expecting the call, somewhat. Her mother was close to Julien and her grandson. Abi had not found the strength to call her, but she had suspected her husband would.

Anna struck a gentle tone over the phone.

"*Agondo*, I got a call from Julien. And one from Max too. How are you doing, my daughter?" she asked.

"Agondo" is a pet name in her mother's tongue, used to refer to daughters who have just given birth. Since Max was born, although her son now had downy hairs over his lip and a somewhat unsettling and changing baritone voice, her mother still called her Agondo.

"Not at my best, but all will be fine," she replied.

"You know it's hard on Max. You should talk to him. He doesn't understand," Anna advised.

"I know, mother," Abi said, downplaying the situation. "We are going through a rough patch, but Julien will be back. I don't see any need to alarm Max. Everything will fall back into place in the flash of an eye," she argued.

Her mother paused for a little too long. Abi asked the question her mother was itching to ask.

"Aren't you going to ask me what happened?" she said preemptively.

"No, Agondo. Julien gave me his version, but he was quite angry. He screamed more than he spoke, and I must admit that I didn't listen to every word he said. Max is confused and sad. I guess you'll tell your own side of the story when you are ready," she said.

She sighed and added:

"You are quite resourceful, my dear. I trust you. You'll find a way out. In the meantime, if things are really so complicated, consider sending Max over here. I understand if you are reluctant, but it would just be temporary while you figure things out. Same as when the pressure inside an airplane is dropping, my daughter, you must first put on your own oxygen mask before you can think of saving anybody else. The same principle applies in this situation. You can send Max here while you catch your breath. Max likes it here in Douala, anyway. He has friends here—Ismaël, Jenny, Tina. It would do him some good to get away from everything, to have a change of scenery, to be in a place where there are fewer problems. Don't you agree?"

Abi did not respond right away. She was hurt and outraged by her mother's proposal. Because she had been unable to keep her husband, Anna wanted to take her child away from her. She responded with false calm.

"That's kind of you but no thanks. We're simply going through a rough patch. Nothing more. Nothing less!" she said before hanging up.

Julien was still nowhere to be found. Abi found herself suddenly surrounded by a void. Friends deserted her. She imagined all the gossiping behind her back. The whispered remarks. Nobody pities a cheating woman—she endangers the stock. The bloodline. Something precious. These couples with their fake alliances, she was well positioned to know, were judging her. Embattled couples act like a repellent to stable unions, everyone steers clear for fear of contamination. For fear that their own imperfections would be spotlighted. Everyone secretly rejoicing that this time around, the axe has not fallen on them.

The high school principal called them. Abi tried in vain to reach Julien to tell him about the appointment. She showed up alone, anticipating Max's disappointment when he discovered that even on this occasion, his father, who had always been very keen on education, hadn't come.

"Maxime is unrecognizable," the principal sighed. "He was an exemplary student, but he is now becoming the most difficult in the entire school. His grades are in free fall, when he even bothers to attend classes or sit for exams. He has a ghastly attitude. Except for the fact that we have known him for so long, we would be quite a bit less accommodating. I have never seen a student's behavior change so radically in such a short span of time. One would think this is no longer our Maxime but an evil twin. Something needs to be done, Madame Achard. We can't tolerate such behavior for much longer," the principal concluded.

Max was staring out of the window, slouched in his chair as if unconcerned. Abi was fidgeting, humbled by this man who was talking to her about the stranger her son had become.

"Our family is grappling with a major crisis," she finally admittedly with a thin voice. "It has affected Max."

She had known Martin, the principal, since Max started at the school. She was the chair of the Parent Teacher Association. Up until then, her son had received nothing but congratulations and compliments during class council meetings. She had adopted the haughty attitude of those parents who have it easy. A little contempt for others with troublesome children. Max was her source of pride. Her ultimate hubris. He had never disappointed her. And never before had she disappointed him.

"A family crisis?" the teenager grumbled. "That's a first. I was not aware. Tell Mr. Martin what the crisis is all about, mother," he said.

The principal reacted firmly.

"Mr. Achard, I will not have you use that tone with your mother in my presence," he announced.

"You are not my father, idiot!" replied the kid before getting up and exiting the room, leaving the door wide open to underscore the total lack of consideration he had for the meeting.

ANNA

I would be dead if not for books. All books.

I devoured every book I could lay my hands on. I read indiscriminately. Entranced by those unsuspected parallel galaxies. Literature gave me the means to escape my reality by inviting me into new worlds. A new way of being that I could access with nothing more than my eyes and my mind.

I read and my world lit up. The scales fell from my eyes. I became more aware. I read and nature spoke an audible language to me.

In my village, the nighthawk was seen as a bird of bad omen that killed children about to be born. Despite its infamous reputation, its even, oscillating song brightened my evenings because it meant the onset of those blessed moments of solitude when I could, released from the constraints of the day and the supervision of the sisters, throw myself, body and soul, into my reading marathons.

Some nights, unable to put down a book, hypnotized by the horrible fates of characters, I felt way more than

I heard in the sleeping presbytery. The silent cries moths made in their already-lost battle against the hurricane lamp. The cackling sound of the wood in the night. The murmur of the wind bumping against the roof, caressing pillars, leading them in a mystical ballet. And I won't forget the frogs croaking and fighting in the nearby stream, and the hooting of an owl out hunting.

I was there, fully awake. But also in the English countryside, where an old madwoman had high hopes for an orphan girl taken in with ulterior motives. Or in a casino in Paris, next to a young man wasting his life in games of chance, ultimately losing it one franc at a time. Or in the Russian winter with a young woman named Anna, like me, who'd left her husband and child out of love for a man who hadn't expected much, and who threw himself under a train out of spite because that's just the way it is. Life and authors severely punish women who fall for crooked men.

I jotted down unconnected sentences in a notebook. I have since lost that notebook. I can still remember some passages by heart. *Vronsky stared at her the way a man stares at a flower he has picked. In this withering flower, he had a hard time seeing the beauty that had made him pick it and cause it to perish.*

Countless worlds offered as a gift! My little room was filling up with ghosts. Crinoline-dressed ladies. Top hat-wearing men. Noisy station platforms. Men trapped in their thoughts as they waited next to a river for the trout to take the bait... Colorful, rich, complex worlds that were all mine and appealed only to me. Colorful, rich, complex worlds created solely for the purpose of this meeting—when another person's creation connected seamlessly with my private world, aligned with my soul in new, indescribable emotions.

Up next was dawn, which I recognized by its perfume. The darkness outside would be stark, but I could feel the already smoother morning breeze coming and the smell of the dew on the grass. The stars went out one after the other, lowering the curtains on my window of freedom. I knew almost exactly, as if tipped off by an inner and infallible clock, when the first cocks would crow. I would have to get up. Take a bath and make breakfast for the sisters. Wait for them to finish eating. Do the dishes. Clean the yard and then head off to school. So, I read faster. Just one more. Just one more sentence. Let me just finish the paragraph. No, the chapter... Please, I pleaded for time, but my body was all too aware of its chores.

The school library teemed with books. More and more kept coming in. Truckloads of them. Somebody back there in their home country was passionate about transforming Africans into knowledgeable beings. Few people took any interest in the library. Students contented themselves with the compulsory textbooks. The reverend sisters contended themselves with their bible and their prayer book. Books piled up on the shelves, but I made sure dust didn't settle on them.

The reverend sisters ultimately noticed my insatiable hunger for reading. This is how the conversation would begin: "Hey, Anna, you like to read. That's great!"

And would continue on, "Do you understand everything you're reading?" Before ending with this part, which I'd overhear: "We must at least monitor what she reads. Such an unsophisticated spirit can't be exposed to some texts." I was saved by the young priest who oversaw extracurricular activities at the school. "Reading can't hurt her, Sister Brigitte. She doesn't have to understand everything, but these books are made to be read, right?" he argued.

I suspect nothing more was said about the matter, not only because he had convinced them that I was accomplishing, by reading them, the destiny of these books, but also because these reverend sisters were sure that I didn't have what it took to understand the nuances of the literature I was stuffing myself with.

Nobody taught me how to analyze a book. How to read from a safe distance. How not to lose sight of context. How to grasp the things left unsaid. About schools of thought and even the basic ideologies that are supposed to underpin a mundane story. Nobody taught me aesthetics, language... All of that, I only discovered in college, where I studied social sciences and broadened my knowledge at the Higher Teachers' Training College in Yaounde, from which I graduated as a French teacher. But it had already become a habit. All my life, I read the same way I had started off. Intensely. Passionately. Primally. And sentence fragments stuck with me.

> *Thing is, we need misfortune for every song*
> *Thing is, we need regret to get chills...*

Books appeased me. Made me angry. Made me strong. They make me laugh and cry. They pushed me to analyze existence. To trust my intuition. To use my spirit to understand, against the backdrop of characters, nature, and plot, the symphony of the intimate time that beams our being to the world.

As a child, I read and felt less lonely. Less insignificant. Less vulnerable. As an adult, I worked hard to understand that although reading had not made me a better person, it had made me more level-headed and aware of my own motivations. Freer as well.

Louis, who would eventually become my husband, was holding a copy of *Discourse on Colonialism* the first time we met. What does a life depend on?

When I received my brevet diploma, the reverend sisters enrolled me in the girls' secondary school the congregation had created in Yaounde, which was now the capital of our country that had been liberated from the yoke of colonization. This time around, I would be in boarding school, with other students. I would no longer have to scrub to pay for my keep.

I am being a bit caustic, but I am fully aware of all I owe these women. They believed in me. They paid for my tuition. Enabled me to access a certain tier of culture that I embraced devotedly. They taught me principles and values. For this, I will forever be grateful to them. I similarly know that they fooled, manipulated, and broke me into a thousand pieces. They behaved like I was clay, and they could me shape as they saw fit. I bear them no ill will. The outcome has been quite different from what they'd hoped. Not that it exceeds their expectation. It is just different from what they could have expected. They gave me the tools to create a perfectly unique mosaic, full of books, culture, experiences, but also of Awaya plunging deep into the forest to harvest her medicinal herbs.

I am the product of the generosity of the reverend sister who was the first to call me Anna and who widened my horizons. I am also the product of the protection of Samgali and my deceased mothers. I am the product of movies and music. Of the contradictions that ripple through my country. The political consciousness born from a covert, dirty war. Covert because it was dirty and set Bamileke country on fire, whose cause I took up, if only figuratively, by marrying a Bamileke man.

Louis thought that Verdi's "Va, pensiero" best captured the tragedy unfolding in his native land. No other song on earth expressed with such keen intensity a people's yearning for freedom. He read Césaire, Damas, Fanon, Sartre, and the Russian greats. Listened to Verdi, Fela, Myriam Makeba, Anne-Marie Nzié, and Congolese rumba. Coltrane, Miles Davis, jazz would come much later. He was also a brilliant product of that hybrid upbringing that bruised and mended us at the same time.

Louis told me stories about the ravages of the war for independence. The Union of the Peoples of Cameroon, a political party fighting for the actual liberation of the country, had been banned. Its members killed. Assassinated. People decimated and terrorized. And the country was offered some semblance of sovereignty with the approval of international bodies. Those who resisted took up arms and moved into Bamileke country. Local politicians, put in power by the former colonial masters to perpetuate the domination, savagely cracked down on the rebellion. Now that the country was independent, every form of protest was considered an act of sedition and punished accordingly.

Louis told me about villages burned down in Bamileke country. About men who were arrested in the night, and whose lifeless and headless bodies were found on the side of the road in the early morning. About the brutal repression inflicted on the resistance fighters and of the residents trapped in the bloody space in between.

A movie released in Europe ten years earlier made headlines in Yaounde. Billed as a classic, it showcased the tactical intelligence of the allies and the bravery of foot soldiers during the Second World War: *The Longest Day* told the story of the Normandy landing from various points of view. We marveled at the unbelievable courage of those young soldiers. In that part of the world, the war was a thing of strategy, courage, virility, *and* victory. Louis flared up when the movie showed three French parachutists blowing up railway lines with the support of the Resistance. "Who will help our own insurgents? While the West numbs our senses with its propaganda, our own people are being killed and nobody cares. According to them, our resistance fighters are terrorists, while their fighters are heroes, even though our land is under occupation, too. A collaborator regime assassinates us mercilessly," he argued.

Louis said, "my people" and not "our people" when referring to the Bamileke. In his opinion, the entire country
had surrendered. Only his people continued the struggle.
Inebriated with Western promises, we boasted about our
sham independence. *Sham* was the right word, recalling
the shameless trade of the past when humans were traded
for worthless glass. Our very own armed forces massacred their own people.

"When will we understand that the purpose of these
manipulations is to pit us against one another? Are we
ever going to see reason?" he lashed out in desperation.

Louis cried, talking about the macabre spectacle of severed human heads. The mystical belief of the
Bamileke is built around the preservation and worship of
the skulls of their ancestors. Killing an enemy is an act of
war. Chopping off his head, pinning his body like a scare-
crow on the roadside was a larger, crueler plan to destroy
even his spirituality. To assassinate him in this life and in
the next. To humiliate him. Defeat his spirit as well as his
body. Destroy him—even his ashes and bone... The final
solution! The puppet masters did not matter so long as
our own government was doing the dirty work.

Throughout my many years in Cameroon, I had several
opportunities to reflect on the nature of our peoples'
bonds and Louis's impressive intuition about the disas-
ters that awaited us.

We had built ourselves on the blood of our brothers.
We had desecrated their spirits. Our country was built
on the Cain syndrome. Although other civilizations were

also built on violence, chaos, and betrayal, they had been able to give meaning to the sacrifices. They had found a rational explanation for it. In fact, from scratch they concocted legends to atone for the horror when they couldn't justify it, and that made it possible to erect a founding utopia. Cameroon contented itself with shrouding its tragedy in silence. Silence laced with an explosive cocktail of sorrow, aggressiveness, self-pity, and mistrust. Trapped in this tight corner, our deep desire to create a nation, our intelligence, our humanity disappeared as if a bad spell had been cast on us. We were our brothers' keepers. We inherited the land of our fathers. What had we done with it? We looted our own property, for others or our own immediate interests. We sold off our judgment, our future, that of our children with our compulsive, pathological greed.

Over the past years, our country has turned into an association of evildoers, where everyone pays tribute to the strongest person and demands ransom from the poorest. The widespread corruption and its targeted retaliation ate away at us like gangrene, fueling our frustration and injustice, helplessness and insecurity. The human spirit adapts to the worst scenarios to survive. The strong desire not to be among those who have fallen to be crushed by the crowd has kept us standing, but at what cost?

Even my Louis's ideal-rich sorrow ultimately gave way to greed, driven by the prevailing rot.

✳

Two weekends every month, the boarding school students were allowed to receive visitors. So family, friends, fiancées arrived for a great moment of joy prepared days beforehand.

Most of my classmates were the daughters of high-ranking civil servants. Some were the second or third generation from their families to attend school. In fact, some of them had traveled from as far as Europe and wore the veneer of sophistication that only education offers. I came from the back country and owed my presence in this place only to the generosity of the reverend sisters. They supplied me with oversized secondhand clothes, toiletries, and each month I had to pass by the clinic to collect menstrual pads. Needless to add that lipstick, perfume, and other cosmetics were not included in the care package. Awaya distilled *manyanga* for me, the oil extracted from palm nuts. I used it as my body and hair lotion. That was the only beauty product I owned. I was conscientious because my grandmother and the reverend sisters had seen to it that I should be. However, the obsession with appearance common at that age wasn't part of my character.

That weekend, as always, I watched as the other girls did their hair and makeup without sharing their excitement about the prospect of visitors. Without even envying them.

Marguerite Tchomté, daughter of a government official, undisputed queen of the dormitory, tried on several outfits before finally choosing the one that fit her best. Her parents and her fiancé, a student at the Advanced School of Administration and Magistracy—where our

top-ranking civil servants were trained—never missed a
visiting day. As I stepped out of the bathroom, a towel
wrapped under my arms, she handed me a dress, saying, "Have this, Agoumé. Try it on. I've worn it a lot
already; I no longer want it." I put on the dress and noticed something strange while pulling up the zipper. A
flash of lightning up my back. I could feel the fabric on
me because the dress was just my size. There were five of
us in the dormitory. The other girls looked at me differently. "Agoumé, when you're not wearing your usual potato sack, you're quite pretty!" they confessed. The dress,
typical of the sixties, was red with white polka dots. The
body-hugging top had a bustier that showed off my chest,
and thin straps tied behind the neck, leaving the back
open. The bottom, wide and pleated, ended just above the
knees. "To think you hide such beautiful breasts!" someone shouted. Marguerite and I had the same slender
shape. Her dress fit me like a glove.

I put on my only worn-out, fitting ballerina pumps,
which were straight out of the Ali Baba cave of the sisters, and was about to hurry with the others to the refec-
tory where the visitors were already swarming, when I
remembered that I was not expecting anyone. I slowed to
allow myself to pick up the book I was reading. I decided
to spend my day in the company of the Joad family on
their quest for a piece of the promised land where they
could settle down and make an honest living from the
fruits of their hard work.

I climbed down the stairs and made my way through
the crowd. I wanted to step out into the garden, sit on

a bench in the sun, and read quietly before returning to my dormitory. I never ate with the others. I had a perfect technique: At the end of the meal, when everyone was scattered all over the garden, I'd head to the kitchen for some leftovers, so I could eat undisturbed. Absorbed in my plan, I didn't hear him call me. He put his hand on my shoulder just as I was about to leave the main hall.

"Maguy, I have been calling you this whole time. Are you deaf? Where are you flying off to? One would think you're trying to escape," he said.

I turned around and he immediately removed his hand.

"Sorry, I mistook you for someone else," he apologized.

"Don't worry," I said smiling. "Maguy is surely in the hall. You won't have a hard time finding her," I added.

I was tall for a girl, but he wasn't for a boy. He was barely taller than me despite the ballet pumps I was wearing. I noticed his muscular body, which would eventually fill out. At that moment, there was no way to guess whether he would get fat. I also noticed his eyes, lively, deeply set in their sockets, and his wide, smiling mouth. He had forgotten to dress in the bell bottom trousers popular back in those days, or the suit and tie so precious to ENAM trainees. He had opted for a pair of jeans beneath a checked shirt with rolled-up sleeves. This detail made me smile. Marguerite would surely have preferred to see him in a suit and tie.

"That dress looks better on you than on anybody else," he said, walking off.

I'm not claiming I have cornered the market on suffering by telling my life story. I'm simply revealing what I really was. A young orphan girl and, except for an old illiterate woman back in my village, nobody cared about me. If Awaya hadn't decided it, I wouldn't be an educated woman. If the reverend sisters had not given me an education, I would now be married to some village man who still wanted me despite my ill-fated ancestry. My life would mainly revolve around bearing children and farming. I have never cared about my clothes. My sole worry has only been that they be clean. For the first time ever in my life, I was ashamed of my outfit. I felt humiliated that someone would recognize another person's dress on me and point it out. I was angry with Marguerite for giving me this poisoned gift and worse still hated myself for accepting it. For having felt so pretty. So different. Cinderella for only a day, thinking I was a princess among other princesses.

I was angry and sad in a strange way. Come to think of it, not much was said. But just enough to unsettle me. In those sorts of moments, I always had only one solution: I sat down on a bench and immersed myself in my reading.

"What are you reading?" he enquired.

I hadn't heard him coming. Breakfast was over. The students and their visitors had broken out into small groups all over the garden. I closed the book, a finger marking the page, and showed him the cover.

"Steinbeck, excellent choice," he said.

I didn't reply. The reputation was that the students

from our school were intellectuals. Or that, in any case, they preferred educated men. Every visiting weekend, I saw them arrive, book in hand or shelved in the pocket, going on and on about Césaire, Kant, Camus, Sartre, or other authors. Flaunting their intellects to young girls whose general knowledge rarely went beyond the picture supplement in *Nous Deux* magazine.

"How far are you into the story?" he asked.

"Where the young Joad joins his family in California," I answered.

"I remember the moment he returns home after prison to discover that the bank has foreclosed on their house, and he sets out to nowhere. In as much as it is a scathing critique of capitalism, the novel opines that poverty is a relative concept. Although they are the ground, and trampled upon, the Joads own a car. They find camps to host them. Their living conditions are deplorable, no doubt. There is death, misery, famine. But take a minute and imagine that same scenario happening here. These people would long be dead. You will see. The end is both splendid and horrible. Quite poetic," he explained.

Okay, I admitted it to myself. He had read the book. I gave him that. One random novel. The other kids in his class did not stoop so low as to read novels. They read philosophical, economic essays, lampoons, newspapers. But no novels, the preserve of girls!

"When you're done reading this, if you can, read *Of Mice and Men*. I think you'll like it," he suggested.

"I read *Of Mice and Men*. Thank you, Sir!" I responded.

Louis sat down next to me on the bench, I can't say

why. The conversation immediately shifted to the political situation in our country. He swiftly swung to the topic closest to him. The planned, calculated massacre of the Bamileke people.

This country is strange. It already was back then. I lived in Yaounde, a secluded place, rather insulated from the external disorder. I knew that we had gained our independence, but I only had a vague sense of the deadly tensions, the ongoing fighting in Bassa country and Douala, or the ordeal suffered by the Bamileke.

"We're at war. Did you know that?" Louis told me. "Do you hear the sound of guns, machetes, executions carried out where you live? In this same country, while we sleep in our soundproof bubbles, some have taken up arms to fight for a fairer, less-diluted freedom. Nonviolent resistance? Um Nyobè believed that and it killed him. You get what I'm driving at. Day in and day out, we are force-fed the ideals of Gandhi, Martin Luther King Jr., and others. But nonviolent resistance supposes that the almighty enemy at least considers you to be a human being, capable of logically arguing why you disagree. It supposes that this enemy is ready to hear your convictions, make compromises. Bamileke resistance fighters took up arms. That's a fact! Did they have a choice? The colonial masters feigned a retreat. Their cruel puppets continue to safeguard their interests through murder. We have been cheated. Our struggle has been used to different ends. And you will see, they'll chop off any head that stands out, and then falsify our history. They won't even bother to write it, our history."

"Who is 'they'?" I asked.

"This 'they' is 'we,'" replied Louis. "We're the ones killing ourselves. Our killers are encouraged, trained, and funded by the former colonial master. But this is what really hurts, we do their dirty work with unthinking enthusiasm!"

That was how Cameroon—not only for myself as an individual and my village, Ombessa, Bafia, and Yaounde, the places where I had lived, but also the multilayered, nuanced, bruised entity called my country—became something quite real to me.

We talked till visiting hours were over. On several occasions, Marguerite, or one of her emissaries, came to remind Louis of his responsibilities. "I'm coming," he'd reply, unmoved, before continuing to speak.

Was I aware of the situation? Did it bring me joy? The prince was not keeping his promise to Cinderella. Sincerely speaking, with respect to those special moments, I wasn't thinking about them. I was as indifferent to them as possible. It's so hard to imagine it now. Now that everyone has friends, when social media and free internet connection makes it possible to speak, even to strangers, night and day. But that was the first time in my life I was having an actual conversation. That I was having an ordinary conversation with someone. Louis latched on to my responses. Answered them with passion. Clearly liked my company. I listened as much as I spoke, and this was a first. I developed an idea. He replied. Enriched it. I interrupted him because I understood what he was trying to say, even before he could complete his sentence. And he finished my sentences. I argued. Constructed and explained my line of reasoning. I discovered that I loved it and that I was gifted.

There would come a time where we would stop talking to one another and, of all the illusions lost during our union, all the things that have humiliated and hurt me, all those disappointments that have followed, that particular one would be the most painful.

I immediately sensed the animosity of my classmates when I returned to the dormitory at the end of the visit. Until then, they had paid me no mind. I was discreet and accommodating. There was no rivalry between us. We were not in the same league. By spending the afternoon with the fiancé of the "star of the school," I had stepped into the limelight in an odd, inappropriate manner. And they let me know.

Marguerite did not have to say it. Her girlfriends made sure I knew immediately when I stepped into the room:

"You! You pretend to be innocent, a bookworm, reading every day, answering 'Yes, my reverend sister,' but you've been ogling other people's boyfriends," one said accusingly.

I kept walking without responding to the young girl attacking me. She moved to block me from getting through. An aggressive attitude that indicated she was spoiling for a fight.

"I'm talking to you, Agoumé!" she continued.

I could fight. Without any doubt! These city girls, coming from the heavily guarded houses of their parents, driven here in chauffeured cars, did not have the slightest idea what it meant to spend your childhood in the village, farming the land and carrying loads weighing more than you on your head. A place where the slightest uncontrollable childhood peccadillo resulted in a proper fight and ended with a beating by your parents.

I pushed her back, *tutting* with aggressiveness.

"Get out of my way or I will beat you so bad your mother won't be able to recognize you," I warned.

I was well aware that a fight could also be won simply by stepping up. You had to display violence, spite, stronger resolve than the opponent, look itchy for confrontation.

"Who are you talking to like that?" she asked.

I could see her coming from kilometers away. I felt the moment when she decided that the insult deserved a greater response. I struck first, with all the violence I could muster. A straight blow to the stomach. I knew that would take her breath away. That all that would be left to do would be to grab her, hold her still by her hands and then, with my foot, kick out her legs and let her crash to the ground. Back in my village, that was known as "sweeping." Game over!

Where I came from, we didn't fight the way girls do. Pulling hair and whining. When we fought, the goal was to inflict as much harm as possible. To extinguish in our opponent any desire to confront us again.

Queen Marguerite, quiet so far, finally stepped in, speaking to her friend.

"Come on, Marie-Louise. I've already told you your altitude depends on your attitude. How can you stoop so low as to fight with an Agoumé?" she asked.

It was still a fight, but this time around with gloves on. The words hit different than the physical aggression, which had accomplished nothing besides angering me. They may have been richer and more sophisticated than I would ever be, but words were my forte and they knew it.

"You better be careful. Don't put yourself in harm's way! To spare yourself a concussion, I'd suggest you use words that you understand before things get out of hand. Your brain might not survive too much complexity," I snickered, using the most formal language I could.

I tsked in disdain before undressing and stepping into my pajamas. I carefully folded the dress and returned it to Marguerite.

"Here you go, and thanks for the gift," I said.

She was talking in hushed tones with her girlfriends and didn't even raise her head.

"You don't really think I, Marguerite Tchomté, will ever wear that dress again. Put it in the trash, or better still, keep it. It's not like you have another one after all," she said.

In her own way, Marguerite was a warrior. She also had some arrows that never missed their target. I had made the strategic mistake of not ending the fight when I'd had the upper hand. She didn't miss me. I placed the dress on the bed and no walk seemed as long as the one I had to take back to my bed.

The days that followed confirmed that I had been ostracized. Marguerite and her friends stopped talking to me. They mocked my worn-out clothes and girls I had never noticed before suddenly took an interest in me. "Agoumé, is it true you taught Marie-Louise Mbarga a lesson?" they kept asking me in the corridors.

The school buzzed like a beehive.

From transparent, I became overexposed. The topic of gossip. But it didn't affect me. My encounter with Louis and our discussion had stirred so much joy in me. A feeling of happiness so strong that nothing could change it. For the first time in my life, a man, and not just any man, had looked at me, chosen me, Anna, over one of these girls who had everything they desired.

Louis came back to see me the following visiting days. He had that kind of courage. He greeted Marguerite and her girlfriends. Then he had lunch with me—now I also had a visitor. I began to like this ritual of eating together. Later, we settled in the garden. A little away from the others, and we continued our discussion from where we had left it the previous month.

I felt anger and tension rising in him every time we met. He brought me news from the Bamileke front. And then one day, the sentence I had been dreading was uttered.

"I should go there you know? I'm angry staying here while my people are massacred," he announced.

"Don't be stupid," I interrupted him.

He stopped talking about leaving but I could feel that it was not the end of the matter.

I found dormitory bullying and gossip to be something superficial. "You offer him caviar but he prefers beans. If his level is Agoumé, really, there's nothing more to say. God has chosen to open my eyes before I would have started my life with this man," I heard Marguerite tell her friends.

Lord, may your name be praised for having chosen team beans over bitter team caviar, I said to myself sarcastically.

After my last discussion with Louis, I no longer paid her any attention. We discussed war. Commitment. The country's fate. We were above those childish things, I thought, filled with my brand-new sense of self-worth.

I went home as usual for the Christmas holidays. Louis came to get me at the entrance to the boarding school.

Back then, holding hands in public, not to mention kissing, was out of the question. We had met during visiting weekends and no physical contact was possible in my school run by Catholic sisters. Louis never said anything out of place. Looks were the highlight of our intimacy. That didn't stop me from fantasizing about the moment when he would place his lips on mine, dreaming about embracing, abundantly fueled by the books I ravenously consumed.

On the way to the bus station, he offered: "Would you mind coming to my place for a drink before you board your bus?"

Louis's family lived in Yaounde but he had a room in the university hostel. It was sparse: a bed, a table, a gas stove for a kitchen, and a curtain rod hung in one corner for a wardrobe. A standard student room with a shared bathroom and toilets.

We dropped my little travel bag and went to a nearby

shop to get drinks. Louis opened the bottles of Coca-
Cola, handed me one before sitting on the bed. "Sit over
here with me. You'll be more comfortable," he told me.

In this situation, just as in many other experiences in
my life, my childhood back in the village collided with
my upbringing at the hands of the reverend sisters.

Most girls from my generation in Ombessa were
now housewives. I understood that my virginity was
precious, easily the most precious thing I owned and I
didn't have to give it to the first guy who came along lest
I mess up my life. Throughout my schooling, I had witnessed girls drop out because of unwanted pregnancies,
or abort in horrible conditions. Those who fell through
the cracks thought, if what they said was anything to go
by, that no guy would respect you if you let him touch
you at all, so why not take the plunge? You had to give
them just the strictest minimum to arouse desire, which
would then be fully assuaged only when they put a ring
around your finger. Guys deployed every possible strategy to make us falter but we, "good girls," had to per-
sistently resist.

I did not feel vulnerable in the arms of Louis. Or
trapped either. Or anything of the sort. It was the complete opposite. I was testing the power, the influence over
others that I hadn't known I had, when Louis put my
hand on his penis. "I have been thinking about this ever
since I saw your low neckline that first time in the refec-
tory," he murmured. The same could be said of Steinbeck
and the revolt in Bamileke country!

We did not go all the way that time. Louis walked

me like a good boy to the Etoudi bus station where I boarded my bus.

But for the feeling of power triggered by Louis's moans as I caressed him, my own feelings were still a haze. Despite everything, far from him, I would embellish, romanticize what was nothing more than a far-fetched flirtation, transforming it into an incident dripping with sensuality and romanticism. That was the first male body I touched. It had had to be an irrepressible amorous encounter, or else what was it? And what did that make me?

Louis came to visit me in the village the next week.

After the year-end festivities that I experienced in a daze, dreamy and frustrated like any self-respecting girl in love, I was ready for what came next.

The bus dropped him off at the Ombessa bus station. He asked some passers-by and was finally led to Awaya's house one fine afternoon in January. We had finished our chores and I had chosen to stay back at the river to have my evening bath, leaving my grandmother to return home alone. She received him kindly and had him sit in the yard, giving him a bowl of water and some fresh ground nuts before sending a little boy to tell me I had a visitor.

"Someone's waiting for you at your house," the child told me.

I knew it was him right away. I had waited, hoped for him. I had dreamed of the moment when he'd appear on the horizon, a knight in shining armor, and he had come. "Bring him here," I said impulsively. We were more or less all related in the village. Anything that happened in a neighbor's house was discussed, interpreted over and over. The people Louis had approached along the way knew me very well. I could trace the splash that this strange young man's visit would cause. Although virginity was not considered sacred in these parts, and at my age a relationship with a man was expected and even wished for, no intimacy was possible under the probing eyes of Awaya and the other women in the village.

Louis sat down next to me, on the cloth that I had laid on the ground. I hadn't stood up when he arrived. I wasn't sure if my wobbly knees would support the tempestuous shiver of my body and my pounding heart.

"They have killed Ernest Ouandié," he told me, sounding defeated. "I came to tell you goodbye. I have decided to go to Bafoussam. I contacted a cell of fighters. They are looking for young men like me, educated and committed, to spread their message. I can no longer fold my arms and do nothing. I am going to join the resistance," he told me.

Is there anything more noble, more glamourous, more exciting on this earth than a young man heading off to war?

I tried to talk him out of it. He refused to listen to what I had to say. His life would have no meaning if he did not go. He could no longer look at himself in the mirror.

Our lips locked. I begged him to take me with him. I too was educated. I too could serve the cause. He wanted me to be safe. To stay far from the turmoil and bullets.

He could not give his best if he knew I was in harm's way.

My breath against his breath, I burst into tears and he drank them straight from my eyelids.

With him inside me, I swore to always wait for him.

Over our intertwined bodies, I made him promise that he would come back alive, because I would die if something happened to him.

That is how I lost my inestimable virginity. On a farm. On the banks of a river. In a swirl of emotions. The heroine in the story of my life. That is how Abi was conceived.

Louis's escapade lasted a couple of weeks. I'd later learn that his father was a bigwig in the Ministry of Interior. Right at the heart of the system that was exterminating the resistance. He soon sent the police and the gendarmes on the heels of his runaway son. Louis's presence, rather than help them, heightened the pressure exerted on the cell he had joined from the forces of the law. He was no longer held in such high esteem. Someone surely sold him out because he was picked up on his way to a meeting of the group. Alone. By chance. Nobody had wanted to go with him. He was forcibly brought back to his family where he had to answer for his actions, not only for him but for the entire family.

The government of Cameroon was waging a merciless war and didn't tolerate traitors. Not only was he risking his life, and if he were hurt his mother would not survive it, but his father would have an uphill task proving his own innocence, too. His father might lose his job. Worst of all, his father could end up in Tchollire or in one of the other prisons littered all over the country where rebels were tortured, about which he was in a good position to know. Is that really what he wanted? Did he want misfortune to strike his family? Didn't he pity his mother one bit?

Family pressure finally won where my passion had only succeeded in exacerbating his desire to distinguish himself. Louis stepped back in line, never to cross it again. I'm exaggerating when I say his last act of rebellion was marrying me.

It's not necessary to revisit the extreme agitation I was in after he left. Awaya didn't ask any questions, limiting herself to holding me more than she ever had before and calling me *Agondo*, without it ringing any alarms in my head.

I returned to college after the holidays with no news from Louis. There was no way I could have had any and that only made me more anxious. He didn't come to see me during the first weekend of visits. I was not expecting him to come anyway, but something died in me at the end of the day once all hope was lost. "Agoumé, has your love already dumped you?" Tchomté's crew asked me provocatively.

I was heavyhearted. My nights were full of nightmares and mornings full of sickness. I lost weight. The slightest thing made me cry. Even my precious books could no longer console me. My grades felt the pinch. The reverend sisters were worried about my health. In fact, I was sick. The ailment I suffered from was called distant love. Unsatisfied desire. Severe anxiety. I was not sure they could heal me.

When the mother superior asked to see me, I hadn't heard from Louis for two months and was but a shadow of myself.

"How are you, Anna?" she asked me.

"I'm fine, Sister. I've been a little tired lately but nothing serious," I replied.

She was silent for a moment, staring straight at me. Barely bothered, I wondered what would come next, eager to return to what I'd been doing. To what filled my thoughts, day and night. Why had Louis not contacted me? Was he alive at least?

"You are doing so fine that for the past two months you haven't come to pick up your sanitary pads?" she ended up adding.

I had barely eaten anything over the previous days because I kept throwing up. My nighttime restlessness only made matters worse. When my mind finally processed the full meaning of what she had just said, I sank into my seat.

I regained consciousness in the clinic and was immediately aware of my situation. Even before I opened my eyes, the word *Pregnant!* hit me like a door closing. Tears welled up in my eyes. The mother superior and the sister in charge of the clinic were standing nearby.

"This is no time for tears. You should have thought about that before," said the mother superior sternly.

"And you don't have to starve yourself," added the nurse, pointing to my ribs, visible under my skin.

I'm not the girl you think I am! I felt like shouting into their faces. *My love is at war. Maybe dead as we speak. Maybe my child will never know her father.*

"Oh, Anna. You are so unique. So intelligent. I had such great plans for you. How could you have made such a silly mistake? How could you have thrown away your future so casually?" sighed the mother superior.

I had just turned eighteen. I guess her hopes for me hadn't included contraception. Or even a clear explanation of my menstrual cycle to help me take care of myself autonomously. The only method known to the girls in my class and myself was *coitus interruptus*. Doubtfully effective given the number of unwanted pregnancies that knocked out my classmates one after the other, forcing them to drop out of school. The hopes didn't take into account my body as a full-grown woman or the possibility that I might meet someone I'd love. Talk less of my own ambitions. They were better situated than me to know what I needed. They mapped out my path. What I owed them in return was submission and abstinence.

"Since when have you been like this?" she enquired.

"January," I answered.

"Well then, you will probably be due late September or early October. This gives you time to sit for your *Baccalaureate* exams. We don't usually host pregnant girls. It's very bad for our image. But I am willing to make an exception because you deserve it and I know you will make good use of it. After that, I will no longer be able to help you. We had planned to send you to France to continue your studies. That can no longer be the case. After your exams, you will have to manage on your own. Is the father of this child planning to meet his responsibilities?" she asked.

I remained silent.

"I thought as much. Always the same old story," she murmured, leaving.

I started long and pitiful negotiations with the Lord.

If He let Louis return, let's say by the next visiting weekend, if He inspired him to ask me to marry him, I would spend the rest of my life singing His praise and blessing His Holy Name. I pleaded with the Virgin Mary. I appealed to the mother, the woman in her. She knew I was not a loose girl. She could see my heart. I asked her to forgive me for my sins. I begged her, she who had God's ear, to intercede with Him on my behalf. I stood at my window and watched cars go by. If the next one was red, Louis would come to see me and ask me to marry him. When the car was black, I changed the bet. If a woman appeared at the street corner, I would marry Louis. If a man appeared... And it was a couple that showed up instead. My catechism classes came to mind. God hates to be put to the test. Like when Jesus was tempted by the devil in the desert. Since I had entrusted my cares to the Lord, I had to forfeit any other intercession lest I irritate Him. So I went down on my knees, asking for His forgiveness for my stupidity. For my lack of belief.

Deep down I understood the anguish suffered by the wives of sailors and soldiers, of Penelope doing and then undoing her magic.

Louis came the following weekend and, elated, I forgot to thank Heaven.

In the *Odyssey*, the studious solitude of Penelope had struck me less than Ulysses's impossible return. He had waged wars. Fought off monsters. Resisted every temptation in order to come home. Upon his return, neither his grief-stricken wife, his son, nor his wrinkled nanny recognized him. Only his dog welcomed him heartily. I too did not recognize the Louis with whom I had parted ways in this worn-out young man. The fire that I loved so much in his eyes had gone out. Even the way he carried himself was less…impressive. Passionate?

He told me about his adventures. I listened half-heartedly, waiting for him to finish to break the big news.

"I'm pregnant," I told him.

Louis was so taken aback that he stuttered.

"What? Already? I don't understand what you are saying," he stammered.

I came to understand that he was not only dumbfounded, but also terrified. Or was it my own terror reflected in his eyes?

"Are you sure it's mine?" he asked.

I immediately went into prayer mode: *Hail Mary, full of grace…*

"Anna, permit me a little doubt. We have known each other for barely a few months and we only did it once," he argued.

I closed my eyes in a prayer so hard that I nearly tore my eyelids… *Blessed is the fruit of thy womb…*

"How do I know I was the only one, Anna? That you're not tricking me?" he continued.

I was a virgin, idiot! Don't you remember the blood? I screamed under my breath, but I summoned myself to calm. Keep praying. Do not further exasperate the Virgin, God, His saints, any other merciful divinity... *Pray for us sinners...*

"Anna, I don't know what to tell you. Anna, I'm somewhat overwhelmed. Have you heard what I just said? My parents... I don't know, Anna. I can't... Listen, I have to go," he announced.

He left me on that bench, trembling... *Now, and at the hour of our death. Amen.* I can't remember how long I sat there, repeating this litany over and over like some mantra.

Louis disappeared for three long months.

When I returned home for the second term holidays, Awaya came to welcome me at the bus station, something she never did.

"*Agondo bamè*, you have finally arrived. I have been coming every day for the past week. How are you, my child? How is our daughter who's growing in your stomach," she asked.

Not even remotely did I feel compassion for the old woman who had come so far to celebrate my return. She had also called me *Agondo*, meaning young mother, the day my child had been conceived. I was mad at her for welcoming my pregnancy with a joy that I didn't share. That she knew I was pregnant with a girl did not surprise me.

The second I became aware of my state, I understood that
the physical and spiritual distance in which I had placed
my hopes had not protected me from Samgali's legacy.

I felt betrayed. I had done everything to escape the
brutal fate of my mothers. I had studied with all my
might. Sweated and bled while scrubbing the wooden
floor of those reverend sisters. I had been insulted, humiliated. Running down the steep path toward a smoother
future, never had I doubted the necessity of those sacrifices, or the radiant future before me. I deserved a better
destiny. I had fought for that. I was Bouissi and life owed
me a new morning. I was exasperated that my efforts
had as such been in vain. Ultimately, I had found myself
back at square one. Saddled with a child I didn't want.
Rejected by a man who didn't want us. All this to end up
giving birth to yet another girl child without any status.
Without a father. Without a future.

I lay, listless, in my room for days. Awaya cared for
me as if I were suffering from a severe disease and living
out my last days, without the drama of such a situation. I
had never seen her in such high spirits. So joyous.

I didn't go with her to the farm and she did not ask
any questions. Every morning before leaving, she left
me a dish with my lunch. "*Agondo*, I've heated water for
your bath. Get up and take a bath before it gets cold. It
will do you some good. You have to get rid of the night
sweats. Then, eat and rest, okay?" she advised. I didn't
even bother responding. Awaya had given birth to eleven
children—five had passed away in early infancy and one,
my grandfather, had disappeared. She knew better than

anyone that a pregnancy was not a disease requiring that a woman lazes in bed. Pregnant women in our community farmed their plots of land and carried heavy loads until they gave birth.

Village life is tough. Only farm work gives you your livelihood and the respect of your peers. Every man, woman, and child plays a part in the family's welfare, and laziness is the worst flaw imaginable. The Awaya that I knew would have quickly scolded me under normal circumstances, but for reasons she alone knew and that—engrossed in my own melodrama—I did not question, she tolerated all my whims and caprices.

She muttered all the time. To herself? No. This is not an accurate description of the situation, as Awaya spoke to ghosts. The ghost of Samgali. Her favorite person, whom she now mistook for the child to be born. The old woman watched over me. Spoke to me kindly. Cooked my favorite meals and, from sunrise to sunset, Awaya sang, "*Oh my sister, I am waiting ooooh. I am waiting for you. I am waiting along the path with flowers, my little one. I am waiting for you. I've put on the white dress that I reserve for church. My friend, I am waiting for you. I am moving my old hips to the Ibassa, doing that ritual dance calling for twins. For you, my other half, my partner, my feet pound the ground. Look, do you see the dust in the distance? That's me. I am waiting for you. I am waiting in dance. In this life, under this sun, my sister, my friend, my daughter, I am waiting.*"

The day before I left, I finally told her what was on my mind. "If I don't have a man, I can't keep the child," I declared.

I only realized the weight of my decision after I had made it known. I had uttered it like a threat. An ultimate challenge thrown to fate. To the deaf gods of my prayers. To the specters with whom Awaya danced. I was taken aback by my own temerity, but my mind was made up. To my grandmother, this child was a blessing. To the reverend sisters, a responsibility. To me, it was nothing more than a withdrawal. Abdication. An unacceptable hurdle on the road to my future. The old woman didn't say a word, but I heard her talking, reciting, singing all through the night. The following day, she insisted on walking me to the bus. I practically hadn't left my room throughout the holidays. But people had seen me arrive and even my oversized clothes could no longer hide my condition. Along the way, women stopped us, broad smiles splashed across their faces, and said, "Awaya, we will be coming to your house soon to celebrate! Bouissi, fortunately it's the good kind of fever that kept you indoors all this time." Awaya beamed with delight.

Come departure time, she told me in the soft voice that she had used throughout my stay," Go in peace, my daughter. Do you hear me? Go in peace. You will have a man." Then she added, a glimmer of pure happiness lighting up her face, "And we will have the child."

The reaction at school was the opposite of Awaya's. There was laughter there too, but the mocking, sarcastic kind. Hurtful comments, too. "It looks like the great footballer has scored the golden goal…" Marguerite and her friends indulged gleefully. "What did she really expect, this poor girl. Now that he has gotten what he wanted, he's going to dump her like an old pair of socks. Come on, girls. Don't laugh. It's quite pitiful. And it's with these villagers and their bastards that we should build the Cameroon of tomorrow?"

I was too demoralized to fight back.

Louis was a duty-conscious man. Nobody could deny him that. He came back on visiting weekend and informed me, without beating around the bush, without even touching or looking at me:

"We are going to get married."

"Thank you," I blurted out in a breath.

My Abi was born and many years have gone by. I have often wondered whether my state of mind then has influenced my relationship with my daughter. Whether this could account for the relative distance she kept from me. Was a lifetime of watching over her and loving her enough to atone for that early rejection? Should I have talked to her about it? Could any mother confess such a failure?

I was terrified by the idea of raising my child alone. The prospect of going back to Ombessa and farming the fields, my baby strapped to my back, froze me with terror, paralyzing any attempt to imagine the future. After all, I could have passed my Baccalaureate and left my daughter with Awaya for a while to look for work in Yaounde. I could have helmed my ship. Taken my life into my own hands, if not like I had dreamed it, but with dignity at least. That possibility did not cross my mind. I had been ready to get down on my knees and beg that man to marry me and protect my child. That said, gratitude is not one of the many violent and ambivalent feelings that seize me when the ordeals I experienced during that stage of my life are brought up.

Abi took up permanent residence in the hospital room where her mother was dying. Only rarely did Anna know what was happening around her. She talked endlessly, awake or asleep, spurred by the urgent need to bear witness. Her words were usually perfectly audible but sometimes all Abi heard was muffled mumbling. She decided to turn on a tape recorder to record her mother. She took her mother's story for what it was: a will. And Abi didn't feel she had the courage to listen to it in real time.

Anna talked more and more quickly as she became weaker. Names from the past rekindled unhappy memories in Abi: Awaya, Bouissi, Samgali… Her mother was opening trenches in an existence that she had talked about only reluctantly. To innocent questions like, "What was your mother's name?" and "Why do we never visit your village?" Anna offered one-word replies. She mentioned Samgali one evening as they were watching a TV show on migrants: "The first one of us also came from somewhere else you know." Her mother often used this phrase, *the first one of us,* as if Samgali had just appeared out of nowhere to create a lineage of cursed girls in a small village in a hidden country in Central Africa.

Abi pounced on this piece of information the same way you might pull on a thread to undo a ball of yarn. She cross-checked suspected dates and studied all the waves of migration her ancestor could have followed. She discovered frustrating information about fantastic sagas, glorious conquests, legends of brave warriors who transformed into leopards at night to combat invaders from the north. She stumbled upon the story of a totem snake on whose back entire clans crossed the river to escape an attack. But no reference to Samgali. Or to all the men and women who were chased from their homes by violence, misery, and fear. There was no record of Samgali in history books. And without the presence of Anna to testify that she had been here, there would be no trace of her left in the world's mind.

Keeping silent. Leaving things unsaid. That is how her family protected itself. Abi came to terms with it when she discovered the inglorious past of her grandfather in a book that exposed the dark underbelly of Cameroon's war of independence. His zealous commitment to combating the resistance was confirmed by the testimonies of both survivors and the archives. Abi remembered it like it was yesterday. She had just moved in with Julien and Max wasn't born yet. From her apartment in Paris, she felt she had been catapulted into this Cameroon, a place where she had grown up but whose essence she didn't really know. Discovering, in a history textbook, her own family's obscure role in a war that she knew nothing about was deeply troubling. It left her with a feeling of incongruity so intense that the discomfort spread to her body. She had plodded through the rest of the reading and then closed the book never to ever open it again. She had only mentioned it to Julien, with whom, back then, she shared everything. "You know, if my own family's silence about the Second World War is anything to go by, there are probably also dark secrets there. Is it any good to revisit the past?" Julien said.

Abi would have loved to ask her father questions, but she didn't. Her memory of her grandfather was quite different from the despicable character described in the book. He would always be the nice old man who had insisted on speaking to her only in Yemba and took her for long walks among the mountain ranches in Bamboutos. Out of cowardice, or—according to Julien—to protect the future, Abi stayed quiet, respecting the gag order like many others before her.

Anna was now breaking these implicit treaties, but her daughter did not feel she had the power to listen. Not like this. Not now. Not at a time when she already had so much difficulty accepting the idea of her mother's impending death and when the old lady was unable to soften the shock of these revelations. She continued recording, nevertheless. For the future. Maybe one day… for Max. As a duty. Because, as it is said, dying declarations are the most true.

Abi went into the office less. She brought her computer and her notes and created a makeshift workstation in the hospital room. Max moved into her house to watch over little Jenny and Abi hired a babysitter to help him. Nothing else mattered beside being close to her mother. Nothing…although from time to time her need for consolation grew too huge. In one of these moments, she texted her lover. "Are you free tomorrow evening?" she asked. He responded immediately. "For you, yes. I'd make time." She reserved a room and sent him the details.

Although her relationship with her son had improved, Max chose to live with his father after spending a year in Cameroon. Abi understood. Julien had suffered from severe depression after their separation and was recovering slowly. Patience was required to heal the wounds. She did not want to rush things. She lived alone with little Jenny and never invited her lover over to their house. She had had major ups and downs in life. Abi didn't feel she was ready to take that step. Even though she had a hard time accepting the distance it created. Once Abi's divorce was finalized, he resettled in Paris even though his family stayed back in London.

"Why?" she had asked.

"To be closer to you," he'd replied.

She had laughed. Skeptical.

"Are you joking?"

"So, let's say it's for work," he said.

Their affair had flourished in previously unknown ways. He had started, in his signature subtle manner, to ask for greater intimacy.

Abi waited for him for an hour, sitting on the bed, motionless, with her shoes on. When he softly knocked on the door, she opened it immediately and embraced him. "I missed you," he whispered to her, his hands, rough, or almost rough, all over her yielding body. Abi closed her eyes. *There is no sorrow a good fuck can't ease*, she thought ironically as he threw her on the bed and spread himself over her... *Even if they don't happen as often as we would like*, she finished when, only moments later, he lay down next to her, breathless. "Sorry, but you turn me on so intensely. I couldn't help it. It's your fault. You are too beautiful. Too rare. Too everything..." Abi laughed at this half-humble and half-proud comment. Her fault, right! Aren't men vain!

She curled up against her lover's chest and he wrapped his arms around her. It was neither the time nor the place, and she had decided not to share it with him, but the words came out by themselves: "My mother's dying," she revealed. He didn't react. Abi had not expected silence. She thought he hadn't heard or that, if he'd heard, he'd chosen to ignore her. She felt tears sting her eyes and cursed her sorrow for dragging her into this room where she didn't belong. After a moment that she felt like a lifetime, he turned toward her. Kissed her wet cheeks, her dry lips, and started caressing her again gently, without the urgency of the first time. He ran his hands through her hair and kissed her neck. He sucked her breasts between his lips while running his fingers along her body. They made love again. Abi shut her eyes, her heart, for a moment of peace.

She left the hotel room to go back to the hospital, where she slept, pressed close to her mother as if to stretch out the tender moments she had just experienced, given that her longing for physical contact was so intense.

Anna sometimes emerged from her drowsiness, looking dazed. "Abi, are you there my daughter? Did I dream? Did I talk? Oh, my daughter, I still have so many, so many things to say."

But her memory had started to fade. The words she said were the only evidence that she was alive. As soon as they were uttered, the very memories she'd mentioned disappeared slowly, like paintings covered over in black. Anna looked for words in the breath she had left. In the firm beating of her tired heart. Abi gently caressed her mother's face. "Mother, I'm here. Look at me," she said. She wanted both of them to share those final moments. Instead, Anna explored marginal lives. A past that brought her pain. Crushed her. Time passed. Abi saw any hope of a connection disappearing. She would get some truths that she hadn't asked for, but the goodbye embrace that she needed so badly would never happen. Abi knew it. Her mother was too away to hear her sorrow and left her as consolation nothing but the story of her life. A brutal legacy that the young woman did not know what to make of.

That day at the hotel, she'd shared her frustration and bitterness with her lover:

"You know I so badly want her to tell me: Abi, I will always be there for you, don't worry."

"Maybe it's unrealistic to expect our loved ones to

console us from the grief caused by their demise," he told her softly.

"But she's not yet dead," Abi replied angrily, "if she doesn't console me now, when will she?"

"You need to accept that this is no longer the time for expectations and demands but rather just being there. Skin against skin, in the breath of your mother. It's a journey, *Mpenzi*. You are only seeing her off. Nothing eases the pain of losing a loved one. Nothing except some form of acceptance," he concluded.

One of the reasons she loved him was his gentleness, his considerate kindness.

✳

Their affair was driven by her mad, senseless attraction to him.

Abi met him at a press conference. A successful sculptor, he was among a wave of African artists whose works were highly sought after on the contemporary art market. And she'd been tasked with writing an article about him for her magazine. She reached out to him after their first meeting for one final tweak to her column—that's the excuse she'd used. Just for the pleasure of seeing him again, she'd had to admit to herself. She was intrigued by him and wanted to understand the unrest he caused in her. He was married. Abi too. As happily married as one can be once passion has given way to a comfortable routine over the years.

Abi knew people who stayed married even though they

didn't have anything obvious in common. Households on which no one would have bet, but which strangely were still on course. She never judged other people's private lives. Despite everything, Abi was proud of the partnership they had formed, Julien and herself. If she had been asked to describe their relationship, she would have said sincere, tender, respectful, and friendly. In this respect, they were exactly the opposite of the couples their respective parents had been.

Her meeting with the sculptor left her excited but undisturbed, their mutual unavailability reassuring her. Abi dressed up for him. Polished her look, her makeup. She couldn't remember the last time she had waited for a man so impatiently. She felt so full of energy. So full of excitement.

Their lunch matched her expectations. They spoke at length. Laughed. She could see in his eyes that he found her desirable and her own desire grew in turn. She flirted shamelessly. Teased. Smiled. Already yielding. Already consenting while ignoring the important questions. Where? And when? She had thought she'd reached a stage where her life, her commitments, her convictions would protect her from falling. Abi allowed herself to be daring and unrestrained like a tightrope walker who, conscious of the safety net between her and the ground, hurries into the emptiness. They went their separate ways after exchanging chaste kisses on the cheek. But he held her close to him for a few seconds longer, sending her heart and imagination into a tailspin.

Back then, he had lived in London. This thrilled Abi,

who considered the geographical distance another insurmountable hurdle. Nothing serious could happen under such circumstances.

She had enjoyed their lunch without any second thoughts. It was an enchanted moment. An innocent, harmless pleasure. They did not have to meet again, or even talk to one another again. She could content herself with fantasizing about what could have been but never would be. Her euphoria lasted days. A somewhat mad, sensitive intoxication. Julien had laughed while making love to her that evening: "Well then, my little wife is all feisty today," he had pointed out. She acted like a cat, burying her face in her husband's neck, biting his earlobe tantalizingly. Never in the world did she feel an ounce of guilt. It had been a long time since she'd wanted Julien this much.

Something in her, dormant till now, woke up hungry for fantasy, pleasure, and caresses. She recognized the desire. Welcomed it with joy. And only then realized to what extent it had been missing from her rather boring existence. The danger had only grazed her, sparking a feeling of urgency. A thirst for life that she thought she could quench without paying a price.

As time went on her excitement morphed into nervousness. Lack. Obsession. He hadn't called her after their lunch. This left her fretting. Had she just made it all up? Had she made a mountain out of what he'd considered a routine, professional meeting?

The day before the column she'd written was due to be published, she wrote him an email, which she hemmed

and hawed over. She typed, deleted, and retyped, looking for the right words to articulate her desires without
overdoing it. "The article will be published tomorrow,"
she wrote after some perfunctory greetings. "I hope you
like it," she added. Then, after some hesitation: "Call
me whenever you're in Paris. I'd love to grab a coffee."
She dithered again with the conclusion. Sincerely? Best
wishes? Till soon? Could she afford to say "Kisses"? Every
word weighed a ton, laden with all the undertones she
didn't dare express outright. He responded very quickly,
writing: "Soon!" Nothing more? No hello? No "how are
you doing"? And no follow-up on the date? Nothing
besides that laconic and anxiety-inducing "soon." "Are
you going to tell me when?" Abi insisted. And then he
wrote back, "That small restaurant over on place de la
République was quite nice. I wouldn't mind going there
again with you."

He did not write her again for several weeks, during
which Abi felt she was going crazy. She was glued to her
phone. Every ring, every new message brought hope,
which turned into acid that burned her sensitive nerves.
She read their messages over a thousand times. Had she
said too much? Not enough? Had she been too explicit?
Could she be any more explicit? Or maybe he didn't like
her. That explanation was the most likely. No man, even
remotely interested in a woman, would behave with such
indifference. She took an unflinching look at herself in
the mirror. "Keep dreaming, poor girl," she murmured to
her reflection, full of bitter self-mockery.

How could she miss him so much? Of what secret,

unknown ailment was he suddenly the indispensable medicine? She didn't have space in her life for the chaos he represented and, conscious of this, she wanted and loathed him in equal measure.

Abi kept a close eye on her phone, but strangely enough still managed to miss the expected message. The alarm clock hadn't gone off. She had had to rush Max, who was dragging his feet. She was fighting over nothing with Julien. She arrived late at her editorial meeting, which dragged on as usual. When she finally glanced at her phone, it was 2 p.m. The message had come late the night before. "I just arrived in Paris. Tomorrow?" it read. Followed by the name of a hotel, the room number, and the address. "I wait for you here till midday." Abi thought of calling back, but afraid that she wouldn't be able to control her voice, texted instead. "Sorry, I'm only just seeing your message. Sorry I missed it. Tomorrow, same time, same place?" The reply vibrated instantly, "Why not right now?"

Because I have a job and deadlines. Because I stepped out in a hurry this morning and didn't wear matching underwear. Because I would like to get waxed. Do my nails. Feel pretty. Because you are skipping steps... "Tomorrow, please," she replied simply.

It was raining. Abi wore a dress too light for the season. She hesitated in the hotel lobby and the receptionist asked her, "Can I help you, madame?" She felt compelled to explain the reason for her visit. "I have to meet Mr. X," she said. The receptionist called up to the room. As the wait dragged on over minutes, Abi hoped that he wouldn't pick up and she would have time to retreat. Everything seemed so unreal. "Do you know the room number? Great, then you can go up," the man told her, hanging up. She shivered as she entered the room, and not only because of the cold.

Their affair went on for two years before Julien found out. They met when he came to Paris. Or arranged for their trips to coincide. They talked or texted one another every day.

He displayed boundless passion for his work. "Folk art museums are filled with masks, figurines, *bas-reliefs*. So many objects looted from all over the world, robbed of their meanings. For those who created them, life did not reside in the object, but rather in the spirit that informed its creation. Even a corpse artistically entombed is still a dead body. They are now no longer art but simply objects. They are beautiful whereas they should be inhabited. From time immemorial, humans have sculpted to magnify their gods. There is a reason why some religions are against any depiction of their gods while others are committed to the practice. There is a form of highly human insolence in recreating the god that created you, and there is the risk of adoring the tangible representation rather than the distant deity. That is what sculpture is. Both a tribute and a challenge to the gods. Some spiritualities tolerate this ambivalence, others don't. Yet others use representations to further tighten control over their flock and guarantee that they will be submissive. They select the artists and dictate the dogma they should represent. Sculpture is both the easiest and the most delicate of art forms. You have to do more than extract a form or reproduce a model when you're shaping a compact block. You have to breathe life into it. That's not something you can learn or improvise. There is always some part of yourself that you inject into the material. In our modern world where art is a business like any other, techniques are taught, but the magic is still a gift, midway between bliss and suffering."

When he was discussing sculpture, his eyes lit up. His voice grew excited. His entire being expressed his enthusiasm. Abi couldn't help but draw parallels to the way they made love. He spiced their lovemaking with the same carnal, inspired intensity. She heard him when she kissed his hands, roughened from manual labor. Magic! She could attest to it.

Did she love him? It's a question she never asked herself. The feelings she had for him were obvious. It is often thought that desire, always just a stone's throw from madness, appeals to the instinctive, animal side of us, while love, that noble feeling celebrated by poets and saints, shouldn't be confused with it, lest it be perverted. She adored everything about him. His voice. The smell of his skin. His charismatic presence in the world. The ease with which he carried himself. His artistic talent. The causes he stood for.

She met up with him in Rome one weekend. He'd been invited to a festival, and she was covering the event. They visited the Sistine Chapel. "What should we think of a civilization that imprisons its gods in artistic genius, magnificent no doubt, but no less human.

See God, stretching out toward that beautiful specimen of a Western male. Notice his full desire to touch him, to graze him with his index finger. Compare his attitude with that of naked, lustful Adam. Notice the relative symmetry of their poses. The painter is telling us this meeting never took place. God, despite his power, despite being almighty, despite his desire, doesn't touch David. And what about the woman, represented even before her creation? Eve in the making? Lilith, the eternal feminine being as old as God himself? How can one interpret the undeniable sensuality of their poses, bodies, colors? I am a huge fan of this place. Here is the most of the self an artist can offer when under constraints. I am a huge admirer of what it reveals and implies. Of the various possible interpretations. There is something deeply pagan about this place, even though this is the place where cardinals meet to elect a new pope. That aborted touch between man and God has become an iconic image in rock and roll and pop art. To the extent that Spielberg used it in *ET*, developing his own understanding of eternity and the impossible contact. The glorious vision of an artist has transformed the Christian omnipresent God into a deity filled with longing for a languid human. Isn't it marvelous?"

He was neither preachy nor professorial. He simply expressed his convictions with passion. Art was all he lived for. When he said, "Notice…" or "Look there…" he'd squeezed her arm, pointing. He was contaminating her with his intensity, his excitement. Through him, Abi saw art in a new and enchanted light, outside of conventional approaches. "Can I quote you word for word in my column?" she asked. He laughed, then replied:

"Do with me as you please."

That evening, they walked through Prati. They passed the piazza Mazzini with its fountains and elegant façades as they looked for a restaurant, which they finally found in Col di Lana.

Julien and Max called her at dinner. Whenever her family life popped up during one of their clandestine meetings, guilt and fear besieged her.

"Sorry about that," she told him, hanging up.

"Don't worry," he replied with a smile, pouring her more of the delicious prosecco they had ordered to accompany the meal.

"No, let me worry. This situation is potentially explosive. We will end up burned like in the *Last Judgment* of your dear Michelangelo," Abi said.

He burst into laughter and, out of nowhere, recited a poem at the top of his lungs, drawing the amused attention of the other customers in the restaurant.

> *Who dares to speak of hell in the presence of love?*
> *May he be cursed forever, that idle dreamer,*
> *The first one who in his stupidity*
> *Entranced by a sterile, insoluble problem,*
> *Wished to mix honesty with what belongs to love!*

She laughed and completed the Baudelaire poem:

> *He who would unite in a mystic harmony,*
> *Coolness with warmth and the night with the day*

Will never warm his palsied flesh
With that red sun whose name is love!

"End of the demonstration," he said, smiling.
"I really like these lines, but I prefer this one:"

I shall strike you without anger
And without hate, like a butcher,
As Moses struck the rock!
And from your eyelids I shall make…

He finished the verse:

The waters of suffering gush forth
To inundate my Sahara.
My desire swollen with hope
Will float upon your salty tears.

An older couple at the neighboring table clapped for
them, smiling, and the waiter offered them another glass
of sparkling wine, saying:

"From the manager. He says any couple that recites
poetry will always be welcome at his establishment."

Her lover was feeling flirty. "We came to the only
Italian restaurant where the manager loves French poetry.
That's a sign," he said, smiling and raising his glass.

He then added: "Your choice was nice, but mine was
more relevant."

She looked at him, more intent all of a sudden, and
asked, "You think this is love?"

"What else?" he asked, a mischievous delight in his eyes as he gestured elaborately. "Do you know what's missing in Dante's inferno? A special circle for women who love poetry. You are too complicated. Too dangerous for us poor men."

"You are avoiding the real question," she mocked.

"No, not at all. But you are. If not love, what then is it?" he asked.

"I don't know. We're an illegitimate couple out for a good time. We know the harm this affair could cause our families, but we still don't end it. I would say it's lust. Don't you think?" she asked.

He laughed so hard that heads turned to look at their table once again.

"Okay, lust, I'm fine with that too."

Rome is paradise on earth for art lovers. He showed her something new at every fountain. Every architectural detail. Every statue from antiquity along the path they walked through the city. He pointed at things, or caressed the cold stone tenderly. He explained. Reinterpreted. Was moved or amused by them. He glowed. He was the poet and her poetry. Captivated, Abi followed him in a circle of light he created just for her. She loved him.

They said nothing more about it. Their relationship evolved in an airtight bubble where she was neither a mother nor a wife. Just a desired, fulfilled woman.

In their private moments, he called her *Mpenzi*, which meant "my lover" in Swahili, his mother tongue. He showed her his devotion every way possible, despite the secret nature of their relationship and she blossomed

in his eyes. Her intimacy with Julien benefited from this
state of grace. She wanted him more. Their lovemaking
didn't have the same intensity, urgency, nor mind-blowing
pleasure—it was just the tender and effective eroticism of
two bodies that held no secrets from one another. She
also loved this domestic sensuality.

That, perhaps, is why Julien couldn't forgive her.
With her head in the clouds since meeting her lover, she
had let her guard down. Abi thought that she hadn't left
behind any concrete evidence, but something in her attitude had drawn her husband's suspicion. Returning from
appointments in a state of bliss. Staring into the distance,
lost. Tiny secret smiles at the thought of a memory. The
suddenly closer attention she paid to her looks. Her increasingly opaque work schedule. Julien had, over time,
put together a body of clues, and he ultimately surprised
her. He still didn't know that she had been attracted to
this man well before he had taken any interest in her.
That, in a sense, he was her trophy and she'd been his
seducer, and not the other way around.

Julien returned and knocked on their door after
weeks of being off the grid. The pitiful state he was in
scared Abi. His secondhand clothes, his greasy hair, his
bloodshot eyes spoke to his helplessness and excessive
drinking. Max flew down the stairs when he heard his
father's voice, but then came to a screeching halt. He was
also frightened by his father's appearance. Julien's anger
had not subsided. He barely looked at his son before attacking Abi. He had only come to get his things, he sputtered repeatedly. He was going to file for a divorce. He

would never forgive her. "Do you hear me? Never!" he screamed. He wandered aimlessly around the house like a caged animal.

"Max, please go back to your room. Your dad and I have to talk," Abi ordered.

Abi was taken aback by the monstrous calm with which she uttered those words. Her voice was smooth, peaceful, as if to defuse the furor and madness being spewed by her husband.

"Please, Julien. Please, sit down," she pleaded.

She filled a glass with water and dropped a painkiller in it to dissolve.

"Have this. Drink. That should make you feel better," she advised.

She was playing her traditional role once again. Soothing his fears. Watching over him. He sat down and drank the medication.

"Should I make you something to eat? I'll cook some noodles. It won't take long. Trust me," she promised.

Her husband kept quiet while Abi frantically busied herself in the kitchen. Her entire being was focused on Julien. The leg he moved compulsively. His hands that trembled and his eyes suddenly teary.

"Is it because he's Black?" he asked.

"I didn't hear you," she replied softly.

To be honest, she had heard him. Clearly. Julien had chosen to run away and had to justify that decision to himself. The reason had to be some insurmountable handicap. A difference so irreconcilable that even the idea of comparing himself was impossible.

"I said, what does he have that I don't have?" he asked again.

"Come on, Julien, please forgive me. Stop this torture, please. The words are all jumbled up in my mind. I'm trying to catch my breath. I have a hard time sleeping." She said these thoughts that were running through her mind, although she knew her feelings were more complex. Had she had the guts, she would have told him, "It wasn't supposed to end up like this. I never planned to hurt anyone, especially not you. Our affair started and flourished in a part of me that I never knew existed before I met him. I failed to cage it in there despite my best efforts. I didn't love him despite you, but rather for me. It happened without any forethought and I organized my thinking so that everyone had their place and no one would suffer pointlessly. The shameful truth is that I had found perfect emotional balance. I was happy." But nobody talks like this under such circumstances. So, she tried to downplay the seriousness of her affair.

"It was nothing really. It has nothing to do with us. You can't compare the two," she argued.

"It was not nothing, Abi. You thought about him every day while sleeping next to me. You traveled across the city several times to go meet him while I thought you were elsewhere. You took off your clothes and made love with him over and over. You lied to me, and you would have kept on lying had I not found out. Don't stand there claiming that it was nothing!" he said.

Julien screamed the final words before leaving, slamming the door behind him.

Influenced by her mother, Abi had a soft spot for women of character. Those who do not give up and do not show any doubt. She didn't have any sympathy for those to whom life had given everything. Those with fortune, beauty, and intelligence, but who became lazy when a cheating man abandoned them along the way.

Julien's rejection had left her so paralyzed that she couldn't breathe. She felt like she had suffered a horrible fall from the top of a building. His crying sounded like a saw in her ears. Julien left because he was full of disgust. Another man had touched, caressed, loved her and she had enjoyed the attention. He knew she was committed. He hated her for that. He used coarse, meaningless words to talk to her, and to cast her affair in the gutter. He wanted her to pay. To crawl. He wanted her adultery to be etched on her forehead. He wanted the whole world to know what a horrible whore she was. In his vengeful fury, he was ready to destroy everything to punish her. Abi knew Julien's flaws. Besides the anger, she felt his pain. His disappointment.

Trapped in that unexpected tidal wave of hate, Max broke down. Only the day before he'd been a loved teenager in a united family. He hadn't doubted the unalterable solidity of the ground on which he walked. But now his father disappeared for days, and then reappeared drunk. He who had suffered so much from his own father's alcoholism and drank responsibly at worst. He spewed the most horrible, rude, racist things that Max had ever heard. Max came home to find his mother still wearing her nightgown, slouching in front of the TV. The house hadn't been cleaned. All Abi did was take a TV dinner from the freezer that she microwaved without even unwrapping.

Max could no longer recognize his parents. Nobody really cared about him anymore. He had suddenly become invisible. He did so poorly in school that his parents decided that he should repeat the third year of secondary school. Only his past behavior spared him outright dismissal. He stopped hanging out with his childhood friends and started spending time with hoodlums. Drank to a stupor. Smoked marijuana. Looked for trouble. He didn't give a damn about his mother, and as if all that wasn't enough to fill the void in him, he started mutilating himself. On his stomach or upper thighs so he could hide the scars. Only the sharp suffering caused by the blade cutting through his skin and the sight of dripping blood soothed his torment for a moment.

Abi saw this by chance. He had forgotten to close the bathroom door and she accidentally came in. "Leave me alone!" Max screamed, closing the door violently.

Abi went away slowly. She had had the time to see that her son was mutilating his stomach. She had seen the traces of old scars, but she did not go back in. The metaphor of her mother under the oxygen mask came back to mind. She wrote to Julien saying, "Please, forgive me for having given my body to another man. Forgive me for having relished like a thief that part of me that I gave up by offering it to you. Our home, from the walls to the roof, is crumbling on my head. Our child is sinking into a suicidal depression. I had not realized that what we had was so fragile or that I was some pillar on which everything rested. I guess there is justice in me bearing the brunt of your anger, but why does Max have to pay for this? In punishing me, have you grown insensitive to your son's suffering? I've stopped wondering why you are doing this. Max is not doing fine, Julien, not doing fine at all. Neither you nor I can help him at this stage. I have decided to send him to Cameroon to spend a year with my mother. He will enroll at the French school. I don't think repeating a grade will be a solution. I will explain the situation to them, and he will sit for his brevet exam there. If this is okay by you, great. Otherwise, it does not change anything. Max has to be miles away from all of this."

Julien called when he got her email and said, "So, now you want to take my son away from me? You want to send him to your shithole country? Are you kidding? I'll never let you do that. Do you hear me? How dare you imply that I don't have a say in all of this. You're the only one to blame."

He was screaming into the phone. His voice was thick.

"Have you been drinking, Julien? It's 4 p.m. and you're already drunk," she said.

"You know what," he blurted, "all the alcohol in the world wouldn't be enough to make me forget the kind of bitch…"

"Yes, yes, bitch, whore, what else? You keep repeating yourself. I've heard it before and understood. Do you hear yourself? You shout. You repeat yourself. Is it too much to ask that we have a normal, calm conversation between adults? Max will leave for a year and that's it. That will be enough time for things to calm down," she said.

"Never!" screamed Julien.

"What is wrong with you, Julien? You love that country just as much as I do. Yes. I've visited the nooks and crannies and not just stopped in Douala like most people do. There's no denying that I have taken a keen interest in Bamileke culture, in my mother's heritage—all thanks to you. You love that place. You even considered going to live there when you retire."

"What you did made me realize that, as a white man, I have no place in your world," he retorted.

"Tell me you're joking? When did you become a racist idiot who explains away life's complexity with stupid skin color? And what about Max? To which world does he belong? Yours or mine?" she enquired.

"Life's complexity. Is that what you call it?" he asked sarcastically.

"Julien, you're getting everything mixed up. Don't mix things up. I made a mistake. A huge mistake, but there is nothing we can't fix. You idealized me too much, Julien. I'm not the woman you thought. I too have a dark side. Is that enough of a reason for you to throw away all that we are? All that we have built? Our memories? Our son?"

Abi sighed. This was so absurd.

"Come back home, Julien. Please come back. This thing has been a nightmare. Give us a chance. Together, we will weather this storm. Trust in us. Come back, dear. Max needs you. I need you," she told him beseechingly.

She heard Julien crying on the other end of the line.

"I can't stop imagining you in bed with that bastard. You want to get rid of Max so that you can be free to see him whenever you want, right?" he asked.

Tears welling up in her eyes too, Abi tried to argue.

"I stopped seeing him, but that's not the issue. Max now does more than behave poorly. He's cutting himself, Julien. He is redirecting his anger toward himself. How far will he go?" she wondered.

She tried to strike a pleading tone.

"What do you need me to do, Julien, so that we can be a family again? What can I do to make things right? Tell me what you need to feel better," she begged.

"Have you really stopped seeing him? I can't stop thinking about all the lies. All the excuses you invented without flinching to go be with him. How can you expect me to believe you now?"

"Did you hear what I said about Max? Stop being so selfish. Think about your son for one second," she pleaded.

"Did you think about your son while you were being screwed by…"

Abi hung up without hearing the rest.

All this violence, the outflow of negative emotions wore her down. Coarseness had become the punctuation in the language Julien used to talk to her. He didn't listen even one bit. He ruminated on his grievances until they became unbearable. He spat his bitterness in her face every little chance he got. It was so unlike him. He had never been so foul-mouthed with her before. She no longer knew who he was.

Explaining it all to Max was a grueling task.

"Things between your daddy and me are not easy, but I know they are even harder for you. We can't go on like this. You'll do the third year of secondary school in Cameroon. Your grandmother has already enrolled you.

"Do I have a say in this?" he asked calmly.

"I am afraid not, my love. None of us does," she answered.

"Whose fault is it?" he asked.

That was a rhetorical question.

When she arrived in Cameroon, she had received a message from her lover. "How are you?" he asked.

He had tried reaching her several times but had not heard back. She replied, "Bad. Everything is going south. Came to leave my son with my mother like a teenager who can't take responsibility for her actions."

He replied instantly, "I am so happy you responded! I've been quite worried."

She did not reply right away—the interaction was doing her some good, too.

He texted again: "Is there something I can do?"

"There is nothing you can do. I'm burning in the limbo of Dante's hell. Nobody can remedy the solitude of the damned."

He replied, "We will burn together if burning is required."

She recognized his caustic humor, and was grateful to him for trying to make the situation less dramatic.

"Any regrets?" he asked when she was slow to respond.

She responded with an honesty that she had not dared since the crisis with Julien broke out, "No! Not one bit, and maybe that's the worst part. No regrets. Only remorse."

"I miss you, *Mpenzi*. Can I call you? Can we talk?" he asked.

She hesitated. Then replied, "Not now. I'll get back to you."

ANNA

There's a Yiddish proverb that says: *Sugar is useless when salt is what is needed.*

A woman's body is way more demanding than her heart. Abi was still coming to terms with that reality in the most unsettling way.

I cannot claim that I was delighted with my daughter's marriage.

Julien was white. From a different culture. Light years away from our experience, and I construed her choice as a confirmation of the distance my daughter was trying to put between herself and me. However, things turned out differently. Julien fell in love with our country. Our culture. The way he viewed us made me look at the circumstances with a kinder eye. Abi and her family came to visit every year. My wonderful grandson made friends in the neighborhood and, like Louis's own father had done with Abi, Louis took it upon himself to teach his grandson the mother tongue and help him discover the richness and complexity of Bamileke culture. My daughter seemed, if not always happy, at peace, in control. The protagonist in the life she had chosen for herself.

That said, I felt that there was a worrying rift in Julien from his childhood, and I knew or guessed Abi's weaknesses. I quickly realized that the dangers threatening their union lay more in the naive faith they had in their ability to exorcise the past than in their cultural differences.

Julien had chosen a woman who was the exact opposite of his mother in every respect. He expected her to give him the affection, security, and stability that he didn't have when he was growing up. He loved her the way hurt children love. With passion and selfishness. Even the affair with his colleague was yet another way of testing the commitment of his spouse/mother. Abi transformed her household into a cocoon. She organized. Consoled. Rebuilt the ties that she needed. She played her role with devotion. Our family had its own flaws. My daughter went about building her perfect home the way a cathedral is built.

When Abi told me her decision to marry Julien, I shared my concern with my old friend, Ma' Moudio. Bonabéri, the neighborhood we had moved into in Douala, was her village. She had always lived there. But like many indigenous families, members of her family had sold off plots of the land piece by piece and now lived all cramped together. Grandparents, children, and grandchildren all in one tiny dilapidated house.

"Really, my child..." She was the only person in the

world who called me that. "These kids, I don't know what they're looking for. Let me tell you, if I had to choose between all the colors on this earth: Red, Yellow, White, etc., I would prefer that my son marry a woman who was Black like him. Preferably Christian. Otherwise, even baptizing your grandson would require UN-style negotiations. May he choose a continental African woman. Not one of those other Black women from the islands or wherever, with their complicated interracial blood—you no longer know who is really who! And while we're at it, preferably a Cameroonian woman. He shouldn't go and pick some fraudster Nigerians or the Sarakoke Malians with their dry skin and gibberish French. Please, even here in Cameroon, I want nothing to do with the tribalistic Bamileke, the broke-yet-proud Beti, the stone-hearted Babimbi, or the jungle savage Deido."

Six billion inhabitants on this planet. Over two hundred and fifty tribes in Cameroon alone, and she had just knocked every one of them out with a sentence!

Ma' Moudio was the oldest person in the neighborhood. She had a strong opinion about everything and anything, her own unique outlook on the world that she never missed a chance to share, whether you asked for it or not. Her sharp and often cruel tongue made her quite unpopular, but I was still very fond of her because she didn't beat around the bush. This senior, still on her two feet and full of life, commanded respect.

She continued: "I don't know why Abi did not marry my son, Ndedi. They both live in France and grew up together. And we know each other well. Should a problem have arisen between our children, we could have sat and said, 'My sister, how will we solve this?' You and I, we are problem solvers. Do you know that Ndedi married a Japanese woman? That woman…even her religion is a mystery to me. What race are my grandchildren? I can't say. Do you think I can sit with her and talk the way I'm speaking with you? I don't understand her language to start with. In all of that France, he couldn't even find a white woman?"

Fully immersed in her diatribe, she had forgotten that my daughter was Bamileke. A fact I refrained from reminding her about. Ndedi, Ma' Moudio's son, played the guitar with near mastery and dreamed of becoming a music star above anything else. He had no interest whatsoever in his education, and after repeated failed attempts to make it in music here, had found himself—I don't know how and don't want to know—in France. There, he was living off his neatly kempt dreadlocks and his perfect body when he met the lovely young woman his mother was complaining about. Imagining him married to my Abi made me change my stance. We were going to try our luck with the son of Folcoche.

I immediately thought about the Rezeau family in the movie *Viper in the Fist* when I met the Achards. Their father would play the role of the evil stepmother, terrorizing his spouse and torturing his children. He was a true reflection of the average man: a cocktail of drunkenness, debauchery, greed, and domestic abuse. Julien's brother had died in a motorcycle accident a few years before.

Before the tragedy happened, he had escaped the family hell at sixteen and lived off of petty jobs and little allowance he got from his mother. No picture of him hung in the parlor. I have never heard his name.

The Achard family lived in a beautiful timber-framed house, typically Norman, as they proudly informed us. Despite its cost, some repairs would have done the building some good. Everything seemed narrow. From rooms crowded with heavy wardrobes from another era to windows that limited the already scarce light and air. Everything would have felt claustrophobic but for the beautiful garden with its winter roses and spruces.

Mr. Achard, the father, was a civil servant and elected council official. His wife had never worked a day in her life. They had inherited their wealth from her family. A fact that didn't stop the husband from a stinginess we experienced right from day one. Although it was February and the weather was dead cold, the heat was not turned on. The fireplace, in his opinion, was enough to keep us warm. "In this house, your sweater is your heat," he informed us as soon as we arrived. The food was bland. A porridge made of tomatoes harvested from the garden, roast chicken with Irish potatoes, and cheese. And for dessert, strawberries from the garden. We were served salad night and day. We were not going to die of hunger, true, but if we'd had in-laws coming from far away, we would have prepared a buffet for them. Louis had brought along a few bottles of good Bordeaux that Mr. Achard hurriedly put away before serving us some cheap wine that he alone liked. Charlotte had insisted on hosting us. First thing the next day, I had a tête-à-tête with my daughter. "I can tolerate your mother-in-law serving us those so-called tomatoes, salad, and strawberries from her garden in the height of February, but I will not sleep one more night in this freezer. We're going to a hotel."

I had had time to watch Julien sit upright when his father was around. Poor Charlotte shuddered when I offered to help her serve and he stepped in to say, "But no, Anna. You are our guests. Let her do it. Let her be useful for once." Mr. Achard didn't try to hide the iron grip he had on his family. He even made it more blatant by openly being disruptive and disagreeable as the evening progressed and the second bottle of wine was emptied. His behavior was even more unbearable given the courtesy that bordered on deference he showed Louis. My husband was an influential man, well aware of his charisma. Our host was visibly impressed by it.

Abi told me about Julien and his brother's painful childhood. The whippings they received for the slightest prank. Zero toys at Christmas—the goal supposedly to avoid turning them into spoiled brats—but rather, worn-out winter clothing. A formal ban on having anyone over to the house. The repeated rebukes unseen by anyone outside the family. Their father's countless affairs. I of course empathized, but was not surprised. I could easily imagine the diabolical inspiration sad people are able to summon to torture their offspring.

Mr. Achard died a few years after the wedding. From a protracted illness. Whether the disease was related to the cigarettes he smoked serially, the liters of cheap alcohol he gulped, or the heinous bile that obstructed his spleen is anybody's guess. Louis and I traveled to the funeral because we come from a culture that has the utmost respect for the dead. And that believes supporting family members during difficult moments is sacred. In the tiny chapel to which Mr. Achard had dragged his entire family every Sunday no matter the weather, there were seven of us, including the priest. The seventh person was an old lady who, I was told, attended all funerals. No office colleagues. No friends or other family members. It was the most boring burial I had ever attended. A beautiful April sun shone. We had only one desire: to get it over with and move on.

When the ceremony ended, we sat on a terrace at the seaside to share a drink before leaving. A calm, almost smooth, silence reigned. We watched boats dock at and leave the Cherbourg port without feeling a need for words. Charlotte, eyes closed, basked her face in the sun. Beams of light illuminated her ginger hair, which Julien had inherited and hints of which could be seen in the curly hair of my Max. She had visited the hair salon, made up her eyes and lips. Her dress for the occasion hugged her slim blonde figure. I realized that Charlotte was quite a beautiful woman. A fact I had missed before. She emptied her glass of chardonnay with relish and, all smiles, turned to us and asked, "Aren't we living our best life here?"

Her son smiled at her.

"No?" she asked again, speaking to everyone.

I couldn't help but chuckle. "Yes, sister. This is the

best life there is," I responded. Julien ordered another round for all of us.

We had rarely spent time with the Achard parents since the wedding. I didn't like the father and had no sympathy for the spiritless woman who let him mistreat her and her children without ever fighting back. I was surprised to see her in a different light. So radiant. So different on this day of mourning. Anyway, who had Mr. Achard been, really? What tragic events had transformed him into the domestic monster whose demise seemed like redemption for his family? I didn't know anything about those people. I didn't know their true story. That said, I could observe the effects on Julien. His severe emotional addiction. His sick possessiveness with respect to Abi. My daughter, who was also fighting her own demons, was reassuring. She kept any possible danger at bay. They isolated themselves, surrounding themselves only with those who posed no threat to their partnership. They had forgotten that life does not care about our safeguards. That none of us is immune to an encounter that will turn everything upside down, deal a new hand, call everything into question.

Abi's affair weakened him by rattling the solid structure that was the backbone of his life. It reopened in Julien wounds that had never scarred over. Another fully grown, clearly cruel, heartless, powerful man was again taking the protection of the woman in his life. A man so different from him that it was a losing battle. His anguish was even greater because the man in question was Black. He thought that this man had an almost cosmic racial bond with Abi and Max, his mixed-race son in whom he no longer saw himself. His analysis was all wrong, but he was no longer able to see that. Abi was the cornerstone of his emotional edifice. Her betrayal rocked Julien's life like an earthquake. Despite his repeated denials, he knew that she no longer accepted the role he wanted her to play, and he punished her for that. Punished all of them.

Every union is built against the backdrop of the world. With its uncertainties and its errors. Not in some ivory tower. But that lesson was maybe too sudden, too brutal for this couple. I prayed for them to find their way, together or apart, and if not for them, for Max at least.

My daughter agreed to entrust me with her child for the duration of the school year. I was quite hopeful that a year spent with kids in our neighborhood would do him some good. There was Jenny, who lived with me along with her mother, and whose adoptive grandmother I considered myself to be. The pretty Tina, a little orphaned neighbor I had taken under my wing, and Ismaël—so intelligent and mature. They were all Max's age and had hung out together during the holidays since Max was a child.

Jenny, Tina, Ismaël, Max. They were my lost children... I will tell you about them. Yes, I will. Maybe that's even the goal of this sudden rambling. I will talk about them. But before I do, I have to explain what we were. How what we were made everything else possible.

What it was in our lives, in this country, that blinded us to the distress of our very own children.

*

I grew closer to Ma' Moudio at a time when I too was having a marital crisis.

Louis's mother hated me from the start. She considered me the schemer I was yet to become, but that I eventually learned to become by her rejection. She and her husband were top-ranking civil servants, close to the regime. She hoped her son would marry a young woman from her class. A more lavish union, more aligned with their traditions and social standing. She was forced to make do with me, less than nothing—no name, pregnant me. What "upstanding" girl gets pregnant before marriage, if not to entrap the poor innocent boy?

She ran her household, like many housewives back then. The children, house staff, relatives from the village, *njangis*—the finances—and other weekly meetings were her responsibility. He, on the other hand, handled relations with the outside world, and the modernity that he hastily shelved when he crossed the threshold back into his home and became an old-school patriarch again.

Cameroon is a rich mosaic of peoples and landscapes. But no place in it compares to the glittering, lush, untamed beauty of Bamileke country. Especially not the cities, where commerce takes place amid skin-crawling filth. All you have to do is step back a few kilometers from all of that. Head out to Mount Bamboutous, where even the city of Dschang has a fairy-world-like charm.

We arrived at sunset for my maiden visit to my husband's village, when the dying sunrays colored the sky with a thousand shades of perfect saffron-inflected azure. My father-in-law had built his house not far from the *Centre climatique* in Dschang, the former getaway of the colonial masters, at an altitude of 1,400 meters on the flanks of the mountain. To get there, we drove past vast plots and fences cordoning off blooming hibiscus hedges. Eucalyptus forests surrounded by creepers. Tiny hamlets of huts with thatch cone-shaped roofs, and walls made from mud and plaited raffia bamboo. As painstakingly put together as a bird's nest.

Seen from up there, even the houses lost in the wild vegetation of Dschang with their hats of rusty ocher sheets, and the towering cross of the Catholic church overlooking the city seamlessly fit into the majesty of the panorama.

"It's fantastic. I have never seen anything quite as beautiful," said Louis when he joined me, bringing in our luggage to the room we had been given.

My father-in-law's house was built at the top of a tree-covered hill that offered, regardless of where you looked, a breathtaking view of the landscape.

"Right?" he asked.

He joined me at the window, wrapping his arms around my waist.

"Welcome to your new village," he added.

We still believed in it.

The area around Dschang was great, but it wasn't exceptional in that part of the country full of lush green hills and majestic waterfalls with their shimmering mists

of water vapor. Its granite-rich soil produced abundant
food. In Cameroon, people grow leafy vegetables that can
be farmed all year round and are ideal when staple food
crops run out. All except the Bamileke, who don't need
to—their soil produces such a rich array of tubers, fruits,
vegetables, and grains that they are spoiled with choice.
Dishes are richly flavored with spices, all of equal sub-
tlety. Every meal is always hefty. Super tasty and flavorful,
even for those less privileged.

The extraordinary beauty of the landscape, and even
the soil's generosity, stood in sharp contrast to the distrust
locals had for strangers, the term sometimes referring to
the village next door and sometimes to the rest of the
country. Louis accurately expressed that feeling when he
said the entire country had forfeited its freedom, prud-
ishly looking the other way during the massacres committed on his land. Many Bamileke had run from their
villages to settle in other cities during that dark period
in our history. A massive exodus that the regime used
to drive a wedge between them and other people. They
were not only framed to be cunning and vengeful terrorists, but also troublemakers, resistant to the progress so
generously offered by the former masters. They were also
labeled invaders, pseudo-Cameroonians unlike the rest of
the people, obsessed as they were with being Bamileke.
In response, they shut out the world. Regardless of where
they were, they clustered only among themselves, both
in association and in marriage. In the economic sector
where they excelled, they worked to eliminate the competition. Sometimes the various clans of the tribe clashed

with one another in deep and irreconcilable ways. They nevertheless made sure none of it filtered out to the outside world, putting up a united front against the rest of the country.

Their unshakable herd instinct had become entrenched with the violence, betrayals, and exoduses they had suffered. The entire country had suffered during the war of independence. But they had not forgotten that they had been hunted down. They protected their language, their customs, and their spirituality with stubborn determination.

But there was a crack. A fault line at the heart of the community, caused by their close alignment, with one side or the other, in the actions of the powers that brutalized them. They had done much more than incur the wrath of others. They had also killed one another.

Some colluded with the government to hunt down rebels. Every family had, among brothers, its own lot of both resistance and collaborators. And in both camps, its own lot of brutes and peacemakers. The armed struggle had gotten worse. The resistance returned every blow they were dealt if they could, never hesitating to attack other villagers with questionable loyalty.

When the war was definitively lost and all hope of freedom subjected to the firing squad or cowardly assassinated with their fighters, they had to coexist peacefully again. The community forgave the "traitors" the government had made rich and respectable in thanks for services rendered. It pretended to forgive the resistance that had slaughtered entire families, torching their farms and their homes. There was a price for resilience. It demanded silence, but nobody forgot.

There, more than elsewhere maybe, the conflicts relating to that dark period were swept under the rug, where they smoldered, waiting to explode.

✳

I was never able to feel welcome in my new family. For a long time, I blamed my mother-in-law. Louis had four brothers, all conveniently married to women from the area, who were all experts in the art of obsequious respect and shameful hypocrisy that characterized relationships in that society where it was necessary to master both outright and latent hierarchies. I came from elsewhere. I know nothing about their customs and traditions. Nobody went out of their way to teach me.

In the beginning, out of a desire to learn, and then over time, out of a fascination with that unique people, I looked at them through what I considered an anthropological lens. I spent every day in their midst, learning their customs and even their language, but I was resolutely an outsider. The Bamileke became my own Dowayo.

I now know that Louis's mother was not the only person behind my exclusion. My own fears impeded my integration, and nature took care of the rest. I was distinctly put off by Bamileke spirituality. One of the most ancient, which is still practiced in our country to this day. This too, they had succeeded in protecting. I, who had fought tooth and nail to steer clear when Awaya invoked her deceased relatives in the forest, was not going to embrace skull worship and the esotericism tied to dealing with the dead and childbirth, in all the aspects of life in Bamileke country.

When Abi was born, I decided not to present her to Awaya and to sever ties with my village. I was finally on a path that would lead me away from the poverty and insecurity of my childhood. I was steering clear of the influence of the dead women who had brought me into this world. I could not handle the idea that my child might slide into the arms of the past. My daughter would launch to conquer the world from the summit to which I would have heaved myself. I was impervious to the many pleas that Awaya sent to me through third parties.

Louis completed his studies and joined the Ministry of Finance, where he was waiting on a transfer to a better position. In the meantime, I studied at the Higher Teacher Training College. We lived in a modest house in a working-class neighborhood in Yaounde. His family had stopped supporting us after the wedding and we lived off Louis's meager salary and my scholarship. Back then the Cameroon government paid students in higher education who would join the public service. Things have changed radically since then.

My daughter had just turned three when Awaya passed away. The still vivid memory of these events is etched in my mind.

I was doing laundry, sitting in the tiny, shared yard in

our housing estate. I had a basin of soapy water in which I scrubbed the dirty linens and another one with hot water to rinse. I had given Abi a small bucket filled with sudsy water and one of her T-shirts, which she was pretending to wash by mimicking my gestures. My little girl was naked on that sunny morning, covered in foam. I was responding to her joyous babble when I saw Awaya arrive.

She came into our yard and before I could do anything, my Abi launched toward her. The old woman stooped with a dexterity uncommon to someone her age and scooped my child into her arms, lifting her high up. They both laughed, the chubby and naked body of my little girl wriggling in the arms of Awaya, who covered her with kisses. This left me paralyzed. Still carrying the child, she came over to me and hugged me warmly. "*Agondo,* you are soooo beautiful. Turn around and let me look at you. Motherhood has unveiled your beauty, my daughter. Samgali, see—our sun has finally peaked out."

Then, out of the blue, she put Abi down and started dancing around her, singing and ululating.

"I have come. I have come, my sister. Do you see how beautiful I am? I waited for you. Did you see me coming? I have missed you, twin sister. Have you missed me too? My sister, here I am. Here I am as promised," she chanted.

My daughter danced along with her, clapping, wide-eyed, laughing heartily. The neighbors came running, drawn by the noise.

"Anna, who is that?" they asked.

"My mother," I responded, mumbling.

What else could I say? The rest was too complicated to explain. Everyone smiled. It was a beautiful scene. I alone was bothered by her presence. "When did she last set her eyes on you? Look how happy she is," people said.

I said nothing in response.

Awaya finally sat down. She sat Abi on her knees and my daughter curled up against her. The old woman turned down the glass of water and food that I offered her:

"I'm not hungry, *Agondo*. I ate on the bus. I even feel a bit bloated, but I'm okay."

She gave me a hand with my chores, without asking about my life. Nor did she quiz me on my silence. She went on and on:

"I'm fine. Don't worry. I was a little bit sick but now I am fine. Everything is fine, my daughter. I'm no longer sick."

She helped me finish my laundry, then cook. My daughter clasped to her hip the whole time. Louis came home for lunch, and Awaya welcomed him warmly in her unpolished English, saying, "Welcome back to your home, father of my granddaughter." Louis stared at her quizzically without uttering a word. I simply shrugged and he never pursued the issue further. People often visited unannounced. It wasn't that strange.

Abi refused to eat and only accepted food when curled up in Awaya's arms like a small mirthful cat. The entire afternoon passed by in that surreal atmosphere. In the evening, Abi insisted that Awaya bathe her, then cried so loud to sleep with her that it exasperated Louis. "Let her be. If she wants to sleep with her grandmother, where is the harm in that?" he shouted. Weary of fighting, worn out by the emotions of the day, I finally gave in.

I was worried, certain that I wouldn't sleep all night and promising myself that I would check in later to make sure everything was fine. However, immediately after getting into bed, I slept like a rock until late the next morning. I woke up with a start and hurried into the room with Awaya and my daughter. I could have killed myself for having been so absentminded. Abi was alone. Wrapped up in the sheets and lying in the middle of the bed. Awaya wasn't there. I immediately noticed the tiny scarifications on the wrists, lower back, ankles, and forehead of my little daughter. I bore the same. Outraged, I stormed from the room, determined to have a word with Awaya. To send her back home. I never ever wanted her to come close to my daughter again.

I looked for her in the parlor, the bathroom, the outdoor toilets that we shared with the other residents in the common area. She was nowhere to be found. I asked the neighbors. Nobody had seen her. My anger turned to anxiety. Had she left? Had she collapsed somewhere? Was she missing? Injured? I hated myself for having been so angry. Sorrow and regret overwhelmed me. Out of pity, some other women joined my search party. We screamed her name all over the neighborhood. Nobody had seen her.

Abi was still asleep. I handed her to a woman who often looked after her when I wasn't around and after a quick bath, I headed to Louis's office. I wanted to go to Ombessa, I explained to him. Awaya had disappeared. I had this bad feeling. "What do you mean, disappeared?"

Louis exclaimed. "People don't just disappear like that. Have you looked for her? Maybe she just lost her way. Elderly people often get confused. You know that all too well. And what would you do in Ombessa? She would never leave without saying goodbye, Anna."

His incredulity did not calm my fears. I had to go to the village. Something there was beckoning me, calling me back there. Some undisputable order that I felt inside, and which I could not resist. There was nothing Louis could do about my decision. He drove me to the bus station in the old Peugeot 504 he was so proud of. "You're worrying for nothing," he reassured me. "I will go back home. We'll search again. She should be somewhere."

I scouted the road for the whole trip, my head leaning against the window of the bus. Attentive to that stretch of road I had traveled so many times. Deep down inside, I knew that I would not see anything. But I shuddered every time I saw a shape—a rock, a tree trunk in the distance—fearing I'd find Awaya lying on the ground. Wounded or worse.

It was Wednesday. A market day. The center of the village was crowded, as it usually was on that day. As soon as I got off the bus, I saw Awaya's daughter. She threw herself into my arms crying. "Bouissi, who told you? I was about to get on the bus to bring you the news. *Nyedi bitcho*, our mother passed away this morning," she told me, hugging me tightly.

At that very moment, the anguish that had gripped me since I'd woken up disappeared.

At the moment of her death, Awaya was stepping

into my yard. Now that I think of it, I think I found her to be...not younger, because the deep wrinkles I had grown up seeing still ran across her face, and her fingers were still gaunt and blotted from old age, and her gaze, grayed by cataracts, had not changed. But she had looked so perfectly alive to me when she knelt like a young girl to scoop Abi into her arms. Strong when she had picked her up without any apparent effort. Sharp-minded when, carrying her on her hip, she had helped me with my chores. I had found her strong. Alive! My mother had come to say goodbye. To connect my daughter to her sister, Samgali. I could now lay down my weapons, the battle was over. The deceased women had won.

My defeat brought me unexpected peace. In my unending battle to protect Abi, I now had allies more committed than I was. My daughter's life now fit into the wider web of our shared history. Yes! I had doubted it. Yes! I had at one point thought that I could wrest myself free. Awaya showed me conclusively that even death can't break bonds wrought by love, as old as the hills.

That said, I grew an instinctive distrust of death, causing me to keep a safe distance from the huge death celebrations my husband's family organized. I had lost the battle against my own deceased family members. I didn't feel I had the courage to face my Bamileke benefactors because I knew more than anyone about how stubborn the dead are in their desire to run our lives.

From November through May, during the dry season, when crops have been stored away and new plants sowed, Bamileke country pulsates to the rhythm of death celebrations. They are a sparkling expression of the complexity and depth of their attachment to their ancestral values. They are also an opportunity to show just how well one is doing economically. I dreaded this period that everyone else welcomed with joy.

The Bamileke had perfected the art of protecting their privacy. My lack of enthusiasm didn't make life easier for me. Even Louis took offense. "I don't understand," I argued dishonestly. "You're all devout Christians. You wear out your knees in church every Sunday. And then you head out to indulge in God-knows-what in your sacred forests. Does that not offend you? Don't you find it incompatible?"

I distanced myself from what my husband's family did together. They held it against me. If only I'd had sons! If I had given them sons, they may have been more forgiving. The things I stopped myself from doing, my whims as a stranger, a *nkwa*, would have been tolerated if my sons had lined up with their forefathers on the long road of timeless traditions. My only daughter wasn't sufficient guarantee of my loyalty, of my commitment to the group. As surely as if tearing my marriage certificate and casting the pieces to the wind, as insidious as they alone were capable of being, my husband's family invalidated my marriage.

I graduated as a teacher. Louis was appointed to head the finance unit of a parastatal in Douala and I transferred to a high school in the city. We took up residence in Bonabéri, a suburban neighborhood on the city's west

side, over the Wouri bridge. I got my driver's license. I
had a beautiful single-story house, equipped with all my
dream amenities. I had a library built to reflect my love
for books. At long last, I was getting the dream life I had
chased with such determination. Despite our best efforts,
I was unable to conceive again after Abi. Although the
real reason is I had no family, and Louis, who had recon-
ciled with his, had had enough.

When the time came, my father-in-law retired. He
took up residence in Dschang, where, during every visit,
I endured the bitterness of my mother-in-law and her
hurtful comments about the second child that was long
overdue. "My daughter, why is your stomach getting big
like that? Should I be expecting good news, or is it nothing more than the big helpings of yellow soup you have
been stuffing yourself with?" she said.

Okay, I admit I was a huge fan of *achu* soup, a
Bamileke specialty made from an emulsion of palm oil and
flavored with a dozen tasty spices. Eaten with pounded
cocoyams and the indispensable grilled pork chop, skin
and fat included. However, my stomach, squeezed into
a body-hugging dress to display my pretty body, wasn't
growing one inch bigger. Later we lived in a place where
being overweight, because of the variety and number
of dishes, was normal, and even my mother-in-law was
bursting at the seams, but nobody made unkind comments. I dreamed of telling her what I thought, but contented myself with clenching my teeth and making fewer
trips to Dschang, so Louis would go alone to take part
in burials, baptisms, and the numerous other events that

attracted the city-dwelling Bamilekes to their village every weekend.

I kept my distance and that was my mistake, because alliances that would directly affect me were being made in my absence.

Louis quickly rose through the ranks at his work and in only a few years became the finance director. In addition to his usual duties, he was now tasked with recruitment and procurement. This wasn't normal. He now had the power to recruit workers in our country where unemployment among the young was endemic. He had the power to choose suppliers and subcontractors, and he controlled the purse strings. It was also agreed that he would replace his boss, who'd been tapped for imminent appointment as a minister in Yaounde. Power was concentrated only in his hands, and the certainty that he was just starting his rise to the top increased his prestige among the people from his tribe. Louis went into "business," a generic term that encompassed winning and awarding fraudulent contracts, which is quite rampant in our country. Jettisoning his former reluctance, he joined the ruling party. He became passionate about politics and started nursing the idea of becoming a parliamentarian.

"You can't accomplish anything in this country unless you are at the heart of the system," he responded to my reservations.

"What are you trying to accomplish exactly?" I snickered.

I wasn't fooled by the torrents of money. Way more

than what he could reasonably expect to be making. Even with a huge salary or his *njangis* with the rich business-people and members of government to whom he awarded contracts in exchange for either kickbacks on profits, or an induction into the *Laakam*, the group of notables who ensured that the chief governed his clan properly and was the hub of the Bamileke lobby in Cameroon. I thought I had a rather clear picture of the situation, but I hadn't fully measured all its consequences.

Louis wanted to move to Bonapriso, a residential neighborhood in Douala. It was way more glamorous than the suburb where we lived. Way more consistent with his new-found ambitions. I refused to move out of my house. We had spent long hours planning our home. The layout of the rooms. The garden. For the first time in my life, I had my own comfortable place that suited me. I was deeply rooted and could not see myself giving it up. Louis stopped mentioning his plan and I thought it was a won battle. From the habitual gossip of my husband's family, I learned that he had bought a plot of land in Bonapriso where he was building one of the kitschy villas highly prized by his nouveau rich compatriots. "And where did you get this money from?" I asked him, worried. My husband had bought land in an extremely expensive neighborhood. He'd started building a luxurious villa, without any mention of a mortgage and without my noticing a change in our lifestyle.

As a precaution, to ensure my future and that of my daughter, I asked that ownership of our Bonabéri house be transferred to me exclusively. Louis was undecided.

To overcome this hurdle, I suggested that he put it in Abi's name. He was so confident of his career path— undoubtedly brilliant and glorious—that it was in some ways, a gesture that brought him relief. He had demonstrated his elegance. His daughter and I had a roof over our heads. Nothing else would concern us.

I rarely went to Dschang after that, except when I couldn't help it. On one such unavoidable occasion, we stayed with my husband's parents. Staying in the house was a pregnant young girl I had never met before. I paid her no mind, all my attention focused on a huge building under construction on the family plot. I smiled, asking Louis, "Which of your brothers wants to become lord of Dschang?"

My mother-in-law replied without giving him the time to respond, "Didn't you know? My son, Louis, has honored his family. This is his village residence," she announced.

I was speechless. I expressed my confusion to Louis when we were alone:

"Oh, come on! This is madness. When will you stop? How are you paying for all of this? What sort of fishy business have you gotten yourself into?"

He got angrier than he had ever been before.

"Do you realize what you are saying, Anna? Do you realize who you are? I'm respected and admired everywhere except in my own house. My wife challenges me. Wishes me evil. Looks forward to my fall. When will you be happy for me? When will you congratulate me? When will you thank me for pulling you out of the swamp you grew up in and transforming you into a rich and respectable woman? Where is my thanks for the house I gave you? For the clothes, the jewelry, the car, the good life? When will you stop criticizing, maligning, and denigrating the things you benefit from the most?"

I envisioned my mother-in-law eavesdropping behind the closed door and responded in a low voice. "I did not ask you for any of this, Louis. Don't use me as an excuse. Be honest for once in your life—deep down, you know I have nothing to do with all of this. How do I know? You have made extravagant real estate investments without even telling me about them."

"Honestly?" he yelled. "You are right. I am dishonest. A thief. Corrupt. What did you say again? I'm involved in fishy business, right?" he added.

"Louis," I tried to calm things down. "Two and two make four. There's no other way about it. You launch gargantuan projects. You're building two houses at the same time. You have just bought yourself a brand-new 4×4; on top of your company car and my car, and now this new car, we have three cars. What would you think if you were in my shoes?"

"If I were in your shoes, I would support my husband, instead of always challenging me the way you do," he replied.

I burst into laughter.

"Do you hear yourself? Do you think you're at a rally? With zero opposition in sight? I am either with you or against you. Is that it? Louis, wake up! We have way more than we need. We do not need all this flashy… You don't have to act like an arrogant parvenu with money that isn't yours. I don't know who you are," I told him.

"Flashy, parvenu, arrogant… Thanks, Anna. I now know what you really think. And rest assured, I won't forget it any time soon. My mother was right. I can't prosper with a wife like you at home," he revealed.

"But what has your mother got to do with this? Would you like us to talk about your mother? The woman who only steps away from the juju pot over which she sits to go pretend in church? The woman who has treated me like a leper since the first day she laid eyes on me? No doubt she supports you! Her husband ignores her, so she stirs chaos in our home in retaliation. You should be ashamed, at your age, to still be a mommy's boy."

"If that were the case," Louis blurted, "I wouldn't have married you, and I'd be better off now. You dare insult my mother? You're the expert in mothers, right?"

Long-standing couples know that, even in the most heated arguments, there are some extremes you shouldn't pass. We went beyond them by a mile.

"The best thing for me to do is return to Douala," I announced, picking up my suitcase. "Could you tell the driver to take me back to Douala?"

"Listen to me carefully, Anna," he said softly, "we came here for the funeral of a dignitary. Important people in this country are making the trip. You'll stand by my side, smiling, meeting people. My future is at stake, Anna. If you mess things up for me…"

Louis didn't finish his sentence and left, slamming

the door on his way out. I decided to stay.

That enraged man worried me, but if I left under those circumstances our fight would become public knowledge. Speculation would run rampant all weekend long. I still believed I could keep up the act. I would do what was expected of me and endeavor to ease tensions with Louis. He was under pressure. I could understand that. This was neither the place nor the moment to discuss it. We would talk about it all later. My conciliatory attitude would be a token of goodwill and the starting point for a calmer discussion.

With that resolution, I went back to join my mother- and sisters-in-law. They had made a fire in the backyard where the inevitable *kondrè*—a dish made from goat meat and unripe plantains—had been cooking since the previous day. It was another richly flavored and calorie-packed specialty. Everyone grew silent when I arrived. Obviously, our voices had carried as far as them, but I overlooked this. All smiles, I took a stool, sat with them, and asked how each of them was doing.

Speaking to me, my mother-in-law pointed to the young girl I had seen when we arrived.

"Anna, won't you greet your co-wife?" she asked.

Quite generic, the term could have meant my relationship with the wife of any man in the village. Back in the old days, women were bequeathed like inheritance. Any of your husband's relatives could thus be your husband. The practice had disappeared, but the custom of women referring to one another as co-wives when they were married to brothers had continued. I looked at the young girl more closely. Spotless light skin, hazel eyes, wide hips, and voluptuous breasts. A typical beauty from Dschang! I gave her, by my estimates, only two pregnancies before those youthful features turned into fat from the combined assaults of *achu* soup, *kondrè,* and lack of self-care.

"Good morning," I said with a friendly tone. "How are you?"

"My name is Geneviève, Auntie," she replied, timidly.

I accepted her calling me "Auntie," which reflected her respect. My mother-in-law continued.

"Géné is a student at the university here in Dschang. You know the Kenfack family, right? The family that owns the big house at the foot of the hill. Their father was a top civil servant in Yaounde. He just retired. He is an important person in our community."

I could read between the lines and noticed the use of the diminutive form of her name "Géné," which informed me that she was under the protection of the old lady. The same way I took note that she was high-born. I became even friendlier.

"And you are the wife of…?" I pressed.

My mother-in-law, determined to steer the conversation replied, "But I already told you. She is your co-wife. Louis's wife. Didn't he tell you about her? We have already paid her dowry. The traditional marriage will take place after she gives birth."

Checkmate!

Only at that point did I notice the silence around us. Acting as if they were highly engrossed in their chores, my sisters-in-law had not uttered a word throughout our discussion. I got to see my fight with Louis from another angle. While I had been trying to lower my voice, his had gone up a notch. He had not only been speaking to me, but also informing his relatives of our fight. I thought I was calming my husband down by choosing to stay despite my reluctance. However, my mother-in-law had construed this as a sign of submission and decided to rub salt in the wound.

The next thing I did still surprises me even now. Abi was playing with her cousins in the yard. I walked over to my child, stooped to her level, and spoke to her calmly: "My dear, Mommy has to go back to Douala right away. Nothing serious. Don't worry. You will come home with Daddy on Sunday, okay?" I then went and got my suitcase and the car key Louis had left on the bedside table.

My husband, his brothers, and their father were there for the funeral, as well as many men I didn't know. They were all seated in the parlor, having drinks and talking loudly, as they waited for the women jam-packed in the kitchen to serve them lunch. Louis stood up when he saw me come in. I have already told you that I know how to fight. When you decide to strike the first blow, no matter the situation and regardless of the opponent's strength, surprise and unpredictable violence are your best allies. My husband never would have imagined that I would hit him. I didn't hesitate for one second. A knee to his private parts. And before he caught his breath, a straight jab, with my hand holding the car key, to the arch of his eyebrow, which started bleeding profusely. Aided by the chaos, I hurried to the luxurious 4×4 parked outside. I locked the car doors and turned on the ignition. The cars had been parked in the backyard, not far from where my mother-in-law was cooking. Alarmed by the screaming, the women had rushed toward the living room. I drove toward the crowd. They scattered in all directions like frightened birds, and I crashed into the pot of *kondrè* that spilled, leaving a huge dent on the new car's front panel. I felt when the wheels rolled over the huge slices of goat meat meant for lunch.

I had to drive past the main entrance on my way out of the compound. I made a U-turn. The car was not easy to maneuver due to its weight. I wasn't used to it. The engine stalled. The men rushed outside, Louis leading, his face covered in blood. He grabbed the door handle as I restarted the engine. I darted off at full throttle, forcing him to run a few meters before collapsing into the dust. I could see, in my rearview mirror, my husband's family rushing to his side where he lay wounded. My mother-in-law was hurling curses, and—the more gripping image—my father-in-law was laughing his head off while tapping his thigh.

My heart was beating thunderously. My legs, from the top of my thighs down to my calves, trembled. My arms were aching from how tightly I'd clutched the steering wheel. The fist I had used to punch Louis hurt. I felt my blood throbbing in my ears as I drove the one hundred and sixty kilometers between Dschang and Douala in hysterics, between giggles and tears of rage.

Louis and Abi got dropped off on Sunday evening. Nobody had reached out to me over the weekend and honestly, I hadn't been expecting any show of concern. I welcomed my daughter happily and ignored Louis. I had had two days to mull over the situation and the long list of grievances I held against my husband. I was expecting to feel sad. I would have loved to make some bold and final decision. I was unable to understand my feelings, to interpret the silence, the blank emptiness. I was sinking in quicksand, losing all balance and reason.

I had thought I was ready to face anything, but Louis's attitude upon his return surprised me.

"Anna, I was planning to explain things to you myself. You know, this union is nothing more than a political move. It doesn't mean anything. You and I chose monogamy when we got married. This other marriage is not recognized by law, but if I want people to support my bid for a parliamentary seat, I must have a wife from my tribe. Do you understand, Anna? You don't have to worry. You will forever be the only woman who means anything to me. You're the one I love."

I did not respond and we didn't speak again for weeks, when he moved into his new house with his "political move."

"Since you no longer want me, I'm leaving," he declared one evening.

My anger finally subsided, leaving nothing but rancor and fear for the future.

It was hard for me to admit it then, but I must now

admit that I was also to blame for the breakdown of our marriage. I hadn't forgiven Louis for doubting me after Abi was conceived. Nor had I forgiven my husband's family for ostracizing me. But I thought my husband would side with me, but he chose his family instead. He took their side and made me feel unwelcome. I blamed him for that, so I grew distant. I shut down. I cast a distant and cruel gaze on his ambitions. Louis wanted to be admired, supported, but all I saw was an ever-deeper immersion into the corrupt system that he had once been able to see with such clarity.

He and his new friends were all alike. Powerful men intent on dipping their hands into the unguarded treasure of the country. Like him, they had influential positions, were into politics, married younger women, and were drunk on their power.

Louis was better than that. I clearly saw the sycophants, the respect he drew with his good fortune. However, I did not measure the extent to which all that could unbolt his convictions, the internal ecosystem of a man such as my husband. My affection for him had turned sour. He was right. I judged and sentenced him long before our marriage collapsed. And even in hindsight, I can't see how I could have remained a part of that deception. It is true that I benefited from it. There's no need denying it. I thought we could live more decently but that isn't necessarily why I left Louis. It had less to do with money or affection and more to do with the dizzying reality of finding myself without the protection of a man to raise my daughter. Or simply without the protection of a man at all.

The devaluation of the Cameroonian franc also played its part. My salary, just like that of all civil servants, was slashed without warning. I was forced to substitute in private high schools to maintain a decent standard of living. Every month, Louis sent us thick bundles of cash, "for Abi," he told me, and he continued paying her school fees in the French school. I opened an account in my daughter's name where I deposited all the money he sent. Our future was increasingly uncertain. Abi would maybe need a little push to start off in life. I wanted to be ready for any scenario.

With the early months of extreme tension behind us, I allowed Abi to have lunch at the new house during her lunch break. Louis lived close to her school, and it was more convenient than returning to Bonabéri. Abi and her father were close. Our separation had already taken a toll on her. I didn't also want to totally deprive her of him. Through our daughter, I learned that my husband's new wife had given birth to the long-awaited heir.

That was when I first seriously considered divorce and Ma' Moudio came over.

My old friend came to visit me one Sunday afternoon, bringing in her basket a huge dish of *ndolè-crayfish-miondo* and bottles of beer fresh from the refrigerator at the store around the corner. Abi let her in and I heard her shout from the hallway, "Anna, come and eat! Abi, kindly set the table for your mother and me. You'll eat in the kitchen—there is something I have to talk to your mother about."

Her tone left no room for dialogue. Abi looked at me

sternly when I stepped into the room. "The cavalry has arrived!" she announced.

Ma' Moudio served us huge portions and opened some beers.

"Ah, *Mùnam*, my child, rumor has it you almost crushed that old witch of a mother-in-law with your car?" she joked. "Rumor also has it that you punched your husband in front of his family? Please, you have to tell me this story."

I burst into tears. Once again, life was bringing me back to my starting point. I had tried as hard as I could. Fought like a devil. But I had ended up alone with my daughter anyway. Ma' Moudio let me bare my soul for a moment, before she interrupted me bluntly.

"Now, can you tell me something? Are you then going to cry all day? Are you so bent on having a man in your house? Don't worry about it. He'll come back, my daughter. All men have a golden age in which life smiles upon them. They think they are masters of the universe. They think they are invincible. If they also happen to make some money, their feet no longer touch the ground when they walk. That's just the way it is," she told me.

"You know, I'm going to file for divorce. You are the first person I've told," I declared.

She laughed, and then hissed with disdain.

"You want to what? Divorce? Why? My dear, you're in the ideal situation. You have the name, the house, a man who takes care of his child. You have the perks of marriage without the burden of a husband. Seriously, my daughter, you don't know how lucky you are. Do you miss your husband's family so much, they who visit all at once and never give warning? Forget that idiocy! You'll see, he will be back. Men always come back. The bubble bursts and they realize that they have hit a ceiling. They're getting old. Competition is harsher. Their health starts to crumble. Their dicks no longer harden like they used to. Who do they turn to for refuge? Enjoy it, sweetheart. Live to the fullest. You know, we beat ourselves up over these things, but it's never as serious as we think. You'll understand when you get to be my age."

My old friend's cynical pragmatism became my guiding light. I built my life around my daughter, my substitute classes at various high schools, and inconsequential affairs. I enjoyed waking up alone in my huge bed, or reading quietly all evening long, while Abi did her homework in the room next door. No man's needs or demands saddled me with a pace that was not my own. No man to poison my nights or days with his mistakes. No man to drive me to the brink of madness with his lies. I found that I was better off this way.

※

Since I have tried it more than once, I now know that failure occasionally offers a welcome peace of mind.

It took us a few years, but my relationship with Louis finally became cordial. The only thing we had in common was our daughter. He didn't try to take her away from me and I let him play the role of her father as much as he chose. I smiled at the tiny seductive gestures he directed at me. "What's going on with you, Anna? You look so fulfilled. Always so slim. Shapely as a young girl," he'd whisper to me when he came for Abi. "You're getting younger while I'm getting older. It's not fair. Tell the fellow who has taken my place that I have my eye on him. You're still my wife, remember that, Anna." His hands would brush against my waist, my chest, almost inadvertently. I didn't give him any reason to go further. Nor did I push him off.

His wife gave birth to their third son. *A downright bevy of heirs over there*, I thought, amused. I cooked and bought a few trifles as a gift, as custom would have it, to welcome the newborn. In doing so, I was telling them that we had buried the hatchet. It had been years since I had laid eyes on my husband's extended family. Quite strange given that Douala is not that big of a city. I think we all made a conscious effort to avoid one another. My reputation as a potential murderer protecting me from unwelcome intrusions. Only my father-in-law called, regularly checking in on us.

I had Louis warn them I was planning to visit and brought Abi to show that I came in peace.

The pretty Geneviève had grown as fat as I'd expected. Her three pregnancies had been one after the other, with no breaks in between. Her body was paying the price. Her formerly voluptuous breasts had collapsed and her hips had thickened. I happily imagined the light skin of her flabby stomach striped by stretch marks. My husband's parents were there, along with my father-in-law's other wife. I was not the only one who had made concessions. They welcomed me with suspicious enthusiasm, hypocrisy being an indispensable ingredient in a dysfunctional family.

In the wake of that visit, my father-in-law and his new wife made a habit of staying with me whenever they came to Douala. "There's too much noise in Bonapriso," they told me. "All those babies crying and running right and left. I'm too old for that. Here at your house there's peace and quiet." I always agreed to host him.

I had seen him at ceremonies, neat, tidy, and sociable. When he was at my place, he asked me to cook him *koum koum*, yellow yams, and *njama njama* cooked with *egusi*. Delicacies from my village. He ate with his hands and drank his beer straight from the bottle. I could sense that he was completely comfortable. He also had a tender way of treating his young wife that made me happy. "Here is a man who has found a walking stick for his old age," I smiled inwardly. Everything about him showed that he no longer cared about societal pressure. He simply wanted to be happy in the time he had left to live. He adored Abi and she adored him back in equal measure. They had long conversations in Yemba and spent a lot of time together. I had a hard time imagining that this charming man used to hunt down resistance fighters. Nobody in the family ever talked about that history.

But we were always happy, Abi and I, to once again be alone when they finally left.

That was about the time my husband won a parliamentary seat and the coveted position of director general of the parastatal where he worked.

They organized a huge party at the villa in Bonapriso to celebrate.

For the occasion, Louis ordered an outfit tailor-made from *ndop*, the traditional Bamileke fabric made from cotton strips decorated with white geometric shapes against an indigo background. The strips are connected by an intricate weave of raffia threads. As a sign of respect, his guests greeted him with their hands together and a slight bow—a Bamileke way of paying tribute to important people. They all called him *DG*, which stood for "Director General" or "Your Honor." Even his new wife and his mother. Well-lit and decorated with fresh flowers, the garden was jam-packed. Tables were covered with the most delicious traditional dishes. Waiters in white outfits refilled your glass immediately if it was empty. Shuttling between jazz classics and local music, a band played quietly.

Louis moved from one group to another with ease. Laughing hard. Accepting the signs of allegiance as if they were his due. In a moment of clarity, I saw him the way he saw himself. He had put on weight. He now had a potbelly, and a neck as thick as a bull's stuck out of his *boubou*. He reeked of the brute power his consecration conferred. Louis was well aware of his power. In every respect that mattered in our society, he had succeeded, and he knew it.

I had taken a seat away from the many sycophants. Louis came over to join me later in the evening. We had not spoken to each other except when I'd congratulated him when I arrived. Talking privately reminded me of other such conversations we had had when he'd come during visiting weekends. I was neither nostalgic nor sad. The thought just crossed my mind. Nothing more. Nothing less. I had initially felt somewhat nervous when I'd seen the crowd. I was only happy in private, in one-on-one conversations. I was grateful to Louis for remembering that.

I smiled when he sat down next to me.

"I'm happy for you," I told him.

Louis leaned back heavily in the chair. I had been drinking but I was not drunk. I was loitering in that gray area where alcohol lifts one's inhibitions but hasn't yet dulled the mind. He, though, was drunk, but less from alcohol and more from his accomplishments and the party, which was his coronation.

"I would very much have loved for you to have experienced this by my side. I've never really understood why we fell apart. I still love you, you know?"

"You abandoned me because I didn't support you enough. Because your mother hated me. Because you wanted to marry a *political move*—the thing that inspired you the most. With me, you would never have accomplished your dreams. I didn't even know this is what they were."

"This is not the time for keeping score," he replied.

"But I am here, right next to you," I said.

"You know what I mean, Anna. We have so much in common. I miss our conversations. I don't really have anyone to talk to," he told me.

We no longer had much to say to one another anyway, I thought to myself silently.

"And what if that was the only thing that mattered..." added Louis, laying his head on my shoulder.

He took my hand, kissing my palm tenderly and inhaling at the hollow of my wrist, saying, "You're beautiful. You smell nice. Your skin is so smooth."

He raised his head and gave me a knowing look.

"Do you still use that body lotion made from palm kernel?" he asked.

I thought about the pretty Geneviève, who was once again pregnant, as if planning to repopulate the earth all by herself. And my mother-in-law, who knew every tiny detail that there was to know, but was powerless. I guessed at their outrage and their impotence. After all, Louis and I were still married. When an alpha male chooses his female, the others run off with their tails between their legs. We made love that night. My husband took me with such passion! I could not help but think that in his mind, he was not only fucking me, but also the world at his feet.

I said that I love all books. That's not exactly true. I have always shied away from African literature. It contains an injunction that I'm uncomfortable with. Foreign authors talk to an inner "me." They explore my race, as well as a history that hurts and humiliates me. I'm a sensitive woman, prone to the turmoil of life. I'm not a concept. A battle lost. A territory to be conquered or an authenticity to be redefined. My identity is self-evident, but if there has ever been any doubt, their imagination has never been able to restore its complexity.

Back when we used to talk about the books we read, I remember that Louis had unbridled admiration for Frantz Fanon, just like a lot of people of his generation. I didn't share his enthusiasm. I surely viewed Fanon through the wrong prism because we just missed each other. Perhaps because he was not a novelist. I can understand that his activism generated a type of exhortation that wasn't suitable for fiction. But beyond the purely didactic comments triggered by the struggle, my dislike for him was anchored in one fact: their wives, who were more invisible than the damned of the earth. And even Fanon, despite all his sensibility and his intelligence, did not acknowledge them.

I completely shun novels that portray Africa a pretty (to a certain extent) wreck, and Africans as nothing but dull children. Or brutes, always poised to slaughter one another in a constant reminder of their atavistic cannibalism. Or helpless victims, who need the protection of cunning and heartless politicians, and even right to their illusion-free indigenous loves that reflect their ugly perception of our land.

That was before I discovered V. Y. Mudimbe and understood the intellectual effort it took—hardly perceptible because it was so deeply entrenched and my spirit had adjusted to the demands, but real all the same—to see myself in all these books whose characters were different from me and existed in a world unbeknownst to me. I adjusted to their respective worlds and they turned my own world upside down, because they spoke to this part of me, in each of us, that transcends affiliations and connects our pure souls.

The novels of V. Y. Mudimbe rattled me like none had before.

It seems strange that he and V. S. Naipaul are referring to the same country in *Before the Birth of the Moon* and *A Bend in the River*.

Naipaul explores the contradictory feelings of fascination and hatred that his character can't help but have for the West. As an Indian whose family had immigrated to Africa several generations prior, the character has a hard time dealing with the loss of his privilege and talks about the spite he feels. Congo is the wild, desolate backdrop that represents his own internal decay, and sub-Saharan Africans are shadows sinking ever deeper into the heart of darkness as they destroy everything in their path.

Mudimbe describes his own suffering in the middle of a disaster. He talks about extreme violence, deprivation, and death. Corrosive love affairs that dry up the heart. Our macabre dance on the edge of the cliff. Our souls that we pawn off for nothing, and the madness lurking in every corner. The hopelessness we all see clearly is what we have in common and is our sole possession. He takes responsibility for the status quo and thus restores our bruised humanity. His African women are complex, subtle, desirable, as if they are women he could fall in love with. He describes the beauty of sub-Saharan men as well as their torments.

To my knowledge, Mudimbe was the only sub-Saharan novelist who did that. The only novelist, period.

I thought about him that night. He would have known how to describe my state of mind—as there is an undeniable pleasure in succumbing to violence and corruption.

II

The plane landed in Douala early in the evening. Max greedily inhaled the moisture-filled air. His skin was covered with sweat from the dusty heat that no breeze could soften. He was used to it. He traveled to Cameroon every year for the holidays, either with his parents, or alone to his grandmother's.

His first memory of Douala was from when he was nine. That's when he first felt the atmosphere like a greenhouse—or like a *hammam*, as his mother would say, smiling—the air hitting you in the throat as you stepped off the plane. He had been distressed by it. The long wait, the wrangling at the customs checkpoint, and the noisy and poor crowd outside had frightened him. He can't remember having been aware of all that before then. His grandparents were waiting for them at the checkout. The air was so heavy when one landed in Douala that your spirit had to brace itself to face the lush and impressive tropical forest. The shanty towns around the airport provided some relief, which quickly evaporated as you sank deeper into the city.

The nervousness Max felt had continued throughout the ride as he watched the scarified beggars who rushed to their car every time it slowed down.

What illness causes this kind of disability? he wondered while looking at the lepers begging for money at the intersections, their purulent limbs ravaged right to the bone. He looked away and made a discreet sign of the cross when a woman in rags, leaning on a small child like a walking stick, knocked on the back window of their car stuck in the traffic. One would have thought that her milk-white pupils had swollen until they occupied the entire surface area of her eyeballs. *Are her eyes upside down?* the little boy wondered, terrified. Max had the impression that her blind gaze was focused on him. That she was looking only at him. That she was stretching out her hand for him.

Happy with seeing one another again, the adults talked excitedly in the car, oblivious to his distress. Max held on a little tighter to his grandmother, slipping his hand into hers. She smiled at him, saying, "*Alougou*, you have grown taller again, eh? Where are you trying to grow to like this? Do you want to pick the stars to adorn my hair?" Max laughed. Here, everyone called him by a different name. His grandfather called him *Ehn Fooh*, meaning "great chief." However, when he was angry with him, which rarely happened, he would then formally address him by his full name, "Maxime Tchoualé Achard, come here, my friend!" The "my friend" part was no indication of friendly tidings to come. His grandmother shuttled between "Dou," "Chou," "Maxou"…with a clear preference for *Alougou*, meaning "husband." His friends in Bonabéri, Ismaël, Jenny, and Tina, despite being mixed-race like him, jokingly called him "white boy." But the strangest was his granny Geneviève who, for reasons unknown to him, had always called him "Belmondo."

As he got older, Max grew to enjoy his holidays even more. He made friends and took advantage of the various opportunities the city had to offer.

The environment, be it for him or for anyone—except for newcomers—fit together to form an incongruous and exciting whole. During his stays, the small group of friends in Bonabéri met to share the latest gossip and stroll around the neighborhood, rediscovering places and people. Later, Max would go on expeditions with his relatives inland, or go with his grandfather who made it his duty to take him to his village.

He impatiently anticipated his holidays in Cameroon because there he had unrestricted freedom. The neighborhood where his grandmother lived was built on a swamp formed after the waters of the nearby Wouri dried up. As soon as the rainy season started, the streets were filled with pools of water as big as rivers. The brown, slippery mud was a distinctly attractive playground for him who lived in such a sterile environment. As soon as the adults left in the morning, he, Jenny, Ismaël, and Tina would quickly swallow their breakfast before wandering around the neighborhood all day, stopping to play football or hide-and-seek. Max was no longer struck by the many languages spoken in the street. Mother tongues. Unconventional English. French littered with funny expressions and unknown words that he nevertheless hurried to learn.

Everyone knew him. They called out to him, saying, "Hey, Maxou. When did you get here? How are your parents?"

Bonabéri was an open-air amusement park. All the more appealing since the young man's parents were not on his case. In Paris, he couldn't do anything by himself. His mother took him to his activities. She came back to pick him up and make sure he was never in harm's way. Here, he followed his friends into narrow unknown alleys. Jumped into stagnant waters. Ate half-ripe mangoes and guavas with the delightful feeling that he was living on the edge.

When they returned, Auntie Astou, his grandmother's housekeeper, would warn them against entering the house as muddy as they were. She forced them to take a bath out in the yard, using the garden hose. The four friends would grumble just for the sake of grumbling. Far from being mandatory, the forced outdoor bath, under the sun or in the rain, was one of the joys of being on vacation.

But this trip was radically different from the previous ones. His mood was darker because his mother, he was sure of it, had come to drop him off like an old parcel before going back to be with that idiot. The teenager arrived in Cameroon with his morale at an all-time low. He only spoke to Abi when he had to, and threw a tantrum every time she tried to get close to him.

By constantly eavesdropping at the door—and he did not even have to strain much given how loud his father screamed his grievances—Max had come to understand what was going on. His mother was to blame for everything. His world had gone up in smoke because of that *b*... He fumbled over the word, unable to use it to refer to the person he most cherished in the whole world—to refer to both his anchor and his lighthouse. She was his own home. More than a person. The place from where he could take a leap without any fear, with the assurance of knowing he was loved. His unwavering light. His inextinguishable source. His invincible bond. She was his mother, but she had betrayed him.

He hated his father, too. In fact, it went beyond hatred, he despised him. What kind of bum lets his wife be snatched and spends his time whining instead of going to smash in the face of the other man? Max thought it would be better to be an orphan than to have such shameful parents. At least they would be dead and everybody would console him. He would not feel like he was struggling all alone in the mud. But everything he felt revolved around his mother. His parents had always kissed and touched each other in his presence. He thought their tenderness was guaranteed. Their recent conversations were so brutal. It bothered him deeply to be so abruptly introduced to a quarrel that revealed his mother's nakedness in a way he considered disgraceful. He couldn't look at her without his mind swarming with images of her like some porn actress. He felt like vomiting, crying, and killing her all at the same time. He felt a growing and irrepressible desire to take a blade and cut his skin to release some of the bitterness and rage that ate him from within.

The decision Abi made to distance her son from their marital storm would prove lifesaving for Max. Although initially it achieved nothing besides feed his hostility.

In the car to his grandmother's house, the teenager relaxed somewhat. Douala was still the same. Noisy. Chaotic. Dirty. At least this one thing hadn't changed, he thought.

Traffic lights worked only occasionally, and nobody respected them anyway. Reckless commercial motorbikes got in your way and the drivers insulted you if you complained. Taxis slowed down without warning if they noticed a potential customer, forcing everyone to drive haphazardly and dangerously. The walls of buildings were covered in mold like wallpapered shit. Hawkers rushed up to you every time you paused, with fruits, vegetables, secondhand clothes. Women all along the road sold puff-puff, beans, roasted mackerel... Groups of children gathered on the sidewalks to steal mangoes from behind the walls of villas. Some scaled the fences, then hung on a tree branch to throw ripe fruit back to their friends on the other side of the fence. At the slightest alert, they jumped from the tops of the mango trees, clambering over the wall and running off with their loot, risking being crushed under the tires of cars forced to halt suddenly to avoid hitting them. Prostitutes sold their bodies, as scantily clad as vixens in rap videos. They wore outlandish wigs in the name of hairdos. They strolled up and down the bumpy roads where lusty men would find their supply of fresh meat for the evening. Giant colonial-era buildings fell into decay amid general indifference, eaten away by moisture, while new buildings with mind-blowing designs sprouted like mushrooms. To slow down the mold infestation, the owners had opted for tiles—those ordinarily found in bathrooms were now used in lieu of paint.

Max had long ago stopped worrying about the state of the city. Nobody came to Douala for the beauty of buildings or nonexistent green spaces—the residents systematically stole the flowers planted by the council, using them to decorate their own gardens or yards. The city was flat, overcrowded, and horizonless. Regardless of where you found yourself, your eyes bumped into the frenzied crowd. For whoever wanted to see it, there was art in the street. Poetry in the people. Douala is one of those African cities that, obsessed with its survival, forgets to embellish itself to attract the foreigners passing through. It's cosmopolitan, noisy, untidy, full of energy, and hungry for knowledge, culture, and sensations. It's voracious and insatiable. The thousands of students still crammed into overcrowded classrooms speak to the faith parents have in a better future. Similarly, the huge number of industrial plants is a testament to a strong desire for solutions. In Douala, abject misery and dirty money are close neighbors to the relentless hard work of the ordinary people. Social injustice is on shameless display. Douala is home to more than one contradiction.

Tourists arriving at the airport hurried to more hospitable cities across the country. Only business travelers or revelers stuck around. To them, the city offered its wares unveiled. Douala neither flashed a smile nor opened its arms. It didn't go to great expense. You had to keep moving. There was nothing to see there. If you stuck around, you did so at your own risk, as the city mercilessly devoured the weak.

Max and his mother reached Bonabéri where a home-coming crowd waited. Tina jumped into his arms, all chatty. The more reserved Jenny kissed him heartily on the cheeks. Jenny's mother, Astou, was his grand-mother's housekeeper. Housekeeper maybe wasn't the right word, Max thought. For as far back as he could remember, Jenny and Astou had always lived with his grandmother.

Tina, the orphan girl, had resolved years ago the confusion that arose when the ever-sensitive matter of names among a large group of friends, family members, and colleagues got intertwined to the extent where they could no longer be untangled. She christened the mem-bers of the crowd effortlessly. Sita Anna for grandmother, Sita Ramata for Ismaël's mother, and Auntie Astou for Jenny's mother. Subtle nuances to show respect by estab-lishing a hierarchy between the women. Neighborhood kids and even some adults adopted the names—a nod to her sound judgment.

Max noticed that his friend Ismaël wasn't there and was about to ask why when his grandmother told them, "Drop your luggage. We're going to visit Ramata. She is very sick."

One distinct memory popped into Max's mind

whenever Ismaël's mother was mentioned. That famous summer when he was nine, he, Tina, Jenny, and Ismaël were inseparable but—for some reason that he now can't remember—he and Ismaël were constantly at each other's throats. They often challenged one another over silly things, trying to argue with one another and getting into fights at the slightest provocation.

During a street football match, Max kicked the substandard ball hard and it ended up in the barbed wire of a nearby fence. "See me some *mbout!*" declared an exasperated Ismaël, calling Max an idiot and shoving him. "You should pass the ball but you kick it into the air instead?" Max shoved him back violently and blows driven by encouragement from the neighborhood kids who had gathered around them in a circle, everyone cheering on their champion. Silence fell without the two brawlers noticing. They quickly stepped away from one another when they saw Ismaël's mother approaching. She chased the spectators away, took Max and Ismaël each by an ear, and dragged them back to her yard.

"You both like to fight. Is that so? You're tough guys! Warriors! Okay. This is what we're going to do. You are going to fight here. Right now. To the death," she ordered.

She went to her room, leaving them dumbfounded. Contrite. Ashamed to look at one another.

"What did she say?" asked Ismaël.

"Why are you asking me? Isn't she your mother?" Max replied with hostility that barely shrouded his fear.

Ramata returned with a leather belt in her hand.

"Didn't you hear me? Fight each other like brave

warriors. Kill one another or else I'll be the one who kills you."

Every word was accompanied by a blow from the belt.

No adult had ever raised their hand to Max. And he would never have imagined that the gentle, kind Sita Ramata could lay a finger on anyone.

The boys resumed their brawl, rather half-heartedly.

"Harder!" scolded Ramata, punctuating her words with new slaps. "Is that how you two were fighting a while ago? Is this why people were cheering you on, 'Mike Tyson, bite his ear off,' '*Ali Boma Ye*?' You're Tyson, right?" she asked. A blow with the belt to Max's back. "And you're Ali, right?" she asked with a blow on Ismaël. "Show me you're real boxing champions," she urged them.

She watched as they had a go at one another before backing off.

"I never told you it was over. Keep on fighting. I want a dead body on the ground, or else I will knock both of you out," she warned.

Night had fallen. They were crying in each other's arms as they continued hitting one another. Snot ran down into their mouths. Sweat in their eyes. Pleasant smells escaped from the kitchen where Ramata had been making supper. Their stomachs protested noisily. Anna found them in this condition. Tired. Sweaty. Max thought his savior had come, convinced that his grandmother would quickly end this absurd situation and even chide Ramata for having struck her grandson with a belt. But she barely even cast a glance at them.

"Ramata, what are these two devils doing in your yard?" she asked.

"They're fighting," Ramata responded jokingly. "Since they love fighting, since they are boxing champions, and I don't want two rascals in my house, I ordered them to fight to the death. So that we can have peace. At long last."

"Ah, okay," Sita Anna said simply, returning to her house. "Call me to congratulate the winner."

Max was now wailing continuously. As was Ismaël.

"Sita, forgive us. We're sorry. We will never fight again. Please, Sita, please," he begged.

"Shut up!" scolded Ramata, a threatening look on her face. "Have either of you ever seen Mike Tyson or Muhammad Ali whining like a girl for her mother? Keep fighting or else…"

She brandished her belt like a threat and turned her back to them. They didn't hear her burst into laughter once she was out of their sight.

The boys were saved when Ismaël's father returned, quite late that night.

"What are you two doing?" he shouted.

They didn't dare respond. He slapped each of them on their heads, "I asked you two a question."

"We…we are fighting," stammered Ismaël, crying intermittently as he spoke.

His father frowned. "You what?" he tsked. "You, go home right away and take a bath," he said.

He kicked Max in the buttocks.

"And you, same. Bathroom!" he ordered Ismaël, who

unsuccessfully tried to dodge the kick meant for him.

Max felt humiliated. His clothes were in pieces. His whole body ached. He was dead hungry. His grandmother was waiting for him.

"If you're here, it means Ismaël is dead, I guess. Congratulations. Take a bath and head straight to bed. I don't feed murderers. Nor do I want them at my dining table," she informed him.

When everybody was asleep, Jenny brought him a plate of roasted fish and tomato stew.

"Are you asleep?" she whispered. "Take it. We've run out of *Missolè*, fried ripe plantains, but I saved some fish for you."

Max had been chewing on his rage for some time by then. He was planning to call his parents the following morning to tell them he wanted to leave. That he didn't want to spend one more day in this place where he was mistreated. And never again would he set foot in this country of savages. His grandmother would be less prideful when he refused to visit her. She would beg him to forgive her. If he were in France, he would call child protective services, the police, and the fire department and all of these brutes would end up in jail. He pretended not to see Jenny. He wanted to keep the modicum of pride he had left. In any case, everyone in this country of mediocre people was mediocre. Everyone, without exception. Even Jenny and his other friends. But his empty stomach finally got the best of his outrage. The savory smell of fried fish wouldn't let him focus on his grievances. He seized the plate. Devoured its contents—meat and even the bones. Then he handed the plate back to Jenny and laid back down with his face against the wall.

The following day, he woke up tired and aching, still feeling the effects of the previous day's events. He was angry at the whole wide world and determined to make everyone pay for their brutality, their betrayal, and their lack of respect.

Every morning, once his parents had gone out, Ismaël came to Max's room, ball in hand. He'd say, "Max, wake up. Let's go play. What are you still doing in bed?" They would drink the glass of Ovaltine made by Auntie Astou in one gulp. And then grab the chocolate croissants that they would devour on the road to the empty field that served as their football stadium. *If he comes around today, I'll finish redoing his ugly face,* Max thought to himself. But then he heard Ismaël shout:

"Max, get up!"

"If you're not careful, I'll punch you again," Max told him, jumping off the bed.

He was so relieved to see his friend that he forgot his pain and anger.

"Who will you punch? Do you even know how to punch? On a serious note, white boy, thank God my father saved you yesterday."

That was the last real argument they ever had. And whenever they fought, which was quite often it must be said, they were squaring off against other neighborhood kids, and made sure they cleaned up and hid their black eyes before the adults came home.

Sita Ramata's health had been deteriorating for some years now. Ismaël and Max had kept in touch on Messenger, so he knew that his friend's mother was ill. However, they never discussed it directly. Max didn't know the gravity of the situation. He was surprised to find her so diminished.

Sita Ramata had once been quite slim. Quite pretty, tall with smooth dark skin. Max thought she could have been a model had she wanted to. Ismaël had inherited his mother's slim figure and charm. Ever so lively, Tina said he was the most handsome boy in the neighborhood. All the girls wanted to be his girlfriend. That former Sita Ramata had disappeared into a pile of bones lying on pillows. She had lost so much weight. Large gray spots appeared on her skin. She looked at them through feverish eyes.

"Welcome, children. I hope you had a safe journey?" she asked.

Abi sat on the edge of the bed and hugged her tenderly. She had brought her favorite chocolates, she said, taking the box out of her handbag. Max was standing a little off to the side.

"Maxou, you have grown so big! But why are you so far away, my child? Ismaël is the same. I have to lift my head to see his face. Are you wondering about your friend?" she asked. "He won't be long. I sent him to the shop to get you something to drink."

She surely noticed his discomfort because she then said, "Go meet him if you like. Jenny, Tina, go along with Max. You all don't have to stay here."

On the way out, the teenagers met Auntie Astou, who was bringing food. Ismaël's mother was in such bad shape that she could no longer perform her daily tasks. Astou cleaned her house and cooked for the family every day. Ramata no longer complained about it, but her husband now came home only late at night, avoiding spending much time with his sick wife. Neighbors had made arrangements to help her. Sita Anna took her to see the doctor when it was necessary and made sure she took her medication. Ramata had already given birth to Ismaël's elder brother, Ahmadou, when they moved into the house next door to Anna's, but it was here that Ismaël was born. He, Max, Jenny, and Tina were all the same age. Both women were bound by a sincere friendship, although Ramata was, by just a few years, older than Abi. Ma' Moudio and the other women from the neighborhood took turns at her bedside to make sure she did not need anything.

Ismaël was coming home with the items he'd bought when his friends met up with him. He and Max embraced emotionally before the clique returned to Ramata's bedside.

They helped serve the drinks and then sat there, silent and embarrassed. Ramata once again noticed their discomfort and suggested, "How about you guys go to the *beignétariat*?"

A proposal they quickly accepted. They couldn't wait to listen to each other's stories but did not dare talk while adults were around. Or in that room, which reeked of medication and the disinfectant Astou used so liberally.

"Lucky that Max came," they heard Ramata say to her visitors. "Ismaël doesn't leave the house. He keeps a close eye on me, like I'm a newborn. Children are so strange. Ahmadou never steps foot inside this room. He stands at the door when he wants to know how I'm doing. But every night, I hear him praying. I hear him beg God to heal me. I don't like seeing him keeping company with that new imam over at the mosque. But Ahmadou has always been a little passionate. If it brings him comfort, all the better. All this is too much for my sons to handle."

✳

The beignétariat was a simple shed located about five hundred meters from Anna's house. Someone had had the brilliant idea of mounting aluminum sheets on four wooden poles in an empty lot and then installing stools and tables underneath. In the beginning, the shelter was meant only for women selling beignets, called puff-puff, and that's how the name came about. Subsequently, other street cooks moved in with different dishes. Roasted fish, barbecued meat, sauced dishes, seasonal vegetables… Women had even set up a refreshment stall with huge coolers, where they stored beer and sodas for their customers. You could eat there or get takeout. The place had become a major meeting point for all the young and not-so-young from the neighborhood: singles and housewives who didn't have time to cook dinner or simply wanted to do something different came by; travelers looking for rest at the end of the day; unemployed people who had stumbled on a few coins to spend or hoped that someone would offer them a drink. The beignétariat was part of the hustling and informal trade so typical of working-class neighborhoods in Douala. It belonged to everyone because nobody owned it. By implicit agreement the sellers kept it clean and that was enough. People gathered under the intermittent streetlights when they came on or by the light of the firewood with which the women cooked. The beignétariat was the place for heated debates about football, politics, and gossip. There you learned everything about the world. But it was most importantly a prime spot for dating. Max, Tina, Ismaël, and Jenny had, over the years, transformed it into their headquarters.

Max was happy to be back there. He greeted the proprietors with kisses to the cheeks.

"Heh, Maxou. What is up with all this handsomeness, my son. Are you trying to kill us or what?" one joked, pressing him in a tight hug against her chest.

He also greeted the customers whom he had known for ages now. "Max, how can you come for a vacation before school resumes?" someone asked.

"This time around I am here to stay," explained Max.

Another one burst out laughing, mocking him, "My brother, we are here fighting to go overseas, and you are coming here? You must have surely done something horribly wrong over there!"

"And how is that your concern?" Ismaël jumped in. "What is the matter with you?"

"Nothing. I was just saying," the customer said, retreating.

"And what were you just saying?" the woman selling food stepped in. "You, who does horrible things here day in and day out. Your parents no longer know what to do with you and you have courage to talk? Please let this be the last time you open your mouth. Finish eating quietly or leave," she ordered.

She didn't have to repeat herself. Her impressive build, arms set on her hips, was a clear sign of her authority.

"My children—is it the usual? *Accra*, beans, and pap?" she asked them.

"Yes, Auntie. Also some *safou* and roasted maize," said Tina.

"Miss Tina, I am only talking to you because Max is here and you know that. What kind of dress is that? Do you now walk around naked?" the woman chastised.

Tina went to her seat mumbling, "That one, always poking her nose into other people's business."

"Did you say something?" asked the seller, not letting the matter go.

"No, Auntie. Well, yes. I was saying that your beignets are always delicious."

"If you have nothing important to say, you might as well be quiet, my daughter," the seller said, rebuking her with a long spiteful *tsk*.

Max settled in, feeling like he had returned home after a long exile. For the first time in months, he felt fine. He was eyeing Tina. She was wearing a rather short jean skirt that revealed the roundness of her butt and a tiny blouse that hung above her navel.

"Auntie is right, you know," he said teasingly. "Why do you always dress as if you were using the last pieces of fabric in the whole wide world? Did your voodoo priest advise you against wearing normal-sized clothes?"

"My voodoo priest said you should go to hell," she said back.

Tina was breathtakingly beautiful. All the men in the neighborhood, both old and young, turned to stare whenever she went by. Since she was twelve, she would disappear for hours with some man or another and only appear later, never giving any explanations. Max caressed her arm, asking, "I hope this year you're going to give me some?"

She pushed his hand away roughly, saying, "Is that how they ask a girl out where you come from? No 'my dear'? No 'your eyes are to die for'? Nothing? Get this once and for all, white boy, I won't be giving you anything. *Nothing*!" she told him.

It was their usual joke. It made both of them laugh, but in truth Max adored Tina. If someone had told him that he was in love with her, he would have laughed in that person's face. Half-embarrassed and half-scornful. He considered her a good friend, with whom he spent hours trading salacious jokes, criticizing those around them, and reshaping the world. She didn't have the same place in his heart that Jenny had. Jenny whom he could not help treating like a little sister he had to protect. Tina was a friend. A little like Ismaël. The problem was that pair of braless breasts under T-shirts that left nothing to the imagination. The quiet excitement dating back to the time when they first bathed in their underwear in the garden had given way to something more restless. Max really did want her to give him what she distributed to others so generously. She laughed, teased him, and deflected.

On the way home, Ismaël mocked him, saying, "You will have to marry her if you want to fuck her."

Max kept up his friend's same lighthearted tone. That is how they broached serious topics, pretending that they did not take them seriously: "Marry Tina, my brother, isn't that witchcraft? The entire neighborhood has slept with her!" Max replied.

"The entire neighborhood except you, or am I wrong? Are you trying to solve your problem or other people's?" Ismaël replied.

"I'll marry her. You marry Jenny, and we'll move in together. Is that the plan?" Max asked.

"My brother, do as you please. One thing is certain: I will marry Jenny!" Ismaël promised.

They walked a moment silently before Ismaël continued, "So you'll stay for the school year, yeah?"

"Yes. Things are tense between my parents," Max answered.

"How tense?" Ismaël asked.

"So tense they'll get a divorce, I think," Max disclosed.

They observed another silent pause, before Ismaël concluded, "You're right. That is really tense."

✳

That year was a difficult one for Ismaël.

His mother died. His father brought home a new wife as soon as they returned from the burial in their village. On the pretext that there shouldn't be motherless orphans, their tradition encouraged new widowers to re-marry right on the heels of the funeral.

The new wife was not wicked, but she took the place of a woman who was still being mourned by her children. They felt attacked every time she went into their mother's kitchen. Wore her clothes. Sat on her sofa. There was no way in the world she would sneak into their good graces. Ahmadou buried himself even deeper in religion. Ismaël spent more and more time at Anna's house, with Tina, Jenny, and Max.

Max was enrolled at the French high school. Tina and Ismaël attended the government school in the neighborhood and Jenny went to a private school in the city center. But they met up after school and hung out together whenever they had free time.

Max found himself wondering daily how their circle had become so inaccessible. No other kid was allowed in. Even if they partied, played video games, or played football with others, it always ended up being only the four of them at the end of the day.

Max's relationship with his parents improved slowly but surely, thanks to Ismaël.

"Bro, my mom *died!* No matter what she had done, I would rather she were alive. You, you still have a mother who cares about you, but you are here playing tough?" Ismaël scolded him when Max refused like often to pick up his mother's calls.

The teenager tried to defend himself, saying, "You're only saying that because you don't know what she did exactly."

"Is she dead? No? Well that is the worst thing that she could inflict on you. The rest can't compare! Not one bit."

A few months earlier, he would have responded that he would prefer it if she were dead, but Ismaël had lost his mother. Max watched him wrestle with despair every day. He saw the gap left by the absent person in his friend's life. He would never have wanted his own mother to die. He wanted her to suffer and then return, repentant and contrite, to continue their family life from the place where they had left it. He wanted to punish her. Not that she should disappear forever. Faced with the reality of grief, he understood the stupidity of his childish acts.

Jenny was so studious and focused that she did not give them any breathing space. They had to sit for the brevet exams: "You'll all pass. This is an order!" she declared.

Max brought back weed to a party Anna was organizing for them to celebrate their success at the exams and to bid farewell to her grandson. They invited other kids from the neighborhood. And their classmates too. Despite their parents forbidding it, they brought beer and whiskey. Once the party was in full swing, Max lit a joint and drew on it once before handing it to his friends.

"Damn, it's been a while! A whole year without the slightest drag. I'm alive again," he exclaimed.

"What is this, *mbanga*?" Jenny asked.

"Oh yes!" shouted a delighted Max, "and good stuff."

"Why? Is the whiskey all finished, bro, for you

to be smoking mbanga like the last *niè-man?*" Ismaël exclaimed.

Max was stuck with an outstretched arm, nobody taking the joint.

"Who here in Bonabéri have you seen smoking this stuff?" Tina asked. "Nobody but failures, idiots, losers, the type you do not even want to say hi to. The same people who wolf down Tramol like popcorn. Who did you take us for? Is this how you guys have fun back home in France? Go throw that thing away, please. If you want to *shack*, drink beer or whiskey like a real man."

Embarrassed, Max did not know what to say in response, so he sidestepped the issue.

"Well, if I throw it away, would you at least give me a kiss?" Max asked.

Ismaël burst into laughter.

"Come on, Tina! Give the guy what he wants and let's get it over with once and for all! What language should he beg in?!" he asked.

"But our one and only Tina has become a good girl," joked Jenny. "Haven't you noticed? She no longer disappears with the first guy who comes along. Her lovers in the neighborhood are going bonkers. They're at their wits end, trying to invent some reason to see their dear Tina."

"That's true," acknowledged Ismaël. "Since Max arrived, Tina, your boyfriends are nowhere to be found. You still dress with nothing but scraps of cloth, but something has changed."

Max laughed, all proud, "Ah, I knew it! I'm your real boyfriend, Tina. The others are just placeholders. You pretend you don't want me, but deep down you do, and just don't dare tell me the truth. You love me. Me too—I love you. Why are you wasting our time?"

Tina tsked, yanked the joint from Max's hand, and stomped on it before heading off to meet her admirers on the dance floor. They were all slightly drunk. There was joy and excitement in the air.

"That girl is only out to kill me or what?" murmured Max.

"Go to the village for a cleansing, bro. You are cursed," Ismaël said and then whisked Jenny away for an entranced *bikutsi*.

The playlist was the usual. Bikutsi followed by a round of languid *zouk*. Ismaël planned it so that he would already be on the dance floor, Jenny in his arms, sparing him the embarrassment of having to invite her to dance to the slow zouk. Max, just like all the other boys at the party, knew how things worked. He cursed himself for having missed his chance to seize Tina from the clutches of her dance partner. At the moment, the guy was contorting to the rhythm of the latest hit in town, drooling in anticipation over the round of zouk songs that would let him hold Tina close for fifteen long minutes. Emboldened by alcohol, Max headed straight for the couple.

"My friend, you've had enough," he told the young man, taking Tina by her shoulders. "Now let me dance with my girl."

The other guy got angry, not ready to surrender this close to the finish line. "What do you mean, 'your girl'? Leave us alone," he responded.

Max was holding on tight to Tina.

"Didn't you know? Well, I'm telling you. Tina is my girl. She won't be dancing with you anymore," Max said.

Tina stood motionless. Everyone knew the special bond that existed between the four friends. Her dance partner guessed that this was a fight he would lose, but dealt Max one last humiliation to save face:

"My brother, this girl belongs to whoever comes along first. Didn't you know? Wait your turn like everyone else instead of…"

Max punched him in the face without giving him the chance to complete his sentence. The guy punched him back. Ismaël rushed to the rescue and the dispute immediately turned into an all-out brawl.

After they had, with much difficulty, chased away their opponents, Ismaël, still breathless and furious for having missed his round of zouk songs with Jenny, lashed out at Max, "I can't take my eyes off you for five minutes without you getting into trouble? What was that fight all about, can you tell me? Explain it to me so that I can know why I split the lip of a guy who did nothing to me."

"He called Tina a whore," Max said without looking at him.

His mind shuttled between his grandmother's parlor, ravaged by the fight—Anna would kill them if she found it in this state—and his despair at the idea that the party ended with him unable to also dance with Tina.

She joined the conversation, and said with a tiny coarse voice, "He isn't wrong, you know? We should call a spade a spade."

She was on the verge of tears. Jenny joked to lighten the mood.

"Max, you should hit her too, so she can get her thoughts straight. Pure nonsense!"

Jenny took her friend into her arms before Max could react. Another missed chance, he thought to himself, disgusted.

"Well, we have to clean this place up!" Ismaël exclaimed.

Tina cried in Jenny's arms, and her friends were moved. She wasn't a girl whose feelings were easily hurt.

Max had only seen her in tears during the wakes in the neighborhood. When someone died, good manners required that their neighbors come assist the bereaved family. On such occasions, Tina cried with a passion that Max found exaggerated. He and Ismaël mocked her for it. "Do you realize that you are more affected by this person's death than those directly affected, Tina? Did you know the deceased well?"

Ordinarily, Tina was cocky. She was a loudmouth with deadly comebacks. She seemed immune to all forms of provocation. Seeing her suddenly crumbling showed Max she had wounds whose existence he'd never suspected. He regretted not having found the right words to console her. The year spent together had amplified his feelings for Tina. He burned with his desire for her. His heart beat restlessly whenever she stepped into a room. He eyed her breasts under her T-shirts and slowed down to watch the fall of her hips when they walked together. He would have given anything to smell her lush hair and pull her naked body against his.

Tina's untamed sensuality unsettled him and made him lose his composure, but it wasn't just that.

He would have loved to tell her that he really did find her beautiful enough to die for. That other men wanting her didn't make his feelings wither. He wasn't only drawn by her face or her body. He was drawn by everything about her. Her luminous smile. Her dark humor. Her generosity. Something intense. Irresistible. Max muted his feelings out of pride. But especially because he thought they had all their lives before them. There would be other chances. There would be more rounds of zouk. Moments of intimacy and carefree laughter.

They were on the good side of history. The time to love one another would come like a kept promise.

Max returned to Paris after his long absence to no groundswell of emotion. No memorable declarations. Only a "Man, good to see you!" directed at anyone who would listen and a pile of plans for the coming months: to take his written driving exam and prepare for his road test; to focus on school; to earn the right to go back to Douala next summer. Thanks to social media, it was possible to stay in touch with his friends online, so he would never really be far away. They could talk to one another every day, like he had never left. Max felt good, sure of himself, confident in the future.

✳

It was nearly two years later that he finally returned, and Max only realized on the flight back to Cameroon the extent to which he was desperate and ready for the worst upon arriving back in Douala. Jenny, Ismaël, and Tina had been the ones keeping his head above water.

Two years, not even, and his life had taken a dramatic, incomprehensible turn. He was coming back once again, but nothing was ever going to be the same.

The man who came to pick up his mother and him from the airport in Yaounde was clearly military intelligence. Max made this deduction from the man's outfit—strict and plain. And the politeness tinged with authority that he showed them.

Abi had cried all through the flight from Paris. Her eyes hurt. For long months, they had gone through every phase of worried confusion, false leads, and disclaimers. They had shuddered at every new phone call or email, but refused to give up. Finally, misfortune fell on their heads with all the furor they had feared and even more, because here—just like in Paris—murder and madness ravaged blindly.

Jenny and Ismaël were dead, and Max was on his way to see Tina again during her interrogation at the State Defense Secretariat in charge of terrorism.

"Stop the car for a minute, please. I'm not feeling well," he said.

The driver of the SUV, wearing tinted glasses, pulled over on the side of the divisional road connecting the Nsimalen airport to the city of Yaounde. Max hurriedly stepped out of the car and bent over a pothole, hoping to empty his bile—that sorrow and fear that left him bloated and breathless. He hiccupped unsuccessfully for a long time, his eyes full of tears, before his mother took him in her arms and brought him back into the waiting car.

He was coming back to Cameroon deeply shaken by the turn of events that had taken place since his previous trip. Jenny, Ismaël and Tina, his friends, had chosen the path of violence and death.

Max judged himself harshly. Survivors tend to. He remembered the sadness he felt leaving Douala. But also how excited he felt about returning to his world. Once he was back home, he missed his friends. The cold of the winter felt crueler. The disorder, chaos, even the random change from intense heat to endless rainfall specific to Douala all seemed preferable to the gray of a Paris winter. Living in Douala, he knew, had helped him successfully navigate a decisive stage of his existence. He now accepted the difficulties in his life—the divorce of his parents, uncertainty about the future—like variables he would simply have to live with. He liked this new Max, already older, more at liberty to move, less dependent on others. His emotions were even more sincere now that he embraced the vulnerability that came with them.

"You're different," his mother had observed a few weeks after his return, without Max being able to tell whether the change made her happy or sad. He had just told her that he would rather go live with his father. "He's quite upset, Mother. I think he needs someone to watch over him."

All she did was agree with him. Before, in their former life, she would have replied that parents should watch over their children and not the other way around. That he was under no obligation to sacrifice himself to support his adult father while he was still just a teenager. And before, he would have been scared to hurt her. Scared that she would think his decision was some form of rejection, which might have been the case given that she had quite a temper. They had gotten past that. The perfect family behind the curtain had gone up in smoke, showing everyone stripped bare before the others. They'd had to reinvent a relationship that acknowledged their respective vulnerabilities. Her son wanted to have his say in this process. Abi understood that without needing further explanation.

At the height of their family crisis, the special friendship that he and his mother had always shared aggravated his feelings of betrayal. Now, the teenager was happy to reconnect with her, because he was able to see her in a new light, consider her in a new light. She was still his mother, but Max was no longer a child. Abi had also accepted this new reality.

His friends had given him with the power to be more resolute in his relationship with his mother. Max wondered, worried over, what he had given them in return. Had he been in Douala when it happened, would he have gone along too? Would he have allowed himself to be convinced to leave everything behind to join the jihad?

Tina was telling a story so horrible that he felt like plugging his ears and screaming. In front of the SED officers and the other families, she spoke only to him. Her gaze stayed glued to him, but her words were shocking, horrible. She spared him none of the details.

They had been four kids. United by friendship. A special bond. Their countless plans for the future. His brain had a hard time admitting that this Tina, hurt, scared, and bald (*What happened to your pretty hair, Tina?* he thought when he saw her. *What happened to us?*) was the lone survivor of the group.

The madness of the world had hit every one of them, stealing their childhoods and their faith in a terror-free future.

Dead, Jenny and Ismaël? In what parallel, incomprehensible, crazy world was such an aberration even possible?

Jenny, so tender, so smart…their Jenny? Everyone's kid sister was no more?

And Ismaël. If he had had to name from among his friends someone strong, someone impervious to all these fundamentalist ideologies, and someone who wouldn't harm a fly, Max wouldn't have hesitated for one second.

He could not believe the story Tina was telling. He was wading neck deep through a nightmare, conscious deep down that he was contending with his own mortality.

TINA'S TESTIMONY

Jenny was my sister. My own bright half. I would have followed her to hell. And I did. Out of love.

Initially, seeing her hanging out with Ismaël's older brother made me laugh. "My dear, what's going on? Is that deviant cleric your new best friend?" I'd ask. She would also laugh, saying, "I don't know what he wants from me."

And then she changed.

We have always been very close, Ismaël, Jenny, and I. People used to call us the Siamese triplets.

When we were younger, Sita Anna used to take all of us to church. You too, Max, when you came for the holidays. Do you remember?

Every Sunday morning, freshly bathed, we gathered around her. It's funny to think about it today. Ismaël's mother, who was still alive then, encouraged her sons to go with us. The goal wasn't to get them to convert to Catholicism. We all bathed and went along willingly to pray with Sita Anna, whom she trusted blindly. For her, this was all that mattered. Ismaël's father didn't care either way, and Ahmadou, ten years older than us, wasn't a member of our crew.

Ismaël and I looked forward to the weekly trip, more because of Sita Anna's pretty car than the mass. We quickly grew bored from the long ceremony. We invented games to pass the time. We played as the faithful gave us stern looks and mumbled their annoyance. Quite quickly, Sita Anna would tell us to go play outside while waiting for the mass to end. We happily complied, sure of meeting other undisciplined children in the yard. Jenny wouldn't join us. She read the Gospel. Listened attentively to homilies. I suspect she was less motivated by faith and more by her desire to please Sita Anna. We'd sing at the top of our voices on the way back home, and Sita Anna would stop at the bakery, asking us to pick any pastry we fancied. We would then have breakfast at her house before going to play outside.

Those mornings together are my fondest childhood memories. While I was away, I revisited them every time I was in the throes of despair.

In our house, nobody cooked. Or bothered with what I ate. My grandparents slept off their drinking till nearly noon, when my grandmother would send her housekeeper to get something to eat from Ma' Moudio. When I came home after school, I'd find dirty dishes in the sink and an empty fridge, while they slumped in front of the television, snoring. There were times when I wouldn't come home. I would go straight to Jenny's, where Ismaël would come meet us later. We'd spend the evening doing our homework under the watchful eye of Sita Anna before having supper, and then later everyone would go home.

Some evenings, I'd stand around outside long after parting ways with my friends, since I didn't like the idea of going home to be alone with my grandparents. Everyone in the neighborhood knew about their alcoholism and disregard for me. Sita Anna did her best to fill the void but it was more complicated than it seemed.

My grandmother already had a daughter when she met her husband where she worked. After they married, they settled in our village in Bonabéri. Rumor has it that all whites are wealthy. They live in the suburbs. I don't understand why this one chose to come hide out in a place as remote as ours.

My mother died when I was five. One morning as I went to take a bath, I found her in the red water of the bathtub. She had swallowed some pills before slitting her veins open. This just goes to show how much she wanted to get it right. No mass was held; no funeral either. My grandparents buried her discreetly. Without informing the family.

In our village, regardless of the life you lived, when you die all your relatives come to your funeral. They mourn your demise and, even if they shunned you while you were alive, claim that you were a saint. It's one way of making peace with the past, of releasing the departed from any dispute that hung over their life and enabling them to rest in peace.

When my mother passed away, I learned that at least one person must have loved you enough to strike up the song of sorrow that the whole community would then sing. But without that person, you went in silence. An indifference that was worse than death itself. My mother left this world without as much as a whisper uttered in her honor. To anybody who asked me, I responded that she had moved to France, just like so many others before her. Nobody bothered enough to inquire further. How many poor people died in similar circumstances in Douala? Dead and buried somewhere without anyone even raising an eyebrow?

If I could, I attended all the wakes in the neighborhood and I cried so hard that people consoled me, thinking I was related to the deceased. Do you remember how that made you and Ismaël crack up? Do you remember how angry you were when you stumbled upon me kissing Ismaël after his mother died?

You lost it, saying, "Can't you express your condolences like everyone else? You know, for most people, an 'I'm so sorry' is enough—no need to offer your body as consolation."

You couldn't understand. My body is my most prized possession. The only thing men are interested in. It only seemed natural to offer it to my best friend when he was suffering and in need of comfort. If I don't console orphans, who will bring me peace? If I don't mourn my mother, who will? She took her own life at seventeen. I was five then. Do the math. Furthermore, I am mixed race. Do you know any other white men besides my grandfather?

Ismaël turned down my offer. In his normal way, firmly

but kindly. "That's not necessary, Tina," he said, and I cried in the arms of the only man who has ever rejected my advances. We both consoled each other over the loss of our mothers. Having sex was completely out of the question. In that situation, it would have been almost incestuous.

My handsome, my gentle Ismaël. My orphan brother. They turned him into a monster, you know?

Sita Anna was the only adult who cared about me.

If I wasn't there when it was time to sit down to eat, she would send someone to come get me. "Tina, where have you been? Come here, have a seat," she would say. She never gave me breathing space. "Tina, when was the last time you changed your clothes? Did you take a bath this morning? Go take a bath. A woman has to pay attention to her hygiene. Beauty is not enough. Have you done your homework? Let me see your books…" She would go on and on. She's the one who taught me about my menstrual cycle. Jenny and I were both her little girls—even if Jenny was her favorite. That made sense, Jenny was intelligent, hard-working, well-behaved. While I was only interested in boys.

The endless attention from men clouded my judgment. I was overwhelmed by their desire.

Do you remember Pa Ondoa? He followed me around like an old dog in heat. Sita Anna threatened to deal with him if she ever saw him hanging around me again. That was all that was needed to deter him. The entire neighborhood knew that Sita Anna, in everything she did, had the backing of your grandfather who was in the parliament. The idea of facing such a powerful enemy made Pa Ondoa retreat.

The day she talked to him, she took me aside. "Tina, you aren't a woman yet. You're still a little girl, but there's something in your eye, your attitude, even in the way you speak that puts you in harm's way. I don't know why our Good Lord gave you such a body. It's too much for a help-less child like you. Bad men notice you from miles away. You attract them the same way honey attracts bees. Don't let them get close to you, my daughter. Only hang out with kids your age. Stick with Jenny and Ismaël. If Ondoa or another old man from the neighborhood says funny things to you or proposes something indecent, do let me know, understood? If for some reason, I'm not around, you can always tell Ma' Moudio, Ramata, or Astou. There's no reason for you to keep it to yourself, promise?"

I never went and complained. And even if Ma' Moudio, the neighborhood watchman, updated her on my every move, Sita Anna couldn't have guessed that the only bad man who scared me lived under our own roof.

When my grandfather started giving me strange looks, lingering in my room or in the bathroom as I dressed, letting his hands stray on my body, I didn't smell any danger in it. But my grandmother did. She lashed out at me. She started calling me a little prostitute. Accused me of teasing him by knowingly failing to shut doors. She said I wanted to snatch her husband, and she told me to get out. He called her crazy, a drunken old hag.

I sought refuge in the streets to escape their scream-ing. There, I felt the gazes of bad men as they stared at me. They all looked at me like my grandfather did, and that's when I understood. I was just like my mother, and Sita Anna was right. Something about me attracted them. It was all my fault. Otherwise, my grandmother would have been on my side instead of seeing me as a rival. That's when I started staying at Jenny's house till bedtime. Then I started staying out until I felt drunk with sleep. Only then would I slip into my room like a thief under the cover of night. I went to bed with a knife and slept with one eye open, determined to defend myself to the death if need be.

Men want only one thing from me. And for as long as I can remember, they've harassed me to get it. I thought that if I gave away what they wanted to buy, if I gave what they were ready to steal from me, if I hand-picked my persecutors, I might, in some way, be in control of my life. You know the reputation I have in this neighborhood. But nobody can say that anyone paid or forced me. I chose what I did. With whom. I didn't get pregnant, and I didn't pick up some nasty infection, because I always demanded a condom. Call that survival instinct if you want. Or maybe the fear of bringing a child into the world in my circumstances was a potent motivation.

It's a miracle that Sita Anna didn't chase me from her house. Or forbid me from keeping the company of her daughter like other mothers had. Even Sita Ramata was nice to me. I thought the loudmouth Ma' Moudio was giving them minute-by-minute updates on my every move, but maybe that wasn't the case. Of course, I know

that even if they had suspected, they couldn't have fath-
omed the scale of the damage. Only Jenny knew all the
little details of what I was doing.

All this stopped when you arrived, Max.

I was falling to pieces. I was falling apart before that
blessed year when the four of us came to one another's
rescue. With you, the sirens of the men no longer lured
me with their deceptive anthem. I finally saw them for
who they were. Hungry, wild beasts. And I was no longer afraid. I no longer felt so diminished, so lonely. I had
friends, a family. I was part of a crew. It feels strange,
you know? Like I stumbled on a glass of cold water after
a long walk through the desert. Or better still, a clear
spring, where I could drink and even bathe. I cried at our
party. Do you remember? When that other guy called
me a prostitute and you came to my defense. I cried and
firmly resolved to end those casual, ugly relationships
that humiliated me and made me vulnurable.

But everything took such a turn for the worse after
you left…

Jenny was my *sis,* but I knew nothing about what she did
every day in school. I told her the personal details of my
life and took it for granted that she did the same. That
was far from being the case.

Secrecy was part of Jenny, of her life with her mother. I
didn't think about Auntie Astou and her, about their place
in Sita Anna's house. I had always seen them there, so I
didn't find it strange. I never wondered how Jenny dealt
with her hybrid status of daughter of the housekeeper and

goddaughter of the madame of the house. I should have, because that's how everything started.

She told her classmates that Sita Anna was her grandmother, that you were her half brother, and Auntie Astou was her housekeeper. Everyone believed her since Sita Anna took care of her schooling—attended PTA meetings, dropping her off and picking her up in the car. Auntie Astou never showed up at school.

After you left, a boy came into the picture. A small middle-class kid from Bonapriso who started asking her out. Inviting her to places. Jenny changed completely. Usually so plainly dressed she now borrowed my mini-skirts and secretly used makeup. She finally felt like she belonged, was fashionable. She was desired for her beauty by one of the handsome guys from Douala's upper class. She was as good as them. I was happy that she was becoming her own woman somewhat. I always found her to be too obedient, but the way she changed surprised me. I had not realized that Jenny envied those rich kids so much. Or the extent to which she felt ashamed of her family background at that posh school.

Your departure, Max, left a crack that turned into a chasm as the days went by. We had already lost so much. We'd been so close. The emptiness created by your absence was a blow. It was fatal to us. Now down to three, our little group lost its balance. Our vulnerabilities worsened. We drifted apart.

＊

Max burst into tears. Tina took his hand.

"No, no. Don't cry, Maxou. That is the way it is. That's life. You're not to blame. It is just life," she reminded him.

The soldier tasked with recording her statement thought he should step in. "Miss, continue, please," he interjected; his tone was kind.

"Thank you," Anna whispered to him.

There was nothing standard in Tina's testimony. The man was there to get her testimony about Boko Haram, but the young girl was telling her life story. She spoke to Max as if there were nobody else in the room. But the soldier let her have her way, contenting himself with recording her statement.

He let out a sigh and said, "You know, I also have kids. Teenagers. We live in terrible times. This right here is key testimony on how youths get indoctrinated. It interests me both as an officer and a father."

✳

Ismaël had always been in love with Jenny. When he saw that she had changed, when he noticed her brief romance with the rich kid, he simply kept his distance. Surrendering was unlike him, but you weren't around. Jenny had new friends. Sita Anna's house had always been our refuge, but we had lost it. Ismaël came face-to-face with his stepmother in a home where he was not welcome. There was no longer a crew, no way out, so he also made new friends at school and in the neighborhood. He left our friendship behind.

His brother, Ahmadou, wasn't even in love with Jenny. He lusted afer her—I saw in his eyes the voraciousness of a bad man. That is why we labeled him the "Deviant Cleric."

When Sita Ramata first got sick, he went to the mosque every day. And then when she died, his passion for religion reached worrying heights. Ahmadou and his prayer beads became one. He stopped shaking hands with women and prayed so much, and with such zeal, that a dark spot formed in the middle of his forehead. All of that, however, didn't stop him from staring at my butt whenever he had the chance, but he blamed me for it. As if the disease was in me and not in the dark force that restrained and unleashed his urges in equal measure. However, his behavior toward me was nothing compared to the way he looked at Jenny. You would have thought he would pounce on her and devour her. Sincerely, we thought he could slice her into tiny pieces and eat her raw. It scared us. We tried to laugh at it, sourly.

Ahmadou changed radically when Jenny started wearing makeup and short skirts. When she started going out with boys. We never really thought that this young man whom we'd always known could want to hurt us. As a precaution, we went way out of our way to avoid running into him, but he always ended up appearing out of nowhere. Prayer beads in hand, he'd give us stern looks. I came to understand that he was monitoring our movements.

One evening, Jenny sneaked out to meet her boyfriend. She came over to my place first to change and

put on makeup. Her guy was waiting for her at the in-
tersection a little farther down the street, in a pretty car
that was surely his father's. Borrowed without permission
for the evening. I walked Jenny to her rendezvous and as
we went by his house, we saw Ahmadou on his prayer
mat. With bloodshot, bulging eyes, he was pointing at us,
mumbling only God knows what. Curses, surely. Jenny
squeezed my hand tightly. "Don't pay him any attention,
otherwise he will think we're afraid of him," she said.

I for one was afraid of him. Jenny was less so—she
just laughed at his outrageous act. She mocked him
openly, taking the threat of him lightly. "We're here
at home in Bonabéri, under the watchful eye of Ma'
Moudio, Sita Anna, and all these people who watched
us grow up. There's nothing he can do to us," she said to
allay my fears.

I could have spent hours telling her about the family
men who harassed me and all the tricks they deployed to
avoid this legendary vigilance and spend a few hours with
me, but I never said a word. I know, personally, the way
bad men's obsessions push them to extremes. But my sis
didn't. Also, danger didn't come from the place we were
expecting. I would never have imagined what happened
to us. I couldn't have predicted it. I didn't have the resources to defend myself.

Sita Anna and your grandfather went to visit you guys
in France for the holidays. Jenny was home alone with
Auntie Astou. It wasn't the first time. Every year your
grandparents went to visit you, but the year after you left

they extended their stay to be with Sita Abi, who was going through her divorce.

Sometimes, even the most trivial events conspire to make the worst happen.

During the trip, parents were asked to come to school to pick up end-of-term report cards, I think. Jenny lied, claiming that her parents were traveling, and that nobody could attend the meeting. However, she left the letter lying around and Auntie Astou stumbled upon it. I did not even know Auntie Astou could read. If Jenny knew, she had surely forgotten given how aloof her mother was when it came to her schooling, the sole preserve of Sita Anna. Maybe Auntie Astou was trying to do well. Prove to her daughter that in the absence of her godmother, she was keeping an eye out. Maybe she even thought she was springing a great surprise on her.

She showed up at the meeting unannounced. I imagine my sis with her friends and her new lover kidding around, carefree. She wasn't worried about her academic performance—always excellent. Her teachers were proud of her.

Jenny told me it was a classmate that noticed. "Jenny, is it your housekeeper attending the parent-teacher meeting?" She turned around and locked eyes with her mother. The poor thing had just met the head teacher who had told her how highly he thought of her daughter and had told Auntie Astou how proud he was of Jenny. Jenny remembers replying: "Yes, it's the housekeeper. She's here because my grandmother is traveling." Her mother paused and then made a U-turn, but Jenny had time to see the disbelief and pain written all over her face. "She doesn't speak French? Why is she leaving without saying hi?" they asked. Auntie Astou, tensed up, continued to walk away with heavy steps, not waiting to hear her daughter's answer.

After that incident, our life took a downturn.

The Deviant Cleric kept scrutinizing Jenny's comings and goings. He felt her distress well before I did and got close to her. For weeks, he sweet-talked her, consoled her. That man I despised had understood the contradictions that had always rocked my sis whereas I had never suspected their existence. He found the words that she wanted to hear. He reassured her by showing her the path to absolution. He served her lies that derailed her. He said she wasn't to blame—that hypocrites and vicious people were responsible for the damnation of her soul. Ahmadou explained to her that there was a way out. Return to her true faith. That of her birth. The one she should never have betrayed in the first place. He promised her a special place in Allah's heart. Jenny did not distrust the Deviant Cleric as much as I did. She listened to him and was convinced.

I now understand how much the idea of finally having a goal in life, a clear-cut path and hope in redemption could have lured Jenny. Her mother's secrets about their past and my loose life made us easy scapegoats for her angst, as well as the selfless kindness of Sita Anna. She dreamed of purity and rebirth, and he was offering that possibility.

I thought the Deviant Cleric was asking her out. I

laughed at the thought; undoubtedly, my sis was rejecting his advances. She would never fall into such an obvious trap. Sadly, he was doing something worse. He was indoctrinating her and against that I didn't know how to fight. None of us did. We were not prepared for it.

Bit by bit, Jenny stopped going to school and started going to the mosque daily instead.

My sis told me the whole story on the night train to Ngaoundere. I didn't understand before it was too late to turn back. To explain. To ask for forgiveness. Things moved at such a dizzying speed that once we were able to slow down and catch our breath, it was already too late. The doors of our prison were firmly locked.

I immediately noticed the change in her behavior, but I didn't know what to make of it. Jenny now wore dark clothes that covered her entire body and she shrouded her hair with a headscarf. I dared to laugh about it kindheartedly, "You went from jean shorts straight to jute sacks. What's the deal?" I asked teasingly. She stopped talking to me.

She and the Deviant Cleric were now inseparable. She followed him to the mosque and came back a whole new person.

I tried to get in touch with Sita Anna but I didn't have her Paris number.

I went and spoke to Auntie Astou. "My daughter is returning to the faith of her ancestors," she told me. "That can only do her good. Better than living in lies and sin."

Which ancestors again? When we attended church,

whose faith was that? In the parlor hung a picture of Jenny in her white gown during her first Communion. Didn't that mean anything? What place did lies and sin have in Jenny's life? I kept my questions to myself. Auntie Astou was narrow-minded, hostile. There was no way you could have a conversation with her.

I searched for Ma' Moudio everywhere in Bonabéri until I learned she had also moved to France to live with her son. I could have you called you, Max, but the thought didn't even cross my mind. I needed an adult. Someone who knew all of us and was a respected figure in the neighborhood. Someone who could put their foot down and end this madness.

✳

For the first time since she had started giving her testimony, Tina turned to the other people in the room.

"I looked for help. I swear! It's as if the world had abandoned me. I was scared, overwhelmed. I didn't know what to do, or who to turn to."

"We know, Tina," Anna said softly. "You don't have to be ashamed of anything. Nothing at all."

Tina continued her testimony to Max alone. This absolution was coming too late. The damage had been done.

✳

Of the four of us, I was the loneliest. You all had an adult who worried about you. Imperfect but present nonetheless. As for me, you were all I had.

Ismaël avoided us. He hung out with boys I didn't know. It was as if our childhood had been scrubbed from his memory as soon as our memorable year together ended. Alone, I watched my sis closely. I asked about her new clothing and headscarf and went to buy the same things in the Hausa quarter in New Bell. I also bought a prayer mat. A little before 5 a.m. one morning, I scaled my grandmother's fence, just like I had done so often before, and went to knock on Jenny's window. She opened it, annoyed.

"What do you want? It's time for me to pray," she told me.

"I want to pray with you," I confessed.

Jenny got angry.

"Do you think it's a joke? Do you think this is some joke? I don't want to see you anymore. I can't be your friend anymore. You are unclean."

My heart ached, Max. I swear, my heart was on fire. If you had seen our Jenny at that moment... Her stern look, her inflexible attitude... Where had my sis gone? Who was this person? I felt like screaming: "Jenny, Jen, it's me Tina. Don't you recognize me?"

I couldn't hold back my tears.

"Sis, don't leave me alone. Please. If I'm unclean, cleanse me. If I'm damned, redeem me. I don't know how to pray, teach me. Do not leave me, Jen, you are all I have in this world. I don't have anyone else. You know that. You know me. Bring me closer to your God," I begged.

She didn't respond immediately. We were more than friends, we were sisters. Adopted twin sisters. Never had I laughed or cried without Jenny crying or laughing too. Our emotions aligned seamlessly. She knew all there was to know about my charged nights, my doubts, and the ghosts I wrestled with. In that moment, she looked at me without emotion, as if I were a stranger and we no longer belonged to the same world. It increased my sorrow ten times over. I panicked, ready to do anything. Absolutely anything to be her friend once again. She ultimately responded in a cold voice:

"Don't you ever call me Jenny. My name is Djenabou. Did you know that my first name comes from Zineb, a flower that grows in the desert? Just like me in this faithless world? The Prophet, peace and blessings be upon Him, loved my name so much that two of his eleven wives and one of his daughters were named Zineb. Whereas Jenny, where does that come from? Some American TV series? And what does it mean? Nothing! No meaning. Only emptiness. Futility. Jenny no longer exists. I am Djenabou once again."

I didn't respond. I didn't even know Djenabou was her name. I had always known her as Jenny. Together, we would once have mocked a man who chose his wives based on their name and married two women with the same name. What did he call them: Zineb 1 and Zineb 2? We would have blasphemed as we cracked up, taking the joke to the extreme by imagining how confusing such a situation would be in daily life and then we would have moved on to something else.

My new friend wanted to be Djenabou. I told myself, fine. Djenabou she will be.

"In regards to your conversion, we can talk about that shortly with Ahmadou and the imam. They will decide whether you should be admitted into the Umma. Now leave me alone. I have to pray."

What is the Umma? I didn't dare to ask. Instead, I asked, "Can I pray with you? Would you teach me?"

Djenabou looked at me the same way Jenny once had. With kindness and friendship.

"It won't count. You first have to proclaim the Shahada in front of witnesses and then undergo ritual purification. But you can stay, if you want, and start learning. For now, I pray in French while I'm working on being able to recite Arabic."

She softened her tone, "You know, when I wash my face and hands, and I kneel on this mat to speak to Him, I can really feel God's presence. I bow down and my soul rises toward Allah. Let Him be praised. That is when I know all my weaknesses, all my pettiness has been forgiven, because He is merciful. His compassion is second to none. I know He has forgiven me the moment my heart goes out to Him."

I did not understand anything about this new way she spoke, but all I wanted was to learn. Jenny...in my heart she was still Jenny...did her ablutions before praying. I, who had always felt dirty, liked the idea of a God who wanted to wash us clean of our iniquities and give us the means to purify ourselves. Forehead to the ground, she said a prayer that moved me. It soothed the

torments of my heart, quieted the keen awareness I had
of my mediocrity:

> *In the name of God, the Gracious, the Merciful. He is*
> *Allāh, One; Allāh, the Eternal Refuge, He neither begets*
> *nor is born, Nor is there to Him any equivalent.*
>
> *I seek refuge in the Lord of daybreak; From the evil*
> *of that which He created; And from the evil of darkness*
> *when it settles; And from the evil of the blowers in knots;*
> *And from the evil of an envier when he envies.*
>
> *I seek refuge in the Lord of mankind; The Sovereign*
> *of mankind; The god of mankind; From the evil of the*
> *retreating whisperer –; Who whispers into the breasts of*
> *mankind –; From amongst the jinn and mankind.*

Jenny had forgotten that I was there. Every inch of
her soaked in the prayer.

I watched her lips, paying attention to each word
she said. I found them beautiful, deep. I too needed a
Merciful God, who would see beyond the sinner and protect me like a loving father.

In my chaotic life, deep in the middle of the night
when I finally fell asleep clutching the handle of a knife,
when the boys who had been hounding me the day before ignored me the day after, when I had no place to go
and wandered aimlessly around town until I got tired,
when I doubted the usefulness of my life and the image
of my mother floating in her own blood left me dizzy, I
hoped for this Merciful God. And He had finally settled
His gaze upon me.

The next day, we spoke to Ahmadou. He got bitterly upset. "I don't believe for one second that she wants to convert. This little slut is pretending. She doesn't deserve Allah," he sputtered, giving me a death stare.

I was wearing the dark clothes and headscarf I'd bought the day before. I was looking at the ground, as submissive as possible in order not to come off as defiant and further irritate him. "You're not the one who decides. Ask the imam," an annoyed Jenny said. Deep down inside I was elated that she spoke to him so sternly. Maybe he didn't have as much control over her as he would have liked.

The imam told us that the doors of Allah's house were wide open to every honest man and woman. To those who turned their back on sin and false gods, and came to seek refuge in Him. Over all those people, Allah stretched His blessing. When Ahmadou tried to argue, the imam told him that the jihad needed good Muslims in the north of the country and that Allah would reward him a thousand times over for having brought us to Him.

I performed all the necessary ablutions before proclaiming the Shahada. The imam asked me whether my conversion was sincere and thoughtful, to which I answered yes. He informed me that I was blessed because I had joined the community of believers. Then the imam said that I would be called Aïcha from then on.

Djenabou beamed with joy. "Aïcha was the third wife of the Prophet, greetings and blessings be upon Him, his favorite. Aïcha means alive. We could not have found a name that suited you better."

My sis held me tight in her arms. I embraced her

back, crying. I clung to her, relieved, so relieved that we were friends again.

Starting the next day, I took classes with the imam to learn the Koran and the obligations of a good Muslim woman. I understood that Djenabou didn't just want to bless and praise God every time that she said his name, but that this was a religious obligation. The imam told me about the five prayers said at specific times and the Surahs to learn by heart, first in French and then in Arabic. He explained the mandatory purification rituals to me. Over time, I memorized the code of conduct I had to live by, owing to my conversion. But as we embraced in the empty room that served as a mosque, I had only one thing in my head—my sis and I once again belonged to one another. Were together in each other's arms. We were all the other had—no longer Jenny and Tina, but Djenabou and Aïcha. None of that mattered because we were together. I wouldn't be alone.

Don't ask me where Ismaël was during all this because I don't know. We sometimes saw him in the distance, but we were no longer allowed to talk to boys. Our old, already strained, friendship was now a thing of the past. However, one evening he came to see us in Jenny's room. He knocked at the door shortly after we'd finished our prayers.

Jenny half opened the door without letting him in.

"What are you doing here?" she asked.

"I came to ask you to marry me," he announced.

I burst out laughing before being cut off by Jenny's

frown. Since she'd started keeping the company of the Deviant Cleric, I hadn't seen her laugh once. She no longer sang either. Not to mention dancing, when we had been so fond of dancing... Do you remember, Max?

"You're playing a joke on yourself, Ismaël, not on me," she said.

"I'm not joking, Jen...Djenabou. They are planning to take you up north to one of those terrorist camps. Have you heard about them? Open up, please. We need to talk," he begged.

We had all heard of the Boko Haram camps.

We didn't listen to the news, but you would have to be deaf to miss it. They found infamy when they kidnapped a white man and his family not far from Waza park in the north. They were released two months later after millions were paid in ransom, rumor had it. The whole country was upset by the kidnapping. These monsters are not Cameroonians but Nigerians. Surely. We have many flaws, we Cameroonians, but even our worst outlaws wouldn't kidnap a white family, risking shame for our country in the eyes of the world. Thieves in our country don't kidnap tourists, even if they stray far from established trails. All they do is relieve them of their belongings before leaving them to their fate. Basic rascals! Not unscrupulous and illiterate savages. We all laughed for a while over the rumors that part of the ransom had been embezzled by those negotiating the release of the hostages. We clearly recognized our compatriots for whom any opportunity is manna from heaven. However, the kidnapping happened in the Muslim region, far away.

It might as well have happened on another planet for us. Everybody had their daily struggles and the story was soon forgotten.

Ismaël told us another story. A reality far different than the street gossip and official version:

"Our village is located not far from the Nigerian border. We're Kanouri. My mother was from Bama, an area on the Nigerian side of the border. In our village, Gance, just like all over the region, people have family in both countries. Maroua is closer to Gance than Maiduguri, but we used to go there on vacation when I was small. My uncles still live there. For us Kanouri, Maiduguri is a traditional, cultural, and religious center. Ahmadou attended Koranic school there. We have a shared history, and bonds of faith and blood. They are our brothers. That is where Boko Haram was born. Ahmadou and the imam are agents on a recruitment drive just like others all over the country."

My best friend was telling me that he was related to the outlaws terrorizing the northern part of the country. I was shocked.

"But...who knows? I mean, the real bad guys, the real terrorists, they are all Nigerians, right? I mean... this...it can't be you, us, Cameroonians...otherwise we'd know," I babbled.

Shocked, I was stuttering. Ismaël continued patiently:

"Along these borders, nationality doesn't mean anything. Nigerians, Cameroonians, Chadians, Nigerois, we are all the same people. We have had the same faith forever. The extremists come from these places and promise to reunite us under their independent caliphate. Does that make sense?"

Djenabou commented bitterly, "That is beside the point. To Southerners in Cameroon, our culture is nothing more than the songs of Faadah Kawtal or the fantasia of the Lamido of Ngaoundere where girls dance bare chested and well-dressed riders on horses charge empty air. To you, we are savage *maguidas*, primitives, soya sellers and nothing more. We interest nobody. Now, they will be forced to see us. This country that's corrupt right to the marrow will witness the fire of Allah, may He be praised."

I knew Faadah Kawtal just like everyone else and even some soya-selling maguidas but I didn't see how any of this was related to Jenny and Ismaël. I'd never thought about Ismaël's religion, except to appreciate it when we got to stuff ourselves with barbecued mutton and millet-based pap every time Sita Ramata and her family broke their Ramadan fast or invited neighbors over for Tabaski. As for Jenny, until recently, she'd been a baptized and practicing Catholic. So where had this "we" and "you people" that revealed old divisions and secret wounds come from? We were frightened by Jenny's passionate outburst. I didn't understand. Ismaël seemed even more worried.

"They slaughter people, Djenabou. They loot the villages of poor people who pray to Allah every day. They kidnap traders and cattle herders and demand ransom from families to release them. They kidnap women and rape them. They are not the idealistic revolutionaries you think they are…"

She interrupted him, angry, "You're lying! You are simply reiterating the government's propaganda. Ahmadou warned me. We know the falsehoods you peddle to slow down the will of the one true God. I don't believe you. Ahmadou told me that I could take care of children there. Help them. Run literacy programs."

"Literacy programs? Are you kidding? Do you know what Boko Haram means? Boko comes from *book*, the Pidgin English word for book, and *haram* is the Arabic word for forbidden. They combat education, teaching. They shoot school children. They kidnap young girls as they leave school and forcefully marry them off. You can't afford to be a child in their midst. You don't know what you are getting yourself into," he warned.

"That isn't true. They are fighting Allah's battle. May Allah be praised. They are carrying out the jihad the scriptures prescribe against miscreants, unscrupulous corrupters. They... You are lying! You're a bad Muslim. An infidel! It's people like you who are dangerous," she said accusingly.

Ismaël stopped talking, deeply hurt by the accusation. We didn't recognize our joyous, intelligent Jenny in this obtuse and aggressive Djenabou. As the name of God and the words *corrupters* and *liars* came into our life, cracks had appeared in our bonds at a mind-boggling speed. How was the merciful, compassionate, and consoling prayer that Djenabou—soul turned toward the Lord—murmured five times daily compatible with such hate?

Ismaël changed tactics.

"Listen, Djenabou, maybe I'm wrong. You know,

to my mother, the jihad was a battle of the soul waged against demons. To her, it wasn't about fighting external enemies but rather confronting the evil inside us. A private and personal fight to become a better person. But you're right, I want to believe it. Let us get married. Head out together to the jihad. To your jihad," he proposed.

"Your mother, mine, your father, you, you all are half-hearted. You have let yourselves be fooled. I don't want to get married. I want to serve Allah. May He be praised."

"You don't understand, Djenabou. Allah doesn't care about the devotion of virgins. You're serving the wrong god. If you want to carry out jihad, it will be next to a man, you husband, your master. You won't have a choice. You either marry me or they'll marry you off to Ahmadou. I overheard him talking about it with the imam. Everything has been arranged. First thing tomorrow, Ahmadou will ask you to marry him, and they won't give you a choice. They think it is your duty as a Muslim woman to contribute to the next generation of the caliphate. My plan is quite simple. You want to join the jihad? Great! We'll all join or none of us will. Here in Douala, there's nothing they can do to us. We can dictate our terms. They can let us marry and go together or you'll refuse to go with them," he said.

She had no response to that, but I could see that Ismaël's words had made her doubt. He continued in a persuasive tone, "If we're married, we can look out for one another. They won't harm you and you will be able to contribute to the fight in relative security," he promised.

"Okay, then marry both of us," said Djenabou, taking us by surprise. If I'm in danger, so is Aïcha. Who will protect her?"

Ismaël turned toward me. Do you remember his look, Max?

"You shouldn't come, Tina…" he said.

"Aïcha. Her name is Aïcha," Djenabou interrupted him abruptly.

"Aïcha," Ismaël complied. "The emir of the group that we will be joining has a thing for light-skinned women. Your mixed-race heritage will make you stand out. Peul women whom he likes are kidnapped during raids and reserved for him. The imam is planning to offer you as a gift to him or to trade you for a favor. When we get there, there won't be anything I can do for you. Everything I'm telling you, I heard from eavesdropping on my brother and the imam. But I don't know when we will leave or to where exactly. I'm not even sure that we will be able to stay together."

"Wherever you go, I will go," I said.

Did we know what we were doing? What we were getting ourselves into? I guess yes. You could say that. Ismaël had warned us. There was still time for us to back out then. The only compromise Djenabou accepted was to marry Ismaël. I think that, even mesmerized by faith, she couldn't stand the idea of being married to the Deviant Cleric.

If Djenabou and Ismaël were leaving, there was no reason for me to stay. I was ready to face hell and its demons by their side rather than my loneliness. But we never had the slightest idea how ferocious the monsters walking the earth are. How could we have known?

The imam quickly briefed us about the journey, and on how the jihad was one of the pillars of Islam. He went on and on about how vice and corruption flourished unabated in our country, how respect and modesty had long disappeared. He was upset by the virtueless women who were paraded as role models. He spoke about our helpless Muslim brothers rotting away in misery and general indifference in the northern part of the country. He said the hour of Allah had come and it was our duty as Muslims to bear His cleansing fire fearlessly. It was our duty to enlist in the armies of God. He preached. Over and over, he repeated the narrative I would hear a thousand times over the coming months. However, I didn't understand back then the unparalleled violence in it. Everything was metaphorical to me. I was far from imagining the extent to which "bear the cleansing fire" was to be taken literally.

For the time being, his words alluded to a reality that I was familiar with. He struck a chord with me.

Ahmadou lost it when Ismaël and Djenabou asked the imam to marry them. He screamed that it was a trap. Betrayal. That Ismaël had never been a believer, and barely knew how to say his prayers. He was a bad Muslim. That I was a nobody. The imam tried to calm his anger and make him see reason. I now know that he wanted to avoid a scandal. He was afraid that Ahmadou would be prompted by his ferocious jealousy to do something thoughtless, which would draw attention to us. I found his attitude reassuring, and actually felt some sympathy for him. *He's on our side. He is a man of God. A good man*, I thought. It didn't take long for me to see I was mistaken. Ismaël was right. As long as we were in Douala, the imam played for time. He listened to us. He had already informed his master about my arrival. He did everything in his power to get us to go with him.

I think even Ahmadou underestimated the extent of that man's duplicity. He allowed himself to be coaxed by his sweet words, calling him knight of Allah—he who was just a lost orphan like us. Ahmadou was too sad to think beyond his blinding rancor. He patiently conspired to drag Jenny into his jihad. He planned to isolate her, to take advantage of her vulnerability and make her dependent on him. To make her love him and crush the terrible solitude that had become his fate since his mother passed away and which no prayer really soothed. So close to his goal, our mass conversion thwarted his plans.

The imam felt it and changed his story accordingly. He flattered, encouraged, was borderline fatherly. "Allah will reward you for your devotion, not only in paradise but as soon as we get to the camp, as soon as we meet our own people. Trust me, son. You will finally leave this place where nobody sees you for who you really are. There, you will be powerful. You will be Allah's sword bearer and you won't regret your decision," he promised Ahmadou, whose will was now wavering.

The imam had a schedule and objectives we knew nothing about. He was here to recruit, something he did clandestinely, with the constant fear of being caught, chased away, or poisoned. The new anti-terrorism laws were quite draconian. The three of us, he hadn't even had to come find us or convince us. He simply plucked us like ripe fruits. He would not let anything make such a bountiful harvest slip through his fingers.

The hatred Ahmadou felt for his brother spiraled out of control. When the time was right, he would make his brother pay dearly for what he considered unforgivable treason.

Ma' Moudio returned from her holidays too late to stop the plan that had been hatched. When she saw Djenabou and me dressed with our black hijabs covering our hair and our necks, showing only our faces, she panicked. She tried to talk to me, but I avoided her. The imam forbade us from talking to other people. He dictated our every move.

I overheard her discuss the situation with Djenabou's mother, who sided with us.

"What are they doing wrong? They pray. They behave with dignity, cover themselves as prescribed by their religion to avoid triggering the covetousness of men. My daughter has never been this respectful. They have found God. Why would anybody be uncomfortable with that? Do you prefer how Tina used to run after all the boys in the neighborhood, dragging my daughter along? Personally, I am relieved to see that they are on the right path. God is marvelous. He has rescued my little girl from debauchery. My prayers have been answered," she argued.

Ma' Moudio countered, using the plans Auntie

Astou had had for her daughter. "I know you have always wanted your little girl to be educated. Those children are no longer going to school. Doesn't that worry you?"

Auntie Astou simply murmured, "Everything God does is good."

Whatever this really means is anybody's guess, but it is an irredeemably unassailable argument.

Ma' Moudio tried to talk to my grandparents, unsuccessfully. My grandfather had recently suffered two hemorrhagic strokes. Since then, he just wallowed in his shit, while his wife continued sinking even deeper into alcoholism. So, Ma' Moudio decided to contact Sita Anna in France, who in turn reached out to Auntie Astou, who then informed us that your grandparents would come back earlier than planned. We passed this information along to the imam. He also knew Sita Anna. She was an authoritative figure in our neighborhood. The influence she wielded in the city was an open secret. He would be in serious trouble if she set her sights on him. He decided to speed up our departure.

We were ordered not to tell anyone, especially our relatives.

They came for us at night, with no luggage except what we had on our backs. A car was waiting for us in the street to take us to Yaounde. From there, we boarded the train to Ngaoundere. Then after two days, stopping several times for supplies or to switch cars, we arrived in Kolofata. Later, we were taken to the Sambisa Forest, on the Nigerian side of the border.

How do I say this, Max? The minute we left Douala, we understood the mistake we had made.

The farther we traveled, the more the imam revealed his true self—aggressive and bad tempered. And the more Ahmadou's hatred of his younger brother reached glaring proportions. From Ngaoundere, groups of young men and women joined us. Girls and boys, just as scared as us. I can assure you that even Djenabou was no longer so proud and arrogant. Our handlers were violent, bad people. When one of these men disappeared with a girl into the bushes, we all knew for sure the kind of abuse he was inflicting on her.

Ismaël watched over Djenabou. They all knew she was his wife. He didn't let anyone get close to her. Ahmadou, whom the imam had appointed as the leader of our group, was champing at the bit and throwing all sorts of tiny jabs at his younger brother. Ismaël endured the abuse quietly, focused on protecting Djenabou.

Even more disturbing, these men avoided me too. They barely said a word to me. I stayed glued to Djenabou. We never left each other's side, but sticking together didn't help the other young girls. However, nobody laid a finger on me or mistreated me. It was a quite relief for me, although it left me worried.

We were taken to some kind of military camp in Sambisa.

Djenabou and Ismaël were taken away together, led off by a troop of armed men. My sis tried to intervene, saying, "She's my sister. She has to come with us." Her attitude angered the men. A heated debate followed

between them and Ismaël, in a language I didn't understand. Then Ismaël turned to Djenabou and said, "Come.
There's nothing we can do." She resisted. I felt her helplessness. "Come," he told her again. "You're not helping
her by drawing attention to her."

I found myself penned in a hall with other young
girls.

A man wearing white overalls that had seen better days joined us. He had prayer beads in his hand and
spoke a language that was foreign to me. He was giving
instructions, I think, but I wasn't reacting, so he turned
away from the others to focus solely on me. He screamed
and kicked me.

I have been subjected to many things in my life, but
never before has a man beat me like that. I have been
slapped. Shoved. But every time, I've hit back. There, I
did not even dare to make a sound. I fell to the ground,
curled up, and tried somehow to shield my stomach
with my arms, where he was kicking me—hard, unrestrained kicks. I was terrified by such unprovoked violence. Nothing in my life had prepared me for such
aggression.

He stopped when we heard machine guns outside.
I didn't know it yet, but that was how the men signaled
their return to the camp after completing a raid in a
neighboring village. High-ranking officers rode in pick-
ups or Jeeps. The other men were on foot. They were not
cautious. Did not cover their faces. They showed no dis-
cretion. Here, they were at home.

A man came into the room where we were being

held. He said something in the language I didn't understand. The imam with whom we had come appeared behind him. I saw him point at me. Although I did not understand what he was saying, I guessed from his obsequious attitude that the other man was a boss here.

The man spoke to me in French, asking, "Why are you crying?"

He was tall. From where I lay, trembling, he seemed gigantic. Black like soot. Dressed in military fatigues. Two enormous vertical scars on each side of his face, from his lower cheeks to his temples. When we were younger, we'd mocked people with such scarifications. We called them *one thousand one hundred and eleven*, referring to the many lines splashed across their faces. Sharing this memory didn't cross my mind at that moment. Even in the antechambers of my heart, never would I have dared laugh at him.

I didn't answer his question. I clawed at the ground with my nails. A senseless, frenetic act, as if I could dig a hole to swallow me and shield myself from his gaze, the smell of musk and sweat that oozed from his body. He kneeled next to me. Lifted me back up. He took off my headscarf and painstakingly untied my hair.

You know how well I take care of my hair, Max. It's the only part of my body that I don't hate. It grows in long thick locks that I never cut. I wash it with scented shampoo. I condition and braid it every evening. That day, I promised myself that if I made it out of there alive, I would shave my head.

He said something in his language and all the men in the room laughed. Our imam sighed in relief. I understood he had just accepted the gift.

The man asked me in French, "Who hit you?" My teeth chattered. I was trembling. Even if my life had depended on it, I wouldn't have been able to respond. The imam indicated my torturer, engaging in a long vindictive tirade that I did not understand. The other man shrank under the weight of their stares. Both hands stretched out entreatingly. His voice shook. His eyes, unable to face his master, fluttered uncontrollably. He tried to explain himself, but he just babbled. Panicked. Sputtered. Then he fell into a murmur before attempting the hopeless exercise all over again.

The man spoke to me again. "Come see what happens to those who disrespect me." He grabbed the arm of his victim, who was now uttering soft moans of terror, and dragged him out of the room. I wasn't sure I had understood the instructions. I barely understood half of what they said, unable to make sense of what was playing out before my eyes. I was slow to comply. "I said come!" the man growled from outside. I hurried, half creeping on all fours, half running. My torturer, kneeling with hands bound, was still pleading. A small crowd, made up of only men except for me, formed. "Come closer!" he ordered me before screaming something to which the men responded in unison. He then removed a gun from his pocket and shot the man kneeling before his feet. One bullet to the head.

That was my introduction to Commander Yacouba. Emir and undisputed head of our base. This ruthlessly cruel man was my husband throughout my detention by Boko Haram.

I'll spare you the sexual aspects of the thing. Simply know that the worst thing you can imagine doesn't come close to reality. "How many men have you been with in your life?" he asked me right from the first time. "As many as the sand on the beach...?" "Three," I replied timidly. He laughed mockingly and said, "Liar. I can tell when a woman has been used extensively. You're still tight because you are young, but your vagina is unctuous, welcoming. One can easily tell that you love it." And then a moment later he added, "It doesn't matter how many men before me have possessed your body, *inch' Allah* I will be your last."

Commander Yacouba lived in a shack made from planks and assorted materials from the forest. It was similar to the other houses but more spacious. Hierarchies were important among the jihadists. He was the head of our camp. The emir, as they called him. His authority was never questioned. His power was absolute. There were always two young girls living in his house. Slim, light-skinned Peuls. Just the way he loved them.

Boko Haram traded with the villages along the Nigerian and Cameroonian border, but also with Chad and Niger. They massacred shepherds, seized their cattle, and then resold them at discounted prices. The women went to neighboring markets and into the refugee camps set up around the border to sell basic commodities—frying pans, hoes, blankets, and other necessities that their men brought back from their looting. I sometimes wondered about the mental state of the women who'd been forced to run away from their home to escape terrorists, found refuge in a camp, and then had to buy back the things that had been stolen from them without daring to complain. For fear of reprisal here, in this place where they were supposed to be protected by the whole world.

Every item was listed. Prices set. Boko Haram women were driven to the gates of cities and completed the rest of the journey on foot. Their movement and bargaining were closely monitored by spies stationed along the way. They used the money they made to buy fresh food.

With these practices, the sect ruined the economy of the region. The real traders had long ago migrated to safer places. So had all those who had some other place where they could seek refuge. Along the border and for several kilometers inside, the villages that were regularly attacked had been deserted by those who had kept them alive and had the means to do so. The only people left behind were the poor who, willingly or by force, paid allegiance to the terrorist group.

Ismaël was right—they obsessively attacked schools. The government, unable to protect children, closed schools one after another, leaving kids idle and their distraught parents grappling with the murderous sect. Governments, whether in Yaounde, Abuja, N'Djamena, or Niamey, didn't act fast enough or with sufficient effectiveness. They gave the impression they didn't understand what was at stake in those peripheral, disadvantaged regions. They were inconsistent; their solutions ill-suited. Governments wavered while Boko Haram had the right ideological narrative. Enough power to strike first and for reprisal. The sect used violence both as a means to communicate and to persuade.

Aminata and Fatou, my "co-wives," went to the market twice a week. Not me. Yacouba formally warned me against leaving the compound. He left every day at dawn or in the middle of the night for his operations. The troops then left the camp too, leaving the captives and their wives to be guarded by a few men and women, since many women also fought by their side. Under the thumb of the widow of a Boko Haram commander known for her ferociousness, they were made available to the soldiers, with the knowledge that they could be taken as a wife for a night and then repudiated in the morning. Exploited at will, even in combat where they carried equipment and transported the wounded. When governments exerted more pressure on men, the women were brainwashed to carry out suicide attacks and they became the ultimate weapon of the jihadists.

One day, we learned that the terrorist group had kidnapped over two hundred schoolgirls from a place in Nigeria called Chibok, located in the southern part of the state of Borno. The international community was scandalized by this news. It was reported in all the newspapers. Yacouba and his henchmen returned quite proud from that expedition. The girls were dispatched to various camps, offered in marriage. They were destined to carry Boko Haram babies and enable the caliphate to prosper.

A victorious and jubilant feeling reigned in the camp.

"Daesh is far less effective than us," Yacouba told me. "Yes. We have sworn allegiance to the Islamic State, but compared to ours, their wins don't really compare. They're lightweights, more focused on politics than on the creation of the caliphate." After that stunt, Boko Haram became headline news. They were finally given their due consideration by the international media and the governments of the most powerful countries.

On walls, they pasted huge posters of Michelle Obama in the pretty interior of the White House, with the hashtag #bringbackourgirls. The jihadists urinated or spat on the posters as they joked around. They also made all sorts of jokes about what they had in store for her if, in her quest for a man, a real one, she ditched her weak husband to join them.

Those men were gross. They spoke and behaved with such utter obscenity. I don't know why I am saying this—compared to everything else this should be irrelevant, but it was…yes, shocking. The basic rules of modesty and decency that governed every human community weren't in effect there. We were savage beasts. What God could tolerate such a mob?

They all talked about nothing besides the Chibok kidnapping. They were pumped up and even more violent. Our already horrible fate got worse.

I prayed ceaselessly, saying, "Dear Madame Obama, stop saying that we're your daughters. It makes them mistreat us now even more imagining that they are dealing with Malia and Sasha. Your daughters are safe. Protected. Not us. If you care about our fate, shut up!

Don't expose us to their punishment. Don't saddle us with their hatred for you. We're already having a hard time with our own yoke. And you, powerful men, stop making declarations. Everything you say is used against us. Come discreetly, at night. Come free us and demolish this cursed place."

However, no savior heard my prayer, and I sank deeper into my daily life as a captive.

Living with Yacouba's two other wives was stressful.

Women are strange beings. Even there, in that hell-hole, we found a way to compete for our master's favor.

Fatou's Peul name was Fatoumata, but here, every-body called her Fatou, and she was the favorite before I arrived. Daughter of a local dignitary, her father had given her to Yacouba as a peace offering. He lost interest in her after he brought me over. She showed her jealousy every chance she could through endless vexations that made life harder for all of us.

I'm not the kind of woman who fights over a man, but it had nothing to do with being the bigger person. When the men I had been with before were spoken for, their partners didn't consider me a rival. In their minds, the relationship wasn't any different than a trip to a pros-titute who was too stupid to get paid. That is to say, they didn't consider it a relationship at all. I did not challenge their position in any meaningful way so they didn't pay me any mind.

Fatou's attitude came as a surprise to me, but I was too frightened by my new life to be offended by it. My failure to react only angered her more. She ended up talking back to Yacouba, something nobody else, neither man nor woman in this camp, dared do during my time in captivity. "Why doesn't she go to the market like the rest of us? What does she have that I don't?" she grumbled. It was not rebellion as such. Just a flare of bad temper. She had not even really spoken aloud, having barely mumbled between her teeth. She was being stupid and jealous. Not rebellious. Unfortunately, the concept of mitigating circumstances is alien to people like Yacouba. Fatou's attitude was way more than he could tolerate coming from one of his slave wives.

Over the prior months, the Nigerien, Chadian, Nigerian, and Cameroonian armies had been joining forces to combat the Boko Haram scourge. Villagers had formed militias. More and more pressure was being applied to the terrorist group. In retaliation, the jihadists had decided to send women out as scouts before each operation. They didn't really care about them, but there was always public outcry whenever a Boko Haram woman or girl was killed or captured. For shock value, no method was off-limits. Shortly after her minor protest, Yacouba woke Fatou up in the middle of the night, saying, "Come with me!"

A mission had been planned to rustle cattle on the Cameroonian side of the border. Nobody knows how or from whom the militiamen and soldiers on duty in the targeted village got wind of the plan. They laid in wait, ready to receive the jihadists. Boko Haram had sent eight women wearing fatigues as scouts. Armed with machetes, they got butchered. Three of them, in critical condition, were left behind and were surely captured by the forces of law and order. The other five were killed. Fatou was among the dead.

The Cameroonian troops, their mission accomplished, didn't hang around because they had to intervene in other hotspots of terrorist violence. Spies informed the terrorists of their departure. The terrorists returned to the village and went from hut to hut, murdering the residents in their sleep, before carting off the coveted cattle and the meager possessions of their victims.

After Fatou died, Aminata and I grew closer, on her initiative. Much to my surprise, she spoke proper French although I had only heard her speak Kanouri, Peul, or Hausa. I hadn't mastered any of these languages. I couldn't even differentiate one from the other.

Just like our fellow captives, we shared our stories, and one day she finally told hers to me. I wasn't trusting enough to share mine with her.

Aminata had been kidnapped in Cameroon, at the entrance to Sanda-Wadjiri, her village. She was going to the market with her friends when armed men stopped them. Commander Yacouba was there. He chose Aminata for himself because she was his kind of woman. The other men had disappeared with his friends. Since then, she had not seen them again. She didn't know whether her parents were looking for her. Regardless, they were too poor to pay her ransom. She had not heard from her family.

I was suspicious of everyone and everything. It took me some time to accept Aminata's friendship, but I was so lonely! I choked on loneliness in the solitary confinement of the compound, which I only left to gather stones. Visitors never said a word to me.

Only Yacouba spoke to me. Everything I know about Boko Haram, he told me. I don't know why he shared every little detail of his planning, his missions, his strategies with me. But, in fact, I do know. I have a faint idea why: He thought I would never have the courage to escape. He knew I was a coward.

We were in the Sambisa Forest in Nigeria. I knew this, but I would never have been able to pinpoint it on a map. I spoke none of the local languages. They would have quickly found me if I had tried to escape. Or worse, I might have stepped on a landmine or been attacked by a wild animal, who knows. Real and imaginary dangers created an insurmountable barrier between me and even the slightest idea of possible escape. Not that I accepted my fate. Not that I had given up. Every day was a torment, but I knew that I would never have the courage to attempt anything, so I waited for a miracle.

The terrorist cell had accomplices all over the region. People came from Maiduguri and beyond to buy the cattle they'd stolen to sell at ridiculously low prices. I saw helicopters land in the middle of the night, and hooded men gave Yacouba briefcases full of euros, dollars, CFA Francs, or Nairas. Technicians came to install telecommunications equipment. I don't know what it means to be heavily armed, but the camp received huge numbers of machine guns, grenades, ammunition, and machetes.

Yacouba was only interested in money in that he

used it to strengthen his domination. It was useful to run the camp given that new captives streamed in endlessly. Many young men enlisted willingly. Clear rules governed sexuality among Muslims in the northern part of Cameroon. Although polygamy was allowed, religion and customs forbade promiscuity. Here, they could have as many women as they wished, regardless of age, regardless of what they looked like. They were strongly encouraged to procreate. Yacouba was aware that this was the sole motivation for many of them, but he didn't care. They were cannon fodder in battle. The more, the better. After a summary religious and military training, they were sent to the front, high on huge doses of Tramadol and other drugs. Armed with nothing but a machete. Carrying amulets made from chapters of the Koran meant to shield them from enemy bullets, they died like flies.

"I like talking to you," Yacouba told me. "It helps me organize my thoughts."

According to him, they started kidnapping women as retaliation when the Nigerian government targeted the wives and daughters of Boko Haram leaders. Soldiers arrested them without cause and inflicted all sorts of violence on them before releasing them. Sometimes they were pregnant, and their husbands, fathers, or brothers were given no other choice than to kill them to cleanse the dishonor. Assert power and domination over the enemy by degrading their women. Boko Haram learned the lesson and perfected the technique. "These days, their women return to blow up in their faces," Yacouba explained to me with the same calm tone he used to describe the worst horrors.

As the armed attacks against the sect intensified, it adapted.

Young men and women were trained and then sent back to their villages to preach. They also recruited sleeper agents, ready to be killed for the cause or to deliver their neighbors to terrorists. Any resistance marked you, and your relatives, for retaliation. Jihadism was imported into the villages, into families, where it became more difficult to track without attacking the residents who were its first casualties.

These people were poor, frightened, and ignored. The power of the new recruits made them envied and created more followers. Even better, the kidnappings and ransoming created "negotiators," a new class of lords that even governments contacted when important people were kidnapped.

The sect didn't shy away from any type of violence. Women, sometimes even children, were suicide bombers, blowing themselves up in public places, markets or churches, first in Nigeria, then increasingly in neighboring countries. A man remotely triggered the bombs.

Their jihad served as a moral justification for large-scale fraud, rape, and murder. Sermons were organized regularly. Imams took turns vilifying their enemies and hardening the hearts of the soldiers of Allah, as they called themselves. The only words they used to describe anyone else were miscreants, infidels, and they completely disregarded the dignity, humility, and compassion that is central to the spirituality they claimed as theirs. Allah featured in every sentence they uttered, but the first people these barbarians terrorized and massacred were Muslims.

I was overwhelmed by this daily, implacable, inexplicable brutality. Inside, I trembled ceaselessly. I was completely unsettled by dread. Diarrhea, vomiting, insomnia, and despite it all, I tried to maintain the calm, harmless face expected of a slave. I would be dead if I hadn't carried the memory of us four to keep me alive. I spoke to you, Max. I spoke to you all the time. You were right there with me. Your presence in my head, in my heart, consoled me every second and every minute of the day.

I hadn't laid eyes on Djenabou and Ismaël again since we'd arrived. I did not dare to ask anybody about them. One day, Aminata, back from the market, whispered to me that she had something to tell me when Yacouba left.

For me, the status quo brought hope. I dreamed of freedom, but any novelty, the least change in routine, could have been fatal. So, I welcomed this news conservatively. Aminata found me, excited, as soon as Yacouba left:

"I met a woman in the market. She told me that she's your sister. Her name is Jenny. She sends her greetings. She says Ismaël also sends his greetings. She told me to mention Max in case you had any doubts. She said you would understand."

I thought I was going to be sick.

"Jenny? She said Jenny? Did she really say Max? How was she? Did she look okay to you? Do you know where she lives? Is she in this same camp with us? Did she really say Jenny?" I asked.

More questions came rushing out. "And what about Ismaël? And Ahmadou? Max? Did she really say Max?" *Is this a trap?* I wondered.

"Yes, she seemed okay, but I can't really say. She's pregnant, almost due," she disclosed.

Pregnant? Jenny pregnant? God almighty! What did it all mean? Jenny and not Djenabou? What was going on? Was she in touch with Max? Oh Max, my Maxou, your name said by someone other than me. Somewhere other than in my reveries and my day-dreams and it sounded like hope, a blessing in that place of desolation.

"Do you know if she is here in this camp?" I asked.

"No, I don't think so. I had never met her before. Not even at the mosque on Fridays. There is a bigger camp deeper in the forest. The one where the great caliph lives. Maybe she's there. Or in the village. I don't know for sure. I've seen her several times in the market now. Is she really your sister? You two don't look alike. She told me your name is Tina. She was worried about you. She wanted to know whether you were being treated properly. Tina, Jenny. Are you Christians? I should have known better. I've noticed that you don't know how to pray. Where were you two kidnapped from?"

I closed my eyes. Aminata's questions tortured me. I didn't answer her, but for the first time maybe I saw our circumstances clearly. The words, which I did not say, flowed within me seamlessly: *We were not kidnapped. We came here of our own free will. Stupid teenagers trying to give meaning to their lives. We came because we thought our suffering was insurmountable. Our sins unforgivable. We came looking for redemption, and because we didn't want to be apart from one another. Because for Jenny, choosing an angry god and running away without looking back, sinking deeper into darkness...all of that was preferable to dealing with the disappointment of one's own mother, one's own shame... We loved her, so we followed. We hoped that, if worse came to worse, one of us at least could save the others. We didn't foresee the possibility that adversity would crush all of us.*

Yes, why did we come? How do you answer that question?

God, have mercy!

The protective walls that I had been holding up with all my might since being imprisoned in that horrible place gave way, and in huge, uncontrollable sobs, I cried.

I cried because of my situation, because I was afraid. There was fear in the air when I breathed, in the blood that irrigated my heart. I could no longer stand being so afraid.

Because of my poor Jenny, whose child was going to be born in this cursed place. About my beloved Ismaël.

Because of Aminata, Fatou, and all the other lost girls that Satan had brought into my circle.

Because of the blood spilled needlessly. Because of the indifference of the gods.

I cried because that particular day was my birthday. I had just turned seventeen. The same age as my mother when she killed herself. I didn't want to die the way she had died. Alone. Forgotten by everyone; nobody on earth caring enough to come to my rescue.

I couldn't stop crying.

It scared Aminata.

"Aïcha, please get ahold of yourself. Calm down, please. Commander Yacouba will be here soon. If he finds you in this state, I don't know what will become of us. What will you say? He'll think I am to blame. He'll pour his anger on me. Aïcha, stop crying, I beg you," she pleaded.

It made her shiver.

"Aïcha, think of Fatou. Do you want us to end up like her?" Aminata asked.

I stopped crying immediately when that name was mentioned. Sorrow listened to fear, a wise counsel.

I lived through the following weeks in shock. Anguish amplified my terror. Unanswered questions kept me up all night, Yacouba sleeping next to me.

Aminata had told me that Jenny was almost due. Had she given birth? Many women died in childbirth given the deplorable conditions we lived in. Was she okay? And the baby, and Ismaël? Lord, would I receive the grace of holding Jenny's child in my arms? So far, all I'd worried about was my own situation. I thought my friends were out of harm's way. Not *safe*—that word meant nothing to us—but at least spared the worst since they were together. I didn't know what else to think.

I was feverish, and despite my best efforts, Yacouba noticed. He was sharp-minded, intuitive, keenly aware of his surroundings. With him, nothing went unnoticed. "You have changed. What's wrong?" he asked. I did everything in my power to put on a straight face. To seem as calm as normal, but he was monitoring me constantly. His probing eyes tailed me every time I left the room, making me even more nervous. "You've been in contact with the outside world, haven't you?" he finally concluded. I denied the allegation with all the strength I could muster. My life was on the line and I knew it. I protested, claiming that if I had left in violation of his orders, it would have immediately been reported to him. He didn't doubt me, but his instincts suggested that he should be suspicious. He didn't need any extra proof.

Every time he took me, Yacouba had a bath afterward to perform his ablutions for purification and prayer before returning to bed. That night, he didn't. He lay on his back for a long time, listless. Every tiny bit of my being was intently focused on him—with every movement, panic made my lungs freeze. I breathed through my mouth. I choked and swallowed, unable to control myself, hoping he wouldn't notice. I knew how cold-blooded he could be, murderously violent. The speed and ease with which he could kill me if he wanted to. I was powerless before him.

"Do you know why I don't have children? Have you ever wondered why none of you get pregnant? I was a student at the University of Maiduguri when Goodluck Jonathan's soldiers attacked my family because my father was close to Mohammed Yusuf, the founder of our caliphate. They kidnapped my mother, my sisters. My father was a respected imam. Young people came to his Koranic school to learn the Word. They killed everybody who was in our compound on that fateful day. Everybody except my father. Him, they sentenced to dishonor, a fate worse than death. My life was spared only because I wasn't around. We negotiated for months and paid mind-boggling sums of money to those corrupt people to get them to release our family members.

"My mother died in detention. My sisters too, except for two, who were pregnant when they were released. My father ordered them to take their own lives. Our religion forbids suicide, but in their case, there was no other way out because, although Allah blesses the pride of Muslims, he does not forgive impurity. The bastards they carried in their wombs spelled doom for them. They had to take their own lives and in so doing they would be performing their own personal jihad, according to Allah's will. My father prepared the poison himself and my sisters drank it.

"We organized and attacked the military base. My father was killed in the offensive, but I can assure you that none of those dogs outlived him. We collected their weapons and took refuge here. Before leaving, I went to a specialist and had him perform a vasectomy on me. Do you know what that is? A surgical operation to make a man sterile.

"My father's troubles taught me a lesson. I had watched that pious and upright man cry as he buried his own daughters as commanded by Allah.

"Nobody will use my children to defeat or dishonor me. I'll perish in the jihad, the same way I joined it.

Empty-handed. Draped only in my skin and with my Kalashnikov."

Oh Max, I have never come that close to the truth. We had all been lured by a fire that didn't come from the sun but which still spread its toxic heat.

That man was mad. Undoubtedly mad, an assassin and a monster, but he was not an animal. For him, just like for us, there had been a point in his life when the answer had been this place. However—and this was where there was a difference—he had followed his dark star fully aware of all the facts. Determined to become the torturer and not the victim. Because life the way he had been made to understand it, the way he had experienced it, offered no other alternatives. His mind had been perverted to the point where he had become a danger for humanity. That didn't necessarily make him an animal or a demon. He was still a human being.

That realization didn't mean a thing in that moment. I couldn't have cared less. All that mattered was the certainty that he wouldn't hesitate to kill me if he deemed it appropriate, simply because he had the power to. And what mattered was that I would slit his throat if given the opportunity.

Such are the recesses of our souls if lit by shadowless light.

My heart was pounding so hard that I was scared he would hear it. Why was he telling me all this? Why was he bringing all this up now? What was he trying to tell me?

He turned toward me, aroused once again. I don't know how else to say it. Taken. He took me. In the way he wanted. When he wanted. I was his thing. During the act, he tightened his grip around my throat. He strangled me. I choked. He tightened his grip even more as his pleasure heightened. I thought he was going to kill me. That he was killing me. That this was my punishment: He was killing me with his bare hands as he raped me. But he ultimately let go of my neck, crashing down on me. And, breathless, he whispered into my ear, "I made a promise to you... Tina, I will be your last man. I always keep my promises." A moment later he got up to go perform his ablutions.

He had never called me Tina before. He never called me by my name. I never knew he even knew my name had been Tina. As an expert in torture, he waited for me to be distraught with fear, pain. For me to lose any dignity I had left to show me that he was the master of much more than my body. That he held much more than my life in his hands. My memories, my past, my childhood, all those pretty things that we had shared, Max, all the things I thought I'd preserved, were now his property. From that day on, I expected to die.

A few weeks later, Jenny came to see me.

Yacouba had barely left when I heard a timid knock on our door. That never happened—nobody came to our house in his absence. A change in routine might be a bad omen. Aminata and I traded scared looks, not daring to move. "Tina, it's me, Jenny. Open up." I bolted toward the door before Aminata could restrain me. My sis and I threw ourselves into each other's arms. Aminata panicked. She shut the door behind us, wide eyed. "You have to leave. You have to leave. He's going to kill us," she whispered as if even the walls had the power to report every little detail to the master of the house. Jenny tried to reassure her, saying, "Don't worry. I know where they are. It's far. They won't be back before nightfall." That was still not enough to allay Aminata's fears. "No, no, please…" she insisted.

But I had long stopped listening to her.

Jenny took off her burka. Under it she wore a loincloth tied at the waist and a large man's shirt under which, against her skin, she had wrapped her baby. I helped her undo her headscarf and took the child in my arms.

"Oh, Jen, she's such a pretty little baby. What's her name?" I asked.

"You're the one who will name her. And if it's okay by you, I want you to name her Jenny," she asked.

I looked at my sis dumbfounded.

"Listen to me closely," she told me, "there is a lot to say. A large-scale operation has been planned for tomorrow. They've been laying the groundwork for weeks now. They went to put the final touches on today. There's going to be a major suicide attack in Kolofata. Several girls will blow themselves up in various places in the town. That will give you a chance to escape."

"But Yacouba never lets me step outdoors. You don't know how he is…"

"He will this time. All the girls in Sambisa will be there. Only the caliph knows who will die. The others will be there only as a lesson. There will be dozens of girls spread throughout the town. Which is why everything has been planned down to the smallest detail. They need to be sure that the villagers along the route are on board. The plan can't leak out. We have to arrive in Kolofata without alerting the police, without drawing attention to ourselves. They'll take us in small groups along different routes."

Terror is a bottomless pit. Did you know that, Max? At some point you think you have seen its rocky bottom. That your heart can't take any more. And then something unexpected happens and the dread and anguish spike as if your brain was taking note of your imminent death, and you realize that you can still fall further than you already have.

That cage in which I was being held suddenly became my safe house. Escape? How? And go where? Yacouba was my curse. He would never let me leave.

"You don't understand…" I told her.

"I do. I understand. I understand way more than you think. Sis, I have seen these people at work. I know commander Yacouba. Everybody knows him. When I learned that you were in his house…"

Jenny spoke in a tiny voice. She avoided making eye contact with me.

"Even worse is that, of all the people that I've hurt, offended, and endangered, you're not the one paying the highest price for my stupidity and my pride. I'm not asking you to forgive me but…there is the little one and…" she said.

My sis was crying. I held her child in my arms.

DAYS COME AND GO

I have never had anyone who was all mine, never been responsible for anyone besides myself. This helpless little being gave me unexpected courage.

"Tell me what you want me to do," I said.

"Ismaël has changed. Do you remember our Ismaël, strong, upstanding, protective? Ismaël has gone mad. Ahmadou put unbearable pressure on him. He always had to do much more than the others to prove that he was not a spy. That he deserved to be here. They forced him to…to live like them, to act like…like a monster. They crushed him."

I didn't want to believe it. Even here, in this violent, unhealthy, corrupt place, I had believed that Ismaël would keep some semblance of integrity. He could not become like them—he didn't have it in him. You need hatred, spite for others, and a huge but fragile ego to turn into the kind of man who hides in the forest and emerges at night to terrorize the innocent. The exact opposite of Ismaël. I didn't interrupt Jenny. I wanted to hear her story to the very end. I was still hoping for an ending that might return my beloved, the Ismaël from our childhood, to me in one piece. But deep down, I already knew that, for Jenny, my friend had already joined the evil side, which he would never have approached of his own free will.

"You know, we used to be happy. Really happy. In the beginning, he was sweet, gentle. We thought we could start a family in this putrid hell. That we hadn't lost everything since we were together. I easily guessed what happened during their missions. When we got here, Ahmadou quickly rose to the rank of second deputy to

the emir of our group and they picked on Ismaël. During
one operation, he made the mistake of yelling to the others, 'Don't kill women and children. Take their stuff but
let these poor people live.' In their opinion, today's petty
miscreants would become tomorrow's enemies. It was either recruit them or kill them. The women would serve
the jihad. For the others, they only deserved to live if they
could be exchanged for a hefty ransom. They threatened
to kill him if he didn't follow orders more enthusiastically.
And you understand, if he died, what would I become?
Ahmadou was looking for the slightest blunder from his
brother to take me back. They left him no choice. Ismaël
screamed and cried in his nightmares. Early on, taking
him in my arms was enough to ease his torment. We
loved one another, you know? Imagine a world without
those porn movies through which we discovered, a little
stupified, sexuality when we were kids. Imagine a world
without the savagery that we experienced. Imagine a
secret paradise where the children of a fallen god wash
up. In each other's arms, we were deaf to the cries of the
women brutalized all night by their "husbands." We became immune to fear, the smell of rot and death that per-
vaded the air in this forest. Nothing existed but the two
of us. We often talked about you, Max, and about the
neighborhood. Our memories were like a photo album
of the happy days that we revisited over and over. Ismaël
was my husband. The gentlest of lovers. My friend. My
brother. You know? When bonds are strong, grow stronger, the walls collapse and then they disappear altogether.
All the gentleness we carried inside was focused on

only one other being in the world. In the intimacy of our nights, we were in a miraculous oasis. And I became Jenny once again in his eyes. Love, that urgent, imperative love was the last, only form of happiness within our reach. That was until they brought back a little girl from their raid. Every man here has several wives. To hurt me, to soil our relationship, Ahmadou demanded that Ismaël should take a new wife as required by their twisted version of religion. I had just found out that I was pregnant. I locked eyes with that little girl packed in among the others in the truck. I felt my heart melt. I should have left her to her fate. You are better off without a heart here. The jihadists chose their wives from among their captives. I asked Ismaël to take Djami, that was her name, Djamila, before one of those bastards set his sights on her. She was eight…only eight years old."

I thought Jenny was going to start crying again, but no. Her voice was only infinitely sad. Nothing more.

"Djamila came to live with us. I thought I had saved her. Who would come to check if we were treating her like our child and not like a wife? My baby was born, and at the same time, Ismaël succumbed to the horror. Moments of intimacy between us became rarer and briefer. He even stopped having nightmares. He slept like a log and wouldn't toss or turn even once in his sleep. A corpse. He could no longer stand my touch, which should have been the final red flag. We looked out for one another, but I was less attentive, you understand? I worried about my daughter's welfare in this place that's so backward that the smallest cold can easily deteriorate into pneumonia and the least bruise can become infected then turn into gangrene. Djamila and my new daughter took up my time, my energy. They brought me the worries and joys of a mother's life. With my little girls, I had days when I could have almost considered myself a normal person despite this horrible place, and I was happy as long as the laughter of my children echoed. Ismaël wasn't so lucky. Every day, he sank a little further into darkness. I didn't notice right away when he stopped carrying our baby in his arms. He stopped getting close to her. Stopped looking at her. As if he was suffering from some disease and did not want to contaminate her. I can confess this only to you: I closed my eyes while he collapsed, hoping like an idiot that what I did not want to see didn't exist, and that as long as the girls were fine, everything might still return to normal. Ismaël understood what I did not dare to express, even deep down to myself. He accepted the sacrifice that I had forced him to make. Unfortunately, we had once again underestimated what we were up against. While giving Djamila a bath two days ago, I noticed she was bleeding from her vagina. God knows that a woman's body is nothing but a rag to these monsters, I just had to live with that, but my Djami? 'Who hurt you, my dear? Did someone come into the house?' I asked. The child shook her head to say no. 'Are you afraid? You can tell me, you know?' I was thinking about what more I could do to protect her. It was at that moment that I realized we had to escape. I had to talk to Ismaël. We had to find a way to leave this place and get our daughter out of harm's way. We just had to escape from this evil forest. When Djami said, 'It is Daddy,' I didn't hear her. 'Who? Who did you say?' The little one repeated, 'It is Daddy Ismaël.' The following day, I went to see the emir. From Ismaël, I knew what was being planned for Kolofata. I decided that I would be one of the women to blow themselves up. Volunteers weren't streaming in, as you can imagine. They left those poor girls no choice—they brainwashed them with religious inanities and when that wasn't enough, they threatened to kill their relatives, or to torture them to death. They all chose to delay the inevitable, to not die right away. To try their luck on the day of the mission, hoping right to the very end for help that never came. Volunteers are rare but when they have any, they take them, no questions asked. They couldn't care less about your motivations. What I am trying to say is nobody asks a grenade about to explode, 'Why?' The reason is obvious. Its pin has been pulled. All they do is pull out our pins and throw us at good people. We are unstoppable weapons. Objects of dread, hatred, and revulsion. Nothing more. The emir accepted my offer without debate. When I got home, I put Djami on my lap. She was no longer a baby, but you know, she weighed close to nothing. She nestled her head against me and wrapped her arms around my neck. A few days earlier, I had given her tiny braids and wrapped them into a bun at the top of her head. I could feel her hair tickle my chin. I sat still for a long time, contemplating the smooth fluff that layered the somber velvet of her arms. I inhaled her warm child perfume. Her sweet breath. 'Oh, Ismaël, may God forgive us!' I thought to myself before chasing from my mind the senseless images that threatened my sanity. I sang lullabies to her in a low voice, all the songs that we loved, she and I. I told her that, in this world, there are places where little girls her age can dance, lick ice cream, play hopscotch, argue on the way home from school, and that I prayed to Allah the Merciful to give her another chance. If she didn't get the chance to lead a better life in return for this, then nothing made sense, and God was an impostor. I asked her to forgive me. She had to forgive me because I was too weak to protect all of us and I had to leave her behind. I wasn't rich enough to redeem everyone. I promised her that, on my journey as an angel of misfortune, she would be my last victim. Djami fell asleep in my arms, lulled by my words, not a syllable of which had she understood. I carried her over to her mat."

I took Jenny's hand.

"She doesn't weigh a thing, did I tell you that?"

Her voice was nothing but a murmur. We knew the fate that awaited Djamila in this place. With Jenny dead, nobody would protect her from the worst.

"Then I waited for Ismaël. He returned from his mission covered in dirt. Had he killed people that day? Raped helpless women, little girls like our Djamila? He had a distant look in his eyes. Ismaël could no longer be reached. I explained the situation to him. I had chosen to die because my soul was rotting within me, but my daughter, our daughter had to live. If he was surprised, he didn't show it. He told me, 'I was able to send a message to Max about the operation in Kolofata. I hope the Cameroon army will be waiting to welcome us.' Then

Ismaël added, 'I'll die there too. There is no redemption
for the children of a fallen God. Also, there is no God.'
Was I delighted by Ismaël's initiative? Yes, because finally I could see the outline of a plan to save my daughter. I immediately thought about you. Tina. If you and
the little one survived this horror, I could die in peace. I
know all the love you have for Ismaël but there was no
miracle, sis. Not even when he confessed to me: 'I had
no choice. Ahmadou has his eyes on us. He guessed that
we were protecting her. I had to prove to him that she
was my wife. It was either her or you two... He watched
the whole thing.' His confession drove us irrevocably
apart. We were just too aware of our decay to even look
at or even brush against one another. We were forever
dead to each other. The Ismaël that I had loved would
never have harmed a helpless person. He was no longer
the same man. The pure evil permeating this forest had
gotten the better of his luminous strength. They forced
him to soil his hands and he let them, hoping that his
sacrifice would protect me. We had become irredeemably corrupt. I died the moment I learned what they
had transformed him into. When you cut off a chicken's
head, it keeps running but that doesn't make it any less
dead. Ismaël had given us a way out. He had acted instinctively, I thought, but he had done it. That's all that
matters. Everything is ready. I hope Max has done what
has to be done at his end. He doesn't know about your
escape. Ismaël hasn't been able to reach him again, because measures have been ramped up to keep the mission secret. We'll set out early tomorrow; I'm going to

leave the little one with you for the night. Carry her the way I was. Tie her against your stomach, directly against your skin. Her mouth against your breast. That will keep her quiet. Wear a loose-fitting dress under your burka. They won't notice a thing. If anyone notices something strange, he'll assume you're wearing a bomb and won't want to get anywhere near you. They don't know which girls will be killed or how many."

I gently lulled the restless child in my arms.

Death and fear are polar opposites. Did you know that, Max? If you're afraid, it means you are not dead. Yacouba was counting on my cowardice. That the shame he inflicted on me would crush even the idea of rebellion. He was right, of course, but he hadn't considered the tiny being I held in my arms. Nor that the courage I lacked to save my own life would be replaced by the need to shield her from their savagery. Jenny and Ismaël were sacrificing the last bit of humanity and nobility they had left to save her. They have always been my compass, the yardstick by which I measure my place in this world. Once again, I decided to walk in their footsteps. This child is ours. The prettiest testament that could exist about the group of friends from Bonabéri. What we had failed to do for ourselves, Ismaël, Jenny, and I would do for her. Yacouba, despite being a genius at warfare, knew nothing about the strength of a friendship like the one we had.

"Aminata!" I called out.

"I'm here," she replied.

She answered from right behind me, though I had thought she had taken refuge in her room. I turned to her. I needed her help. Alone I would not be able to keep the child out of Yacouba's sight for the whole night.

"Have you been listening? We are going to do it. Are you with us?" I asked.

"Yes," she said.

They forbid us to hope. They forced us to kneel. We trembled before them, but in a sense, we had nothing to lose.

"Can I carry her?" she asked.

Aminata stretched her arms out to me, already bent over the child. A smile on her lips and her face shining. I put the little girl carefully in her arms.

"Be careful, support her head. Jen, has she had something to eat? Have you thought about…"

I turned around just in time to see the door close. Jenny had slipped out quietly. On the table, she had left milk in a bottle and a note.

Name her Jenny if you want to. That was my name when a future was possible. I was wrong to have tried to change it. I have strayed so far that this mistake seems benign, but it is the only one I can repair so… You decide. Tell Sita Anna…that I was not worth the trouble. That's all. That she should not blame herself. She isn't the one to blame, I am. Tell my mother… Find the words to console my mother. Please. And Max, my brother, tell him… Take my little girl to them and may this marvelous little being atone for all my wrongs in their eyes… Live, my sis. Live to bear witness. Live to forgive.

"Goodbye, Jen, my sis, my dearest twin sister. My beloved forever. Go in peace. Forgiveness will never be necessary between us. Not in this life or in any other."

I didn't try to run after her. We had said all that we had to say to one another.

Aminata and I hatched a plan. If things were as serious as Jenny claimed, then Yacouba would want me in his bed tonight.

He didn't touch Aminata often. In this house, she was treated more like the help than a spouse. We decided that she would watch over the child for the night. When he finished his ablutions, Yacouba often walked the compound to be sure all the exits were closed, that everything was safe for the night. Sometimes, he would open Aminata's door. The few times he had spent with her, he had come by incidentally, and then stayed longer. We prayed that he would not do so that night.

Yacouba came home exhausted and angry.

In his opinion, the entire operation was utter stupidity. A large-scale operation had to be organized with as few people as possible and with meticulous care. Too many people knew about it. It would be difficult, almost impossible, to gather so many burka-wearing women in one location without drawing unwanted attention.

A lot of girls had escaped recently. Not from our camp, but all the same. A handful of girls blowing themselves up in Kolofata was large enough to cause panic. No need for more than that. It was supposed to be a commando operation, not a show. There were countless ways to subjugate women without risking everything. The reward was just not worth it. And those escapes would never happen in his own camp.

Carrying out a large-scale attack in Kolofata was meant to demonstrate the group's invincibility and send a clear message: "Your army can't protect you from us."

The caliph wanted to terrorize citizens. Something Yacouba found stupid and counterproductive. According to him, Boko Haram had to strike one of the major cities in the southern part of Cameroon, Douala or Yaounde, to shake things up, instead of limiting itself to remote areas in the far north. But Yacouba was Nigerian. Back in his country, he had spearheaded the attacks in Abuja and even in Lagos, the economic capital, causing considerable political instability. He did not know Cameroon well enough to be so effective.

He was furious. His infallible instincts warned him that they were heading for the slaughter, but he could not back out.

"We won't be traveling in the same car, but I will watch over you. Don't worry, I'll make sure you get back here."

Yacouba didn't join Aminata in her room. He spent the night with me.

The following morning, I found Aminata as Yacouba prepared for the trip with the other men. My friend beamed. "See how pretty she is, and such a good baby. You would think she understood everything. She didn't make a sound all night long. When she woke up, she looked at me with her big eyes, as if I was an old friend.

This little girl is not your average child." *No,* I thought to myself. *She is no average child. She takes after her mother and her father.*

We proceeded as agreed about the baby. Aminata helped me tie the loincloth that kept the baby hanging to me tightly. We had just finished when Yacouba, in a firm voice, called Aminata to the yard. We immediately understood. They chose the girls at the last minute and strapped an explosive belt to their chest. Before stepping out, she whispered to me, "It's okay. Don't worry, I'm not scared. Save yourself. Save the baby."

I was struck by her voice. Her attitude was different than how I knew her. Ordinarily, Aminata was so scared of Yacouba that she trembled when he was in the room. She never looked up around him, was never the first person to speak to him. Even when he wasn't around, she kept her voice low if she was talking about him, as if he had the power to strike her down from miles away. She told me again, "I am no longer afraid," before leaving the room with a type of pride in her posture. I finished dressing quickly. I was afraid. I was terrified.

The night was barely half-over when Aminata and I were separated and it was time to go.

We were a dozen girls in the back of a pickup truck covered with a tarpaulin to hide us from prying eyes. Several trucks headed out in a convoy before breaking off in different directions through the forest. For the first time in my life I might have felt at peace with myself. Inner peace had crept into me stealthily. The knots of terror were loosening under the soft but powerful pressure of the child's little heart beating against my chest, and the warmth of her skin radiating into me. From time to time, I felt her lips on my breast and I smiled in response to the tickling of her suckling, as smooth as caresses.

My fellow travelers knew nothing about the plan for the day, except maybe that they were destined to die. They all wore defeated looks. We knew that nothing good could come from this. Some cried. Some prayed. Most did both. We were cattle being driven to the slaughterhouse.

I curled up in a tight corner. Tried to keep warm and consoled myself, strengthened by the web of harmony the child had spun around my heart. Not once did I look up at the forest. I promised myself I wouldn't come back here no matter what. One way or another, everything would end today.

The trip lasted several hours. We arrived at dawn and they packed us in a tiny cabin at the entrance to the market.

The first people to arrive were the food vendors who had come to set up shop. The regular customers soon followed, and then bystanders, just strolling. The place quickly filled up.

I wondered where you were, Max. The soldiers, all of that. Where was the rescue team?

I had thought that they would be there when we arrived. That the terrorists would be overpowered by an impressive and courageous operation, like in some action movie, and the girls would be rescued and sent back to their homes. But I wasn't seeing any sign of your presence.

And what if the message hadn't reached you?

What if nobody was coming to free us?

The child moved against me. Nothing major, just a tiny movement. One would have thought she knew, that she understood the situation and had decided to help me in her own quiet and warm way.

By 8 a.m. the market was teeming. Vegetables, fruits, grains, meat, and kitchen utensils on display gleamed in the sun. Sellers beckoned to their regular customers. Young boys carrying buckets filled with pouches of water advertised their products by screaming. Other boys rushed at customers to offer their services as porters. The mooing of animals meant to be sold or slaughtered added to the joyous hum.

Suddenly, a Jeep carrying Ahmadou, Ismaël, and a burka-wearing woman—surely Jenny—arrived, and my pulse raced. Why were they traveling together? What did that mean? I didn't have time to consider all the possibilities. Jenny got out of the car and slowly headed toward the market. Then, all of a sudden, she turned and started running in the opposite direction.

From an unmarked car that I was only now noticing, a woman stepped out and screamed her name. I recognized Auntie Astou. Jenny stopped, undecided, then took a few steps in her mother's direction, then stood still once again.

And that's when I understood.

Jenny was wearing the bomb but somebody else had the detonator. She wanted to get as far away as possible to protect the crowd from the blast and limit the damage. Her mother ran toward her, arms open, screaming her name. Jenny didn't hesitate again. She turned her back to her mother and headed straight away from her in a desperate attempt to put as much distance between herself, her mother, and the crowd jam-packed at the market.

Auntie Astou rushed after her, got tangled in her skirts and tripped, but then got back up. She called out her daughter's name with a voice laced with confusion, her anguish. Then Sita Anna got out of the car and headed out after both women, also screaming. Jenny turned around once again when she heard the familiar voice of her adopted mother, and that's when someone triggered the bomb.

Everything happened so fast.

I watched my sis die. For the first time, I heard the sound of an explosive muffled by a human body. The sound would resonate several times that day and will litter my nightmares till the end of my days.

Soldiers sprang out of nowhere and pounced on the two women, pinning them to the ground. The two women resisted. They wanted to run to Jenny, as if they could still save her, put together the pieces of my shredded beloved.

I heard the sound of fighting in the Jeep that Jenny had arrived in. I turned in time to see Ahmadou, still holding the detonator, and then Ismaël pulled his head backward and slit his throat with the confidence of a career butcher.

The crowd, petrified, screamed, "It's them. There they are!" before rushing the Jeep, determined to lynch the terrorist. Ismaël grabbed a machine gun and shot a salvo into the sky. The crowd stepped back, and then the army fired. They killed him on the spot.

That's when the girls started to blow up…

Max sprang to his feet and hurried outside. They heard him vomit and gasp in the yard. His mother and grandmother came over to help him. Not Tina, who sat motionless, an entranced look on her face. "They didn't suffer, Max. It all happened so fast. They didn't suffer." She spoke as if she hadn't noticed that Max had stepped out.

The boy finally returned to the room after several long minutes. He was still in tears. Astou and Abi were also sobbing helplessly. Anna who had made it her duty to be strong for her relatives throughout her life was overcome by grief. For once, she was downcast, completely stunned. Louis buried his head in his hands, trying to catch his breath. Even the two soldiers who had seen and heard others' testimony seemed shaken by what Tina said. Only the young girl was calm.

Max returned to his seat next to his friend. She took his hand and said once more, "They didn't suffer."

✳

I felt calm as I dashed out toward my relatives. I screamed over the tumult. "Sita Anna, it's me. It's Tina." She was holding Auntie Astou in her arms. The women, grief-stricken, were trying to comfort one another. She heard me, sprang to her feet, and opened her arms as if to block bullets:

"Don't shoot! Don't shoot! She's my daughter," she declared.

"Stand back, madame. She's wearing a bomb!" screamed a soldier, pointing his gun at me.

"It's not a bomb. It's a baby. Sita Anna, this is Jenny's baby," I screamed at the top of my lungs.

Auntie Astou battled to break free from the grip of the soldier holding her back. She added her pleas to Sita Anna's, "Don't shoot. Please don't shoot!"

The soldier kept aiming at me as I ran as fast as I could, my arms over my stomach to protect the child.

Yacouba, my god! He was surely somewhere nearby, with another group. Lord, make sure… I didn't have time to complete my prayer. I heard him shout my name, his voice standing out, and in my fear I froze on the spot. Out of breath and unable to move another inch. All the courage I thought I had deserted me. I crumbled. I don't know what reflex kept me in one place, forced me to crawl. I think lying on the ground is what saved me.

I remember sustained fire. Unable to differentiate between those who fired the first shots and those returning fire. I remember human bombs exploding in the market, the town. I remember dust rising all over, hurting my eyes, ending up in my mouth, my nose. The insane crowd running in every direction. Some stepping on me as they escaped. I dragged myself as best as I could. I protected the little one as best as I could, with my only hope being Sita Anna and Auntie Astou who, still restrained by soldiers, screamed my name and reached their hands out toward me.

And then there was silence. Complete. Surreal. I couldn't hear a thing. I saw people open their mouths and guessed at the cries that came from them. I saw people shot and imagined the sound of hails of bullets. The world was melting noiselessly before my eyes.

To both my regret and relief, I thought that so close to the goal, this was the end. I saw Jenny and Ismaël again with a strange clarity. Not their bodies reduced to shreds barely a moment before, but the way I had always known them. Loving. Intimidated by each other. Radiant. I saw my sis once again dancing as he watched her hungrily.

Sorry, sorry my friends, there was nothing I could do, I regretted.

I was so, so sorry but I was happy. At last, it was over. I wouldn't have to go back to the forest. That man would never touch me again. I would die. I would return to my friends. We would once again become, for eternity, the pack we had been when we were children.

An instinct that came from God knows where made me take refuge under a pile of corpses. There, defeated, I passed out.

ANNA

We looked for the children for months. Without finding a trace. Unable to imagine the truth.

Ismaël's father seemed more frightened than worried, which made me believe he knew more than he was willing to admit. Soon enough, he and his wife moved out to a new neighborhood. We never heard from them again.

Astou didn't get any news. She shrank from worry and regret. She had been so hurt and angry after the incident at school that she had given her daughter the cold shoulder. She had noticed the changes in Jenny but didn't think there was any reason to worry. Worst of all, the changes had made her happy, which is what mortified her the most.

I met Astou and her daughter at the local church over ten years ago.

Tides of migrants settled in an empty field in Bonabéri, living in tiny huts made from makeshift materials and cast-off planks. They had been among these migrants.

They had come there after escaping from God knows which conflict at the border. Our turbulent neighbors, Central African Republic, Chad, and Nigeria, regularly released a horde of hungry fugitives into our country. That's what everyone assumed but they might have simply come from the northern part of the country—overlooked compatriots forced by misery to hit the road.

The women got hired as housekeepers in wealthy households. The men got work as security guards, or went to work on the docks every morning at the Douala port. Quite often though, they weren't able to find a regular income, so they loitered in the city's markets for random opportunities to load and offload trucks, compelled to accept the single meal the drivers gave them as compensation. Or they hung around street corners, waiting to change a tire or help free a car stuck on the impassable road in the rainy season. They mowed lawns, did odd jobs in homes. Neighborhood residents unscrupulously exploited this manpower that was helpless, paying whenever and whatever they chose.

Astou cleaned the church and lived off the charity of the faithful. Every day, she and her little girl attended morning mass. The parishioners ultimately got used to their presence. From the hesitating way she responded to the orders of mass, I understood that she wasn't Christian. Catholic rites cut across language, class, sect, and practice. For the faithful, it's evidence of their membership in the same spiritual tradition. Astou hadn't mastered the relevant codes. She imitated us with a discreet clumsiness that I alone noticed, I think, and which didn't matter to me. Mass began at 6 a.m. Dressed in their clean yet threadbare waxed clothes, Astou and her little girl attended every mass, seated at the back of the chapel. Some days the little girl, exhausted at that early hour, fell asleep in her mother's lap.

Eventually I invited them for breakfast at my place after mass. It became our routine. Abi had long moved out of the house. She was a wife and mother. Louis sometimes came around for a few days or a weekend, but the rest of the time I was alone. Not that solitude was burdensome. I had become used to it. I had my work at various schools in town. I hosted friends, my own or people my daughter recommended I meet. I had close relationships with my neighbors, Ramata and Ma' Moudio, and with the other women in the neighborhood. I helped young people who were struggling in school, mentoring those who were interested in reading; I took part in church activities. Simply put, my life was fine. But I was moved by this woman and her daughter. The young woman who had been helping me with the household chores got pregnant and wanted to move in with her fiancé who lived in another part of town, so I suggested that Astou should replace her.

Except when I hosted guests or Louis was around, there wasn't much to do around the house, but Astou quickly found ways to make herself indispensable. She cleaned, shopped, cooked, washed, and ironed. Slowly but surely, she came to handle all the logistics relating to my various activities. She watched me attentively, trying to anticipate my needs, respond before I even voiced a request. She learned to spice meals to my taste. Figured out Louis's favorite dishes, the way he wanted his clothes folded, the number of sugar cubes he wanted in his coffee. Astou took it upon herself to make him orange juice in the morning. I didn't get the same, except when I formally asked. That made me smile. She was a woman—no need to explain things to her. She understood that even though he was around only every once in a while, Louis thought of himself as the man of the house and loved getting special treatment.

I loved how efficient and reserved she was, and most importantly I grew fond of Jenny.

The little girl had just turned five. The same age as Max, who was finishing nursery school near Paris, but she wasn't in school. I noticed it but did not dare meddle. I guessed it would cause problems and avoided having to handle it. But Jenny did not let me keep distance. She waited until she heard me walking in the corridor and would jump into my arms as soon as she had the chance. In church, she sat right next to me, mimicking my gestures. That little girl reminded me of my own girlhood fascination with the reverend sister in my village, the only difference being that she did not hold back her overwhelming affection. She touched me whenever she could, caressed the fabric of my dress, my hair. Inhaled my perfume. Snuggled until I held her close and hugged her. She'd return my embrace with a strength quite unexpected from her thin arms.

I hadn't had such a tactile, physical relationship with my daughter, Abi. Little Jenny showed me, and no one else, not even her mother, her hunger for tenderness and physical contact. She indulged in a type of physical closeness that unsettled me and it got me thinking. Had she felt in me the poor and hungry girl that I had once been? The one I had pushed to the back of my conscience to become Abi's strong-willed mother? Maybe I had let my guard down now that my daughter was an adult, out of the woods, and Jenny caught glimpses of the former Bouissi in Anna. I don't know. Every time she walked toward me, my arms would, almost by themselves, open wide to welcome her.

On Saturdays, I woke up late. Astou knew that what I wanted was a heavy breakfast before settling down in the library to read and grade the essays of my students. She'd then use this opportunity to make progress on her chores. I would read while eating on the terrace, never really in the mood to chat. Jenny would come out and loiter around me until I put her on my lap where she would make herself at home.

"You can stay, Djenabou, if you keep quiet. You know I don't like being disturbed when I'm reading," I'd tell her.

"Okay, Sita Anna," she'd reply.

Sometimes she would stay like that for hours without making a sound, then would end up falling asleep, head on my chest. But one particular Saturday, she was full of life. She ate a piece of toast, jumped around briefly, and then finally whispered into my ear, "Do you mind calling me Jenny?"

Playing along, I murmured back in reply, "Why? Djenabou is a pretty name."

"Yes, but I prefer Jenny," she said.

I smiled, "Okay, agreed."

"And would you mind buying me a doll, and a pair of jeans, please, Sita Anna. I would really…"

I feigned anger, saying, "Jenny, didn't I tell you to be quiet?"

A mischievous glimmer flashed in her eyes, but she didn't say a word, contenting herself with settling even more comfortably on my lap. So far, I had not bought anything for the little girl, out of some sort of modesty. Her mother worked for me, and I paid her more than a decent salary to raise her daughter as she saw fit. To enable her to give her daughter what she thought was good for her. I was afraid I might make the same mistakes the reverend sister had made with Awaya. The little girl wanted toys and modern clothes, which I understood, but Astou was her mother. I wanted her to know that I respected this bond.

I was trying to keep a safe distance, but Jenny was a stubborn and endearing child.

I clearly remember the book I was reading the day that little girl read hesitatingly, "*The…digits…that…he… mani…manipulated…* What does 'manipulated' mean?" she asked.

We always spoke in whispers. My eyes grew wide with surprise, as if I were witnessing a unique phenomenon.

"You can read?" I asked.

She smiled, proud of herself.

"Well, yes. When you teach the neighborhood kids to read, I listen in. I don't get what's so difficult about it. *D-i di, d-igi, digi...* But what are digits?" she asked.

I knew that I could no longer avoid the topic of her education.

I talked about it with Astou. She was excited. She wanted her little girl to go to school, but the mission had asked her to bring the child's birth certificate and an identity card—official documents she didn't have.

"Why don't you have an identity card? Everybody has one. Did you lose it? We can fix that, let me have your birth certificate. We can have another one issued to you. And even if you no longer have a birth certificate, even if you also lost that, we can just apply for a duplicate in your place of birth, and the same for Jenny. Where did you give birth?" I asked.

I was suggesting obvious solutions, as I couldn't imagine how this woman and her little girl had traveled across the country without official documents to identify them, but I hit a brick wall every time.

Astou spoke above average French compared to the other inhabitants of the camp, and even compared to some of my educated neighbors. She was very careful, learning and adapting at breathtaking speed. From this, I deduced—perhaps incorrectly—that she had attended school. At the very least, that she knew the basics. I was never able to know for sure, though. The fact remained that neither she nor her daughter had any official papers. From a purely legal standpoint, they didn't exist, given that they couldn't be found in any record anywhere. If they had disappeared during their migration, nobody would have known or gone looking for them. I could not even fathom the number of predators hovering over people in such dire situations.

Astou never talked about her daughter's father or the circumstances of the girl's birth. I never learned where they came from. Or how and why they finally ended up in the makeshift depot that was their shelter. I didn't ask any questions.

To give them an identity, we were forced to take the back channels of our corrupt administration. I spoke to my parliamentarian husband, who forwarded the file, along with the money needed for the transaction, to one of his associates.

When biometric identification wasn't yet a reality, births were recorded in a logbook that was later used to draw up permanent civil documents. A loophole that created a juicy trafficking ring. Conscious of the fraudulent gains generated by the situation, councils in regional cities left blank pages in their logbooks for people like Astou. This practice was used extensively by civil servants to postpone their retirement date, or for students past the age limit to sit for official exams, or for athletes to play internationally, all of whom needed a new birth certificate. We had one made for Astou.

I had no control over the accuracy of information that she provided, her real name, her date and place of birth, her parents. She was offered the opportunity to turn a new page thanks to a new identity, maybe even a new life. All I did was stand beside her throughout the process.

Astou and I had a rather strange conversation about Jenny's birth certificate.

"Take my child," she pleaded with me as I filled out the documents with the information she provided.

I didn't understand.

"Sita Anna, you're alone. Your daughter is now all grown up and married. I am giving you mine. Take her. Write on that piece of paper that you are her mother."

I stared at her closely. Maybe for the first time since I'd met her. Was she beautiful? It was hard to say. She was always draped in several layers of clothing that made her look thick. Hard to say beyond her pretty ebony skin tone and the somber but expressive eyes her daughter had inherited. How old could she be? I knew nothing about that either. She had said thirty, but I suspected she was younger than my Abi. What had this woman gone through? What horrors, horrors inevitably, had she experienced to want to entrust her child to a woman she barely knew? She continued:

"Sita Anna, I don't have anything. I don't have anyone. What you see here is all I am. There's nothing more and nothing less. I've watched you for a long time. I have seen how you live. With you, my daughter will be loved, and she will get an education. If you let me live with you, I'll try not to disappoint you and you and I will be there to raise her. But if, one never knows, you no longer want me to keep working in your house, you would still have to continue raising my child. If not, all of what we are doing today would be in vain. Don't make us a promise you won't be able to keep. I want you to make a commitment today to my daughter—to support and guide her until she's able to fend for herself. God alone blesses us. These papers will enable me to protect my child, to keep her beyond the reach of want forever. That is why I'm telling you to write that my Djenabou is yours. Take the child. I am giving her to you."

Awaya had also chosen to let me go because she'd wanted me to become an educated woman. She knew from my birth that if I stayed with her I would be exposed to the dangers that the helpless faced. Rather than risk losing me, she accepted the sacrifice that would come from opening my eyes to a new world. I was aware of the love, selflessness, and hope woven into Astou's request. I was also aware of the powerless rage, sometimes unconscious but inevitable, a mother carries when life forces her to cede her place to another woman, and the lifelong stamp of guilt that such a decision embosses on a mother who steps away like this from her child who has dreamed of a new world. Because I knew, I refused.

"Astou, I promise you, I swear to you before God that I will never abandon your daughter. *Your* daughter, not mine. I love her because she's just like you. Because you raised her properly. Despite the obstacles, you miraculously protected her innocence. She's your child. She will be forever, but I will do my part. I swear to you."

"Sita Anna, life is complicated. Promises can be made and unmade. Take the child," she insisted. "If she is yours, you will love her that way. You will watch over her."

"You know what we'll do?" I finally suggested, "You two will come live with me and we will name her Jenny. I will be her godmother. You will be her mother, the one who carried her in her womb while I, her mother before God, will be the one who guides her through life. The commitment I'm making today to you, I will also make to our Lord God. Are you okay with that?" I asked.

Every time those memories come, my heart breaks. Every time my shortcomings, my arrogance, our inability to shield our children from our own negligence comes up, my heart bleeds.

I should have known the heartbreak my little girl would feel. I should have. I, more than anyone, understood the deadly game she was playing in school, pushing her mother into darkness, rejecting any relationship with Astou in her yearning for the fool's gold that I unwittingly dangled in front of her. Jenny had believed in my embellished truth—had become caught up in it to the point where she lost all sense of self.

My little mirror girl, somewhere along the line, I let go of your hand. You didn't deserve that. I did. My life is an inextricable knot of compromises. I have been battling with it for so long now that I was unable to see the danger to your innocence. What your mother did when you were still just a helpless baby, when the cruelty of life was clear to us, we forgot about it because comfort and privilege veiled your suffering. We thought we had given you everything, opened every door, signaled the road to follow, and we left you all alone to face evil. We didn't hear you cry out for help.

I now know what I should have told her, now that it's too late, now that Jenny is no longer here to hear me. I now realize that the words no longer mean a thing:

Take a deep breath. Take the time you need. No need to rush. Days come and go. If you are strong and courageous, if you give it time, life will show you how to love yourself. How to love it.

＊

Ma' Moudio was dying right before our eyes.

She told me that Tina was her great-granddaughter. She had given birth to Tina's grandmother when she was only a child herself. Her family had forced her to a marry a man who refused to take care of the result of his new wife's past mistakes. The little girl stayed with Ma' Moudio's family, and also got pregnant shortly after she became a teenager. And then she ran off with the first man she came across. She settled in town, on the other side of the bridge, found work as a receptionist, and left her violent partner for a white man who was visiting the company she worked for. He was one of those expatriates with a murky past, determined to hide in the tropics, one of the thousands Africa attracts.

Ma' Moudio was happy to see them settle in the neighborhood but quickly became disillusioned when her attempts to get close to her daughter yielded no fruit. "She had come back here to flaunt her wealth, her white husband, her beautiful house. She wanted to mock us, to have her revenge. She didn't want to reconcile," she revealed. Tina was born, and a few years later her mother passed away. Ma' Moudio accepted, just like we all did, the explanation that she had moved to France. From a distance, she watched her great-granddaughter grow. She pleaded with me to protect her, keep an eye on her, and every day that God allowed, she cooked for her daughter. The latter always sent a housekeeper to collect the food and returned the dishes dirty without even a word to her mother.

Over the course of a couple of months, the husband suffered several heart attacks. His condition was critical. He was transferred to a hospital in the city, then evacuated out of the country. Ma' Moudio forced open her daughter's door and found her in an alcohol-induced delirium. She had a hard time coming back to her senses. My old friend cared for her daughter with devotion, but she was exhausted and troubled by Tina's disappearance. "Will God forgive me? At this stage, there is nothing even God can do for me," she lamented every time we met.

We started losing hope when Max suggested that we should talk to a woman working at the beignétariat. "They know everything that happens in this neighborhood," he said.

My grandson had returned to Paris after staying with me for a year. During his time here, I had given him the freedom and space he needed to pull himself together. I hadn't guessed that they would bond together so strongly. The four teenagers roughly handled by life had interwoven their loneliness. Replaced failing family ties with a lovely friendship. Then Max left, breaking the chain, reopening old wounds that we thought had healed and evil stepped into the gap. My grandson felt terrible about it. We discussed it every day. He called his friends unsuccessfully. Sent messages on Messenger, WhatsApp, on all the apps and platforms where they usually met, but nobody replied. His friends seemed to have vanished into thin air, without him, without telling him what they planned on doing.

The woman from the beignétariat opened my eyes to a whole new reality. To the changes that had taken place around me that I had missed.

I invited her to my house, but she turned me down, laughing, "Oh, Sita Anna, there is no denying that I live in the *elobi*, the slum, but I can still afford to host an elder sister. You come over to my house anytime you feel like and we will talk."

I went there one evening.

"Sita Anna, I couldn't come to your house. I don't know if you understand, but your house is a complicated place. Even the woman you have living with you is not who she claims to be," she told me.

I hadn't come to listen to her spew neighborhood gossip. I shut her down.

"Do you know that our children have disappeared?" I cut in.

She sat quietly for a long moment.

"Everybody knows, sister. But who pointed you in my direction?" she asked.

"Max, my grandson. He says you know everything that happens in the neighborhood," I revealed.

She laughed.

"Oh, that child! I wasn't in school for long. You yourself know that. That big intellectual stuff, I know nothing about that, but I have always lived here. I know everyone in Bonabéri. Even those who don't know me, I know them. If you've come this far, you have to listen to me right to the very end. I understand that you don't want me to talk about the woman who lives in your house. So we won't discuss that, okay?"

She gave me a stern look, but I didn't respond. She exhaled and set out to educate me:

"Sita Anna, Muslims have changed. Have you noticed that the women no longer mingle with us in the neighborhood? There used to be a time when everybody met in the street. They invited us for the feast of the ram and attended our baptisms. Girls and boys played together. Now, they no longer talk to us. They stay locked up in their houses all day long. Here, every woman tries to make some money. Even me, I cook food to make just a little bit of money. It helps me raise my children and send them to school. Lately have you seen any Muslim women running a business? Even a tiny call box? Even a small roadside stand to sell candy or cigarettes? In our poverty, where even children are forced to help out after school, can we do without a woman's salary? Before, they used to wear their pretty embroidered clothes and colorful headscarves. They were so pretty that we imitated them. It became so fashionable that we also started wearing them to major events. On the eve of celebrations, tailors and seamstresses embroidered night and day. Come and see how they dress these days... Huge black gowns from head to toe, headscarves worn right to the edges of their eyes. What is that supposed to mean? Do you think that's a reasonable outfit in Douala where it's always so hot? What was wrong with the dresses? Sita Anna, when a woman stops leaving her house, can no longer earn her meager five francs, puts on clothes that even a corpse wouldn't want to be buried in, how do you interpret that? Me, I think there is reason to be worried. There are other prisons besides New Bell. A woman's prison can also be her husband's or her father's house. I am not saying this applies to everybody, every family—when that poor Ramata was alive, she often came to sit with me and talk, and there's Garga, who lives close to the main road, who works in an office in town. She hasn't changed her clothes. She walks around every morning and drives her car. Her eldest daughter will sit for the baccalaureate exam this year. I have not heard that they will marry her off. I heard instead that she will go to continue her studies overseas. In any case the Ramatas and the Gargas, those are the Muslims we already knew in the neighborhood. We called one another *sista*, my friend. Their children were our children. Where did these other Muslims, the evil ones, come from? What do they want? When their new imam arrived, things only got worse. I don't know what he's preaching, but many more people started avoiding

us. Women cover themselves from head to toe, walk in
groups, and ignore us, the men pray morning and evening. But that alone isn't so serious. This isn't the first time
that we've dealt with religious differences here. When it's
not those from the Pentecostal churches with their white
robes and their bare feet who pray, sing, and scream all
night while disturbing their neighbors, it's those Jehovah's
Witnesses springing up on you every minute because the
day of the Last Judgment is close. Or leaving your house
one morning you stumble upon a dead chicken in a circle
of twigs in the middle of the road and you know that
ngangas had been performing rituals in the night. That is
the life of the neighborhood. It doesn't bother me. Times
are hard for everybody; everybody is hunting for luck the
best way they can. The problem since their imam arrived
is that some of our brothers have cut themselves off. They
are isolating themselves. They are the only good people
and everyone else is ostracized. Overnight, Ahmadou
whom I watched grow up, and who used to come here
with his mother, stopped talking to me. After Ramata's
funeral, I cooked. I went over to support them. I wanted
to tell them that they could come here and eat for free.
Was I going to let the orphans of my friend die of hunger? That little clown had the guts to tell me to go away
with my infidel food... I am not educated but I don't need
to know exactly what infidel means to understand that to
him, I am nothing. Me, a woman his mother's age. And
his father was right there, along with the woman he went
and married in their village after Ramata died. They were
present and didn't say a word, as if Ahmadou was the head

of the family and they were afraid of him. Your daughters went with those men, and then they disappeared. I was told that this isn't the first time this has happened here in Bonabéri. Other young people left last year. I don't know where they take them, Sita Anna. I'm simply telling you that they are not good people."

Only at that moment did I make the connection with Boko Haram. Even when we knew that Jenny and Tina were visiting the mosque before they left, we didn't connect the two, as if we were shielded from the fundamentalists' arrival because we had always lived here.

Bonabéri was a typical working-class neighborhood in Douala. Middle-class families lived next to indigent and poor households. There were many intertribal couples and the lady from the beignétariat was right in pointing out that we had our fair share of religious idiosyncrasies. Just like elsewhere in the country, Pentecostal churches were popping up out of nowhere. It wasn't uncommon for a neighbor you had known for ages to unexpectedly proclaim that he was now a pastor, transforming his parlor into an improvised place of worship. Misery and lack of opportunity made people more religious. People yearned for an accessible god, who gave clear instructions, performed palpable miracles, and provided the quick hope they needed to feel better about their lives. The new pastors understood the economic potential of despair and gullibility.

Although I knew all this, I was taken aback when I heard that Muslim extremists had recruited our children. I was convinced that our diverse beliefs, the harmonious coexistence we had would shield us from the danger they represented. Their claims sounded so absurd to me that I thought my loved ones were impervious, protected from them.

Jenny was Christian. Her mother and I made sure of that, and although I found her skeptical, I didn't see any danger in it. Ismaël and Tina were typical youths, religion didn't feature among their priorities.

How could we have imagined what happened?

We had thought they'd run away. Every neighborhood has young people who take off for adventures to Europe. That was all the media reported, day in and day out. We might just as well have switched on streetlights to illuminate the road leading to the Mediterranean. Even me, just from listening to the news, I learned how to go about it, who to talk to if I had wanted to migrate. Max was expecting a call from Libya, Morocco or, even more likely, Italy, Spain, or Greece. I thought that their aspirations and education would have pushed them more toward the West. We hadn't envisaged the alternative. That other route, just as clearly signposted, which led to jihad.

Upon contacting the *gendarmerie*, we were informed that disappearances were more frequent than we had imagined.

So far, they had mostly occurred in the northern part of the country where dozens of girls were regularly kidnapped and just as many young men joined the sect out of conviction, personal interest, or coercion. Some villages were so badly plagued you couldn't tell who was a sympathizer and who wasn't. Major cities in the South thought they were out of reach, but the sect was widening its sphere of influence. Recruitment was carried out primarily within the ranks of homeless children or children from broken homes, but worrying disappearances had also taken place from more stable families. Young people left for Europe or elsewhere, and nobody knew their whereabouts until they reached out to their family once again. Parents no longer bothered to report the disappearance to the police, convinced that they would not get any help.

Was there no way to stop the bleeding, to protect our children? Nothing was done. No communication. No plan to inform families, to direct them to support groups or provide tools to combat the indoctrination. Any form of indoctrination—be it the longing for Europe and traveling through Maghreb countries with openly racist smugglers and modern slave traders, or the calls for jihad, which nobody cared about because, so far, it had only affected Muslims.

The government of Cameroon didn't care about those who exiled themselves. Prospects were so slim, the limits of opportunity so real, that the discontent and disappointment of this generation of young people easily became insurrectional. They were not just a burden, they were also a danger. If they died on the perilous crossing, only their relatives would be sad. If they survived, like all migrants, they would have only one obsession: work to help their family back home. In any case, those protecting their own wealth by blocking the future were winning.

It's no surprise that Boko Haram's strategy was to

fish from the inexhaustible pool of social rejects.

Although it seems disorganized, our country is mostly a police state. The slightest disturbance of public order or to the regime—which is basically one and the same thing—is repressed. It's a well-lubricated machine. Merciless repression is first, next is the subjugation of opposition figures, and last is ongoing threats to discourage repeat offending. It's a procedure that's so effective that every protest movement is suspected of corruption and nobody trusts the government to solve everyday problems, let alone act to protect our children.

And what is there to be done? In places like this, newcomers are immediately noted because everybody knows everybody. How had that imam been able to operate without raising suspicion? I knew the issue wasn't thought of in this manner. My discussion with the lady from the beignétariat convinced me of this fact. People knew. They knew and talked about it with one another, but some form of despair impeded any collective action. When misfortune hit, everyone found themselves alone with their helplessness.

The forces of law and order accommodated us because Louis was well connected. We were received by some bigwigs with knowledge of the situation, but nobody offered to help us. Our children had run away of their own free will, which made them potential terrorists and not victims. Being minors didn't matter.

We had run out of options, and hopelessness was taking over when Max finally received Ismaël's message:

We are in the Sambisa Forest in Kano State in Nigeria. It is the stronghold of Boko Haram. This is where a strike needs to be carried out. January 7 is market day in the town of Kolofata. A large-scale operation has been planned. Several suicide attacks will be carried out by women in the market and in other locations. Be there.

Not only was this the totality of the message, but the line immediately cut off.

That is when we decided to go to Kolofata.

Max and Abi were to board a plane to join us as soon as possible. Our plan, admittedly rudimentary, entailed getting our children and returning to Douala. Astou wanted to head out as soon as possible, before the January 7 mentioned in the message. Louis informed us that it was unrealistic to go to Kolofata without security and hope to be successful. "Where would you stay? There are no tourists in those parts. No decent hotels. You would immediately stand out. And even if that weren't the case, what would you do once you got there? Where would you start looking? No. That is not the right approach. Anyway, this message is important. We have to share it with the relevant officials."

He efficiently did what was needed and updated us on the results. We would travel to Kolofata under escort and would stay in the town's military base.

I was not surprised that Louis would be joining us on the trip.

When we returned from France, Astou, desperate, had not turned to me for comfort. She had found solace

in him instead. She had thrown herself into his arms, crying, and he had embraced her with…how can I put this…
familiarity? As if her body was no stranger to him. As
if he had already held it against his own during another
sort of private moment. This is what the woman at the
beignétariat had wanted to warn me about. I had evaded
the topic because something deep down in me had already
known for some time now but I had chosen not to find
out more about what my instinct was telling me.

Louis had been coming to my place more frequently
and finally ended up staying there almost permanently.
Geneviève, her children, and the rest of their family lived
in Bonapriso, where all of his family and professional responsibilities were. "Here, I am more at peace," he explained like his father had before him.

My husband had had a long career as a parliamentarian before an ambitious youngster unseated him. Next
was retirement, which pushed him further away from the
spotlight. Louis was bitter, disappointed, more critical
than ever of the system that he had been a part of all his
life. "We weren't saints, Anna, but this generation fears
neither God nor the law. They have studied overseas, in
Europe, the United States, Singapore, and what have you.
They know the rules. In our time, we took kickbacks or
overbilled, but the job got done. But them, they collect
money and don't even bother about the work getting
done. They content themselves with borrowing from
Peter to pay Paul, siphoning billions to stash in offshore
companies all over the world, an endless Ponzi scheme.
They ruin banks without any consideration for the small

savings accounts, and all this for what? For nothing. They accomplish nothing with all this money. They build nothing solid. Invest poorly. Create only unstable jobs and regularly fail to pay their workers.

"Even those who inherited successful companies from their fathers have squandered their inheritances. Show me one single company in this country that has lived past the second generation. Is it still controlled by family members? You wonder whether they use their skills and knowledge for the country? They lack the discipline of their fathers, who were for the most part illiterate. They talk about globalization, diversification. They delight in grandiloquence when in fact all they do is run corrupt schemes. Nothing more, except women, stays in five-star hotels, dozens of luxurious cars in their garages, debauchery, and vulgarity in utter impunity.

"Impunity. That is what is killing this country. Even those who benefit from it are uncomfortable. They are stuffing themselves, aware that their good fortune only hangs by a thread, the goodwill of the prince. They keep pushing the envelope and no one is telling them to stop. They grease everyone's palm along the way, so we let them waste our resources, ruin the country, all the while thanking them for the crumbs they share with us.

"We are all shackled by this system where predation, favoritism, and indiscriminate self-enrichment are the only path to posterity. We are heading for an unprecedented disaster," he said.

I couldn't have agreed more. Louis had lost his parliamentary seat to one of the young sharks he was complaining about. The new politician organized a party at his villa and we were all invited. He and my husband were both from the same village. There was no way he could wriggle out of attending. We had to make the best of a bad situation. I found Louis's house in Bonapriso flashy, but this one was way beyond compare. I was flabbergasted at the parquet floor. "Walnut," the happy owner pointed out to me. Crystal chandeliers. Oriental rugs. Everything in the house beamed our host's desire to splash his wealth. On a table set for thirty people, fine China dinnerware and real silverware dazzled. Flowers were artistically laid out here and there. The entire menu, along with vintage wines, had been ordered from a Parisian caterer and delivered that very day by air. Not to mention his wife's jewelry, brought straight from Place Vendôme, the bespoke suit he wore, or his handmade British shoes.

Louis's little party years earlier paled in comparison to such abundance.

There would be two separate receptions, the couple informed us. This one was for distinguished guests, and the following week they would host five hundred people at a major hotel in town.

"Do you now understand what I'm saying?" Louis said to me as soon as we got into the car. "Where does all this money come from? What has he done in his life to have all this? Nobody is asking him any questions. Nobody wonders about the source of such sudden wealth. On the contrary, his guests are just like him or would do whatever it takes to be in his shoes. They have no shame.

None whatsoever! Corruption at this level is basically irresistible. When you open the doors of a plane in flight, every human being, regardless of their strength or their desire, is sucked out into the emptiness. Here, the same principle applies. I hope that one day, those keeping open the door of this bloody plane in our country will be punished fairly," he ended bitterly.

I knew my Louis quite well. He had numerous flaws but envy and jealousy weren't among them. Now that he was no longer part of the system, he was regaining his customary clearheadedness, but it was too late.

We had known a Cameroon where brave men had died defending a certain idea of freedom. I will always remember Louis's anger and emotion on that day of January 16, 1971, when he joined me in Ombessa to inform me that he was joining the *resistance*. "They shot Ouandié yesterday," he'd said, sobbing. I'd consoled him the best I could. "Who was he? A member of your family?"

I knew nothing about the last leader of the maquisards. A leading figure of the Union of the Peoples of Cameroon party in the fifties, he'd launched a rebellion against the government that was formed when the country became independent, and he had continued the fight underground. He was arrested, accused of plotting to assassinate the sitting president, and shot to death in Bafoussam by joint forces from France and the Cameroonian government. His death would not have meant anything to me had it not been for how downcast Louis had been. Had my daughter not been conceived from that.

We lived through that era. Those men *brave to the point of recklessness*—as was acknowledged by the French commander tasked with hunting them down—had left their mark on us. The new generation could barely remember the ruthless repression of the government of Ahmadou Ahidjo and were happy with the subordination, the venality of the new regime.

In Cameroon, the bureaucracy, the law, every mechanism that protects individuals and enables responsible citizens was corrupt. Distorted. Even our borders were porous. In this accommodating blur, a class of oligarchs, who hoarded all the resources and transferred them to their "customers," thrived while the people were left to gnaw at the crumbs of the riches taken from them. They were the vampires of their era. The same way we were those of our time, all of it being more or less subjective. And, whether owing to the magic of grift or the skill of the prince, the tribalism they preached to us day and night wasn't a problem in that close circle. All the tribes in Cameroon were duly represented there.

Louis was a shark in his own way. He had pounced on the housekeeper simply because she had been within his reach. That's all. I had caught him staring at her, like someone with means choosing an item in a shop. He hadn't yet gone through the checkout, but there was no doubt in his mind that the item was his, as he was plenty rich enough to buy it. Had Astou resisted? I don't think so. He was the master of the house. That was reason enough. "*Bend skin massa like you,*" sang André-Marie

Tala in pidgin English, which basically means "Kneel before your loving master." Somebody in Astou's position had no choice but to comply, right?

I was content to look the other way. The same way I had with all the unpleasant hardships in my life. I holed up in my fortified castle with my books.

The body of a woman is way more demanding than her heart. Have I said this before? It has only one life and never forgets that. It keeps the marks of blows the same way it does the memory of kisses, wounds that we self-inflict and those life deals us. It does not heal. Does not get replaced. Evolves as dictated by its burdens. Only the past and present matter; it is unconcerned with the future. Consequently, it can't accommodate any form of hypocrisy. The body laughs at our gimmicks, unceremoniously dismisses our deadlines, those tiny deals we strike with ourselves. It does not entertain excuses and punishes without appeal the lies that the heart tolerates.

A lump appeared in my breast a few months ago and grew as the days went by. My body did what it wanted.

※

Louis's connections really made our trip to Kolofata quite easy.

I will be the first to admit it. He had the skills and authority needed to handle this type of situation.

We boarded a plane right to Garoua where a squad from the Rapid Intervention Battalion, the BIR, made up of the elite members of Cameroon's armed forces, took us via helicopter to the Maroua airport. Then we made the eighty-kilometer trip from Maroua to Kolofata by car.

I discovered that one of Louis and Geneviève's sons—how many did she have in all: six, eight? I could never remember the exact number—was a member of the BIR. I knew the kid. Within the family, we called him Junior, because he was named Louis just like his father, but I hadn't known that he had enlisted. Another surprise for me was that the commander of the Kolofata base was one of my former students. Both men had insisted on coming to pick us up in Maroua.

Our convoy was made up of two four-wheel-drive trucks with tinted windows and a pickup carrying six soldiers armed with machine guns. We had stepped beyond the safe zone and were now moving through an area where an unconventional war was raging. Violence and death could happen at any moment. If we'd had any doubts, this deployment of so many military resources was enough to prove it.

Louis had handled the administrative part of the trip. I didn't know the exact details but understood that being received like this meant that our authorization had come from high up.

The journey to Kolofata was almost fun. The young commander called me "Madame Tchoualé" and, laughing, told stories about his days back in my class.

"I can clearly remember only one thing from your class: *Les Femmes intelligentes*, by Molière. That book and the fact that you were the most beautiful teacher in the whole school."

"*Les Femmes savantes,*" I corrected him gently. I was grateful to him for lightening the mood.

"Isn't it the same thing, madame? In any case, you made us memorize a passage I will never forget, *Il n'est pas bien honnête, et pour beaucoup de causes / Qu'une femme étudie et sache tant de choses. / Former aux bonnes mœurs l'esprit de ses enfants. / Faire aller son ménage, avoir l'œil sur ses gens / Et régler la dépense avec économie / Doit être son étude et sa philosophie.*" Louis could not help but laugh.

"You remembered what mattered, son. That's good," he said.

"Yes, father, because that one right there, it's the truth," the younger soldier responded.

Five of us were in the car. The commander in the passenger seat, Louis and me flanking Astou in the back seat, and Junior driving. He did not participate in our artificial lightheartedness. I saw how stiff his neck was in concentration. His tense calm impressed me. How old was he? Twenty-one? Twenty-two? Not any older. Just a child! Louis noticed my curiosity. He was also watching his son closely. Was the boy reminding him of his own aborted enlistment with the resistance? "Maybe, after skipping several generations, bravery has finally returned to our country," he said to himself.

That statement would haunt me throughout our stay in that disaster-hit area.

Grown men send youths into battle. That's what happens all over and all the time. Old men create the reasons for conflict, fueling hostilities and pretending to defend their core values—good against evil. But all they are doing is ferociously defending their privilege while coveting the riches of others. They hatch toxic strategies, then send their children to attack the enemy.

To hide their deadly greed, they speak with conviction about courage and patriotism while bunkered in their headquarters, in offices or on television sets while the blood of young people is spilled in combat, their innocence vandalized in the ferocity of battles that would forever pollute their soul.

And this vicious cycle starts all over again with every generation, because no war has ever been won. Hatred feeds the desire for vengeance that is transmitted through genes. The first drop of blood spilled when the world began triggered the bleeding that we stubbornly perpetuate all over the earth.

I would think about this again when, days later, Tina would give her statement to the State Secretariat for Defense, tasked among other things with terrorism. She told her story at length, her eyes set steadily on Max's, speaking only to him as though throughout her captivity she had dreamed of seeing him again one day to tell him about her fall and the death of their friends. An official started off by asking questions but then gave up when he understood that he would learn more from this traumatized little girl by listening, rather than being heavy-handed.

They were all young enough to be our children and even our grandchildren. Not just Max, Tina, and Junior, but all those young soldiers—the commanders and top officials included. Three quarters of the population of this country were young enough to be our children. If such desparate audacity was what we expected from our youth, if this right here was the only choice we gave them, then we were showing them way more than spite.

The BIR had taken the information we had given to them quite seriously.

The Sambisa Forest had been a focus of the army ever since Nigeria, Chad, Niger, and Cameroon had decided to join forces to combat terrorism. The place was huge. Sixty thousand square kilometers spread over at least six States in Nigeria. Its dense vegetation, made up mostly of thorns, made it difficult to penetrate. Terrorists had also planted land mines all over in a murderous mapping scheme. The military hierarchy of the allied countries had been discussing the best way to launch an attack. Ismaël's message, albeit short, provided precise and precious information on the enemy's location.

The commander of the Kolofata base told us all this over dinner when we arrived at the military camp. The operation for the next day had been meticulously prepared. The soldiers hadn't ruled out the idea that this could be an ambush or a trap, but they were prepared for every possible scenario.

"How are you planning to deal with civilians? Have they been told not to come anywhere near the market?" Louis asked.

"No. That's not possible," the commander replied. "You can't know who works for Boko Haram and who doesn't around here. If we share the slightest bit of information, it will be forwarded to them and the operation will fail."

"But the message mentioned several suicide attacks in various places around town. On a market day, all the villagers, traders, and shepherds from all around will be in Kolofata to trade. You can imagine the potential death toll. All these poor people…"

"We are at war," the soldier said coldly.

"At war, true, but who are we fighting? Are we fighting terrorists or our own citizens? What is the population of Kolofata? Five thousand, ten thousand? How many come from neighboring towns on market day? Is there really no other way than to use them as bait?" Louis said.

"We are at war, and that's it!" the man repeated. "A dirty war where the enemy hides behind ordinary people, where we can't move one step confidently because there are land mines, where women and innocent children are used as human bombs. This area has been ignored for far too long now. People have been isolated in their poverty and discomfort, and have kept up archaic ideas and old rivalries that have become social norms. They are illiterate and practice old-fashioned customs. Misery wreaks havoc. The yawning gap between this place and the rest of the country is unfathomable if you haven't experienced it. To Boko Haram, recruiting people is child's play here, because they at least offer a tangible, immediate solution. As shocking as we might find it, their message can be appealing. Dying for God is more thrilling than dying of hunger, humiliation, or because the neighborhood pharmacy has run out of antibiotics. Maybe one day someone will study the level of personal distress where faith can be transformed into a weapon directed against one's own people, but that isn't my job. During our last engagement, the wounded were waiting to be transported to the health center but were blown up—doctors, soldiers, and civilians were killed indiscriminately. Do you know how many young soldiers we have lost here? Oh yes, Mr. Parliamentarian, that's what happens when you fight an enemy who has no regard for human life, their own even less than anybody else's. It is a dirty war as I said, a widow or an orphan are just as dangerous as a soldier armed to the teeth. Didn't you know? What were you told in Douala and in Yaounde? Why did they send me simpering civilians who dare to lecture me on humanity? Where have you seen humanity here? We are fighters, Mr. Parliamentarian, the last line of defense between barbarism and you. Because they will die in Kolofata tomorrow, because my men and even I too may die, the citizens of Douala and Yaounde will be able to sleep like babies and philosophize about civilian casualties and human rights. There, you are an influential man, sir. I can easily imagine the effectiveness and power of your connections, given that you are here in defiance of all military logic. In defiance of basic common sense. My superiors ordered me to receive you and keep you safe. I am a soldier; I don't question orders. But know that here, you have to obey me without question if you want to get home safe."

From every indication, there would be no more jokes. No more first name basis. No more "son." No more "father." We now knew who the boss was. We were not welcome here.

Louis continued in a more conciliatory tone, "Our children are in the hands of those monsters. We have to save them. For that, we need your help, sir."

"We'll do our best," the man said simply.

"I'll come along with you," said Astou in a tone that did not allow any room for debate.

"Me too," I added.

The commander looked at us, confused.

"Where do you think you are going, prom? Didn't you hear any of what I just said? Don't you think my men's hands will already be full just with being on patrol, countering attacks, and trying to save their own skins? They will also have to be saddled with the protection of two women? No, ladies, you won't move an inch. You have done your good deed. You have come this far. You will wait in this camp, safe, for events to end, and then you will go home with the feeling that you have done what you were supposed to do..."

"Listen," I interrupted him, "we clearly get your point, but listen to me one minute. Our children have been holed up in the Sambisa Forest for close to two years now. They have accurate, firsthand information that you will need in your fight. But we are the only people who can recognize them. Do you know what that means? We aren't asking you to deploy a special security detail for us. Simply take us along because we are the only ones who can do the thing that will enable you to win this fight. If you refuse to accept our offer, you will be forfeiting an opportunity that may never come again. That is why it is absolutely necessary that we come along tomorrow.

For you. For our children. For the country that we are all defending in our own unique ways the best we can."

"Anna, the commander is right," Louis stopped me. "It's just too dangerous."

"I know he's right, Louis, but that doesn't affect my decision in any way. I will go to that market tomorrow. I will go get my daughter," I declared.

"But if…" he tried to say.

"I will!" I interrupted him once again.

Our generation has failed woefully, Louis. I'm not looking for excuses, but maybe we don't know how to go about changing it, quite simply. Maybe we don't have the right tools. We were the first somewhat free generation in this country, but we carry the burden of buried centuries of servitude wrapped in silence and in shame. The freedom granted to us was incomplete, laden with hurdles. We were smart enough to understand our limitations, but how could we have the courage for more combat after seeing *The Suns of Independence* drowned in a blood bath? How could we have a renaissance without the pride with which to nurture it?

We had to learn, to internalize in the course of a single lifetime what it took others generations to comprehend, to master a modernity that they took millennia to understand, while also trying to reconcile the contours of our own contradictory, conflicting identities. And we did it. We are here while other countries have disappeared. We are eminently modern. You said it yourself. Imagine if all these intelligent, educated, globalization-friendly Cameroonians used their skills to develop the country instead of sacrificing everything for their selfish desires.

There has been a price to pay! We couldn't rely on a past that humiliated us, so we freed ourselves from it. By taking refuge in only select memories, we severed ties with our roots. We discarded our identity to create space for knowledge that then brutalized us as much as it appealed to us.

We forgot how to start families. How to connect with our own, worship our gods. All that was left was but a hollow shell of superstition, prejudice, and materialism. Corruption was the only prospect. We were the first generation of people to be free in centuries, and now we have failed. But *reality maybe had to be more violent for the dream to triumph*, Soyinka would have said. But I'm not making excuses, simply observations.

We have now come to the end of the road. We are carrying new generations on our weak shoulders. They will learn from our mistakes if, with courage and humility, we finally break our silence so that they don't fall into the same traps we fell into. Maybe our presence in Kolofata should be thought of as the logical end to the lives we have led. Here, we've come within the reach of the consequences for our failures.

I kept all these thoughts to myself, and Louis didn't say a word.

"Daddy, take your medicine," said Astou handing him his tablets.

Of course she called him Daddy, I thought, without

even cracking a smile. *After all, why not? She's younger than our daughter.*

She watched over him. Maybe he loved her. Louis was kind, protective, always concerned about "his women." We could have been less fortunate.

My feelings for my husband had long been ambivalent. I'd never admired him, except maybe on that long-ago day when he came to tell me he was joining the resistance. He didn't impress me with the things he'd done to swell his pride. On the contrary, I held a grudge against him for having so quickly given up on the ideals of his youth, because by doing so, in a certain way, he'd been giving up on me, on what we'd been the day we conceived Abi by the riverside, the happiest day of my life. However, Louis was always ready when disaster struck. He took risks for those he loved. He was aware of his duties and his responsibilities, especially in periods of crisis. In this way he's been honorable.

I learned to accept that he'd left when he moved in with Geneviève. The hurt and the resentment finally gave way to friendship, partly because Louis still offered his protection, friendship, and respect to me. He was a great father to our daughter. Abi had a less turbulent relationship with him. He trusted her, encouraged her to venture out, while at every chance I had I'd stood in her way thinking that I was protecting her. Our daughter grew up beneath the watchful eye of a kindhearted father. I was of the opinion that Louis had answered the silent prayer that I had asked when I'd married him. We were even.

Those qualities that he maybe wasn't even aware of

were what made him precious in my eyes. Although I had no illusions, and was quite clear-minded, my affection for my husband had survived our fighting and our torment.

For him too, the years had taken their toll.

The excesses of his life had started to catch up with him as he aged. Diabetes. High blood pressure. Doctors had advised him to watch his diet and to avoid stress. Despite that, he hadn't hesitated to come along with us. I was happy that he was with us during those challenging moments. As often was the case, his presence comforted and reassured me.

The trip had exhausted him, strained him. He looked tired.

We had come to the end of the road, my old husband and I. Paths spread out before us, meeting again, overlapping, and disappearing, leaving us lost just when we had thought we were right on track with our lives.

The commander, who had long been silent, stepped forward once again:

"Okay, this is what we're going to do. Louis is exhausted and won't be coming, but you ladies will be with me in the car. I'll do my best, but I can't guarantee your safety. You just have to follow my instructions to the letter. You are courageous, there is no denying that, but courage is useless where we are going tomorrow. Staying alive is all that matters."

Blood!

Scarlet splashes spurting from falling bodies, oxidizing when they come in contact with the air and take on the color of purpurin, like puddles choked with dust.

The smell!

The acrid, metallic stench of blood and crushed vegetables rotting on the ground carpeted with intestines, the metallic scent of the rifles, breath, sweat, excrement, fetid emanations of our distress.

The sound!

Men, women, children, anger, madness, horror, cries from another age when the earth was populated by hordes of monkeys, those barely human shrieks, drenched in a magma of raw hopelessness, firearms crackling, sowing desolation, human bombs hurled at the crowd, and the sun hidden by the crimson dust.

Death like a toxic cloud of blood, pestilence, and screams.

If I should forget you, Kolofata, let me be rightfully forgotten, too! May my tongue stick in my mouth if I dare to not remember you.

But I won't forget. For as long as I live, long after if there is still a memory, I will testify.

BIR soldiers flanked Astou and me, dragging us out of the reach of enemy fire. They simultaneously wanted to protect us and prevent us from running toward Tina. Every bullet seemed to be aimed at her. A towering man dressed in a uniform, face covered with a black handkerchief, was emptying his machine gun in the direction of our little girl, downing anyone who ran close to her in the mad rush. I saw her crawling and taking refuge under a heap of corpses. She was covered in blood but not dead, at least I hoped. The man didn't even bother to protect himself. Soldiers finally got him with several bullets. He came crashing down, still clutching his gun, shooting into the void, the sky, targeting God himself.

"Cover me," I heard Junior scream.

Defying the danger, he lurched toward Tina, lifted her into his arms, and brought her back to safety. An army vehicle brought us back to the base at full speed. A second vehicle led the way, loaded with soldiers firing warning shots to clear the road for us.

I would have said that this had lasted a lifetime, but only a few hours after heading out and we were back. Louis was waiting for us on the doorstep. I ran into his arms and we cried for a long time, holding each other, trembling like frightened children.

Tina only regained consciousness late in the afternoon.

After the last suicide attack, which had targeted health personnel, the infirmary had been moved to Mora, about twenty kilometers from Kolofata. Only a doctor and a nurse remained at the base to provide triage for the soldiers.

And the others? Civilians, wounded by the dozen, who took care of them? And the dead? Was it up to each family to look for their loved one in the rubble?

I didn't know. I didn't ask any questions. It was all too much. Too much for my terrified, bereaved, devastated spirit.

They examined Tina who had miraculously come out of that hell unharmed. Astou undressed her and found the baby, naked against her naked body, eyes wide, calm—an unnatural calm. She gathered her into her arms and walked away without a word. I took it upon myself to wash away the blood Tina was covered in.

In her testimony, Tina would give her version of events precisely. In such powerful and accurate words she described the absurd, the insane. I would come to understand the hurt I had caused her. The guilt that I caused in thinking I was protecting her. How could I have been so blind, so selfish? How could I have thought I was saving a lost child just by giving her bread and some attention? Those things that cost nothing and protect my good conscience. There was nothing dirty or depraved in her. Nature had simply made her too beautiful, without giving her a guardian or protection. She had blossomed like a magnificent wildflower, arousing lust, and she ultimately got caught in the dragnet of a group for whom despising others and brutalizing women were nothing but a macho shroud over their deep misery. A man had subjugated and mistreated her, but even he had failed to turn off the glow of my little shining light.

And what about Jenny? Will I one day be able to say the name of my dear Jenny without seeing the horrible image of her body exploding before my eyes again?

Tina woke up with a start, waking me at the same time, as I had fallen asleep next to her.

"Yacouba," she exclaimed with bulging eyes, "Commander Yacouba? Is he dead? Did he die!?" she asked.

I unsuccessfully tried to calm her down. She grew increasingly angry. Her screams drew the attention of the soldiers on duty and the base commander who, since his return from the front, had been updating his commanders in Yaounde.

"What's that?" he asked.

"He was the emir of our camp. Is he dead?" she asked.

"If he's the man who was shooting at you, wearing a huge headscarf over his face, yes. My men shot him," the commander replied.

"I want to see him. I will only believe it when I see his dead body. I want to see him now!" she said, springing to her feet.

I am glad I thought to dress her in a *kaba* I'd brought

in my luggage. She didn't care one bit about what she was wearing and would have gotten up even if she had been naked.

"Going out is completely out of the question, it'll soon be nightfall," the commander replied to her.

"Don't you understand? He can't die. He'll come for me. He will be back. Please, I want to see him. Show me his body," she pleaded.

"Who is he?" the man asked again. "Was he a leader of the group?"

"He was the leader. The emir of our camp. The right-hand man of the caliph. Everybody obeyed him. We were all scared of him. He promised to kill me if I tried to escape. If he's alive, he will find me. He will keep his promise. Please, I need to see his dead body."

I think one of the reasons the commander agreed was to fuel the government's propaganda and his own ambitions. To be able to tell his bosses that one of the leading figures of Boko Haram had been killed in combat that night.

He put us in the care of four soldiers, one of whom was Junior. I insisted on going with Tina and for the second time that day, I found myself at the bloody scene.

Tina got out of the car running, turning over dead bodies. "Aminata…" I heard her murmur, falling to her knees next to the battered body of a young woman. We passed by another corpse, a little girl. "It's Djami? Sita Anna, do you think it's Djami?" she asked.

I didn't know who these people were, but she didn't really expect me to respond. Her voice was frightening.

Ghostly. When she wasn't talking, she made a continual moaning sound. An unending *oooooooh*. An expression of immeasurable grief and terror.

Junior and I ran after her. The other soldiers, weapons in hand, followed us with their eyes combing the area. I did all I could to keep up. Not to fall too far behind, I stepped over rotting bodies, disrupting the clustered, feasting flies. My heart was racing. I was afraid I would pass out. "Not now. Not now. Hang on just a little longer," I said to my contorted, tired body.

Tina finally found the body she was looking for. He lay in the midst of the rubble. His bullet-ridden body was far from human. She took off his scarf, revealing his scarred face. "It's him, Sita Anna, it's him," she murmured, kneeling next to the dead man. Tina picked up a knife. Did she pick it up or had she brought it with her? I couldn't say. Everything was so confusing. I only saw it when she lifted it before stabbing the man's remains.

"In the name of Allah, the Merciful," she screamed. "In the name of a god you never knew. This is for Jenny! This is for Djamila! This is for Fatou! This is for Aminata! This is for your sisters! This is for your mother! This is for all the women that you terrified, raped, killed!" Every name she called out was followed by a stab with the knife. "This is for my hair that you loved! Have it!" She used the bloody blade to cut off a thick lock of her hair and thrust it into his mouth. "Have it!" she screamed again. "Take it with you to hell. I'm alive and you are dead. Me, nobody's daughter. Your object. Your rag. I survived. Not you! You lost and I won! I am Aïcha, the Prophet's favorite. I am Aïcha. The girl who is alive!"

I can't remember what I did then. How I reacted. Did I try to stop her? Was it the soldiers who, overwhelmed by disgust from watching this, forcefully pulled her away from the corpse on which she was venting her anger? I don't really know. I felt like vomiting. It felt—like a promise of deliverance—the call of the abyss, madness, actual madness. The type that pushes you to take off your clothes. To twist and writhe on the ground while clawing your own face with your own nails. The one that breaks your spirit like glass. *Not now*, I told myself, *hold on a little longer...* All I can remember are those words playing over and over in my head.

Sitting next to me in the car taking us back to the military camp, Tina shook like a leaf. I took her hand, and finger by finger, with all the gentleness I was capable of, started to release her grasp on the knife that she was clutching in her fist. I threw the weapon out the open car window and only then did the young girl calm down. She laid her head on my shoulder and, so abruptly and unexpected, she fell so profoundly asleep that Junior was forced to carry her when we reached the base.

"Do you think I should wake her up to have her take a bath?" I whispered to him as I got out of the car.

"No," the young soldier replied confidently. She was in shock. Her body had to rest a little. Everything else could wait. And it seemed as if she hadn't really slept in a long time.

Tina joined us much later in the commander's parlor

where we had gathered, just like the previous evening. It had been decades since then, we were spent.

"You are expected at SED in two days—just enough time to transport you to Yaounde," the commander informed us. "You'll be questioned, the young woman mostly. Later, we will see if there's anything we can do with your testimonies."

Astou held the baby against her body as if that baby was the most precious thing in the world. I had not even dared to ask to carry her.

"What's her name?" I asked Tina, trying to break the tension.

"She wanted us to call her Jenny," she replied.

She was sitting on the sofa next to Astou, gently caressing the little baby's hairless skull.

"Jenny was just like this, you know? When she was little, she didn't have a single strand of hair on her head," Astou said, speaking to nobody in particular.

Then, seamlessly, she asked Tina, "Had you seen her recently? How was she? What was my daughter doing the last time you saw her?"

Tina replied without hesitation, "She was determined."

A long silence followed, eventually broken by Louis's phone ringing. It was Abi. They would catch a plane the next day. We would meet them in Yaounde when we arrived. Her father gave her the name of someone who would come pick them up at the airport, and then walked her through the procedure to follow. Given the gravity of the situation, Max would also be questioned, since he was the one who had given the alert. Louis spoke to her a bit longer and then handed me the phone.

Tina got excited.

"Max is there? Is Max with her? Sita Anna, can I speak to him, please?"

I was having a hard time concentrating on what Abi was telling me. My day had been a long nightmare. I was on my last legs.

"Charlie is dead, oh Mother. They killed Charlie," is what I thought she said.

I didn't understand. Who was this Charlie? Who had killed him? My daughter was weeping, heartbroken, but the words to console her came instinctively.

"*Ashia* my dear, *Agondo Bamè*, my little mother, *Ashia*. Be strong. Be strong for Charlie's family."

"What is she saying?" enquired Louis. "Who died?"

"I don't know," I whispered. "I am not sure I understand. Somebody named Charlie."

"Not Charlie," protested Astou. "Not Charlie. My daughter's name was Jenny. My daughter is the person who died. Her name was Jenny! Jenny? Jenny?"

She ran out of the room without giving me time to react. Abi was shouting at the top of her lungs on the other end of the line.

"Jenny's dead? Jenny? Our little Jenny?" she cried.

I heard Max crying in the background. I hastily handed the phone to Tina and dashed off to find Astou.

Frightened by the screams, the baby started crying. Later, Tina would tell us about the baby's incredible calm when

Jenny had entrusted her with the baby and the comforting sensation of that tiny body against hers on that horrible morning. Back to being an ordinary baby, surrounded by her family, the little one was able to cry at last. To calm her, her grandmother had started to breastfeed her. She made a silent *shh* sign to me, index finger pressed against her lips. I quietly slipped into the bed next to her and pulled the covers over us.

"I once watched a show on TV, a documentary shot in a village in Uganda. It said that all the girls in the village had died from AIDS, leaving their children to their grandmothers. Since there wasn't much food, the grandmothers gave the babies their empty breasts to suck on and do you know what? The breast milk eventually started flowing again. By sucking with all their might, the babies made those old mammary glands start lactating again. Do you think it's true, Sita Anna?" Astou asked.

She spoke with such a low voice that I could barely hear her. I couldn't take it any longer.

"Call me Bouissi," I told her. "My mother used to call me Bouissi."

The weariness of life sets in and takes root when we realize that we are the flesh that feeds a history we've had no hand in writing. Unable as we are to align our lives to the rhythm of the world.

We are at the center of a heartbreaking tragedy, caught in the dark axes of the stars and we have no control over our bleak mornings.

Who would want to annihilate helpless villagers,

faultless, poorest of the poor, the ones chosen by any god worthy of that name, who?

Which perverted, bastardized spirit had conceived the idea that my little, gentle Jenny could by herself be a perfect, unstoppable weapon?

Had secret, monstrous collusions made all this possible?

Who was benefiting from these horrible crimes?

Even in our vice-infested country such an aberration seemed improbable, and yet…

One hundred and forty people died in Kolofata, according to the official figures. After almost one month to the day, there was another attack following the same M.O. in Fotokol, a town farther north, on the border with Chad. Officially, three hundred and fifty people lost their lives in that attack.

In any other country in the world, such a tragedy would have at the very least discredited the current government. In our country, all these people died without leading to anything except brief articles in the press and whining on social media. Government coalitions hastened to strengthen the military that had a hard time differentiating between terrorists and victims. Measures were taken to ban wearing the burka in public. Anti-terrorism laws were hardened, drastically curbing already challenged personal liberties.

Later, when the *Charlie Hebdo* attack happened, I would be dizzy watching the whole world mourn in unison. We mourned both Jenny and the staff of *Charlie*, but why were we so alone in mourning our own people?

In places the West considers to be the center of the world, every death is worth a little more. Every grief is amplified tenfold. The entire universe comes to a standstill and covers itself in ashes as a sign of desolation. I watched, alarmed, this discriminatory attention to misfortune. This unequal commiseration, bereft of solidarity. I pointed this out without the energy to feel acrimonious about it.

Jenny, Ismaël, Ahmadou, Aminata, Fatou, Djamila, and so many others.

I would love to name all of them. All these people. Men, women, children, our people cowardly assassinated. I couldn't accept putting away these deaths and all the others into the bottomless pit of our country that never remembers.

I would love to write their individual stories in indelible ink in the book of our lives because, if we can't compel the world to share our pain, we still have a duty to honor our dead.

Tina said it: All it takes is for one person, just one, to burst into grief for the song of mourning to be taken up by others. That's why we are here. That is our duty as survivors. We are all survivors in this country, to varying degrees. To them, may the Lord, in His slow mercifulness, grant them many years of contrition. This is what's necessary, otherwise where would the salty water in the ocean come from?

And even after, even beyond death, I imagine my pretty Ramata reconciling the enemy brothers, Ismaël and Ahmadou, her sons, in the warmth of her arms.

If the display of grief is a key stage in the mourning process, it isn't the ultimate goal.

We will still have to describe the pain. Revisit our mistakes. Call out our excesses. Understand our anger and our humiliation.

We will have to empty the cup of our defeats right to the dregs and accept its bitterness.

We will have to understand the evil eating away at us to hope to defeat it and finally find peace.

We will have to release our dead, unshackle them from the weight of our anguish, render justice for them so that we can have their support.

Too much blood has been spilled. Pretense is a luxury we can no longer afford.

The grieving process is this brutal confrontation between the unavoidable end and life that has to go on. Only under these conditions does loss strengthen the community rather than impoverish it. It consolidates and safeguards. It gives back the right to celebrate life.

Isn't this the profound meaning of the traditional funeral ceremonies that tribes in our country have practiced since time immemorial?

As a country, for our dead and for our living, we have to return to what matters.

✳

I was drifting off to sleep when Astou continued in a whisper, "Do you agree that we should name her Jenny?" she asked.

"If you think we should, I do too."

She lifted the little girl who had fallen asleep from her chest and put her in my arms.

"I tried to give you a child before and you didn't want her. That child is no longer alive. Here is another one. Take her. Have her. She's yours."

The tiny warm bundle curled up in my arms. I thought of telling her that it was already too late for me. That this time around I would still have to say no. I felt my heart beating in my chest, just below the lump eating away at my life.

I could not bring myself to admit it to Astou, how I was unable to take care of our Jenny that she'd protected as she crossed the world holding her in her arms. She did it better than me, and that is what being a mother means. My god, what had all of that meant? Was I condemned to face this same dilemma over and over?

Astou continued speaking:

"You are kind, Sita Anna. Children love you because you are a good person. You are strong. You know how to protect those you love. I'm not entrusting this one to you the way I tried to with the first. I still want to be her grandmother. I want her to know who I am and where she comes from. Who her mother, my daughter, was. My little Jenny died without knowing her history. She died because she didn't have a past to hang on to. I never told her anything about me or where we came from. I wanted to give her a life completely free of any past suffering and for that I lost her. God is giving us a second chance. We won't make the same mistakes. We won't hide anything from this baby. We'll tell her who we are. Together, we will transform her into a kind, strong person. Do you understand? A child needs a community to grow confidently. Every one of us will have a role to play."

It was as if Astou were applying a soothing balm to my wounds. She was providing answers that I had been unable to see. But in my condition, I wouldn't be of much help.

"I'm going to die, Astou. I don't have much time left," I told her calmly.

"I know," she replied, unmoved.

She finished what she was saying, amid my surprise. "I don't know what's killing you, but for a while now, you have been behaving like someone saying goodbye. When I ask you to take the child, I am not only talking about you. There's Abi and Max. Your relatives who have also become mine. I'm asking you to give us a place on your family tree. This little girl is for Abi. She will watch over her the same way I'll watch over Louis when you're gone. That's family."

A song from the past echoed in my mind:

I have come. I have come, my sister. Do you see how beautiful I am? I waited for you. Did you see me coming? I missed you, twin sister. Did you miss me too? My sister, here I am. Here I am as promised.

The stranger had already come for me before, and I had turned her away. She was showing up at my door once again.

Yes, start with a family. The one we come from. The one that joins us along the way. The dead and the living, start with them if we want to have a better world. That's the lesson from Samgali, Awaya, the reverend sister who saved me from misery, Ismaël, Jenny, Tina, Astou, and all those ancient souls who roam the earth without ever giving up on hope.

EPILOGUE

As she packed her daughter's documents, Ma' Moudio had stumbled across an identity card and a French passport issued to Tina. Her grandfather had, unexpectedly, left her his nationality as inheritance.

Abi offered to host her. "Tina, my home will be your home whenever you're ready, think about it. You're a survivor, and I'm horrified by the suffering wrapped in that simple word. I'm horrified by what you went through; I can't begin to imagine the state you are in mentally, but don't overestimate your strength. You will have to heal after this. I'm not saying that I would be hosting you in a palace. You know that times are hard right now in France, too."

Abi had known the *Charlie Hebdo* journalists very well. They'd been colleagues and met at conferences or other events. She had been devastated by their cowardly assassination. No, she didn't approve of their editorial policy, their ideas, or their positions. The only thing she had in common with them was the profession they had chosen, each for their own reasons, and the opportunity to live in a country that allows, even encourages the peaceful coexistence of contradictory, conflicting ideas.

But maybe she should talk about it in the past: "had allowed, had encouraged"? Abi was no longer sure of anything. The sad coincidence of the timing of their deaths and those of Jenny and Ismaël had broken the pillars on which her universe stood. What she'd once thought unchangeable no longer was. Not anymore. The Republic of France, overwhelmed by fear, was curling in on itself. Extremists were pointing accusing fingers at both the culprits and others. The public was splitting into factions.

The whole world was going mad, but despite everything life had to go on, even if that meant joining the resistance.

"We're not safe anywhere anymore, my dear Tina, but if you need me, if you want to start all over again, I will be here for you."

Tina turned down the offer; she wanted to stay with Ma' Moudio and her grandmother, she explained to Max.

"My family is complicated, but it's the only one I have. Ma' Moudio still has a lot of things to teach me. I need to know who I am, where I came from. I want to hear that story—I have missed it all my life. And they are old, in poor health. Who will take care of them if I leave?" she asked.

"And little Jenny?" Max tried desperately. "She too needs you."

"She isn't mine. You know that. She is Sita Abi's now," she replied.

"And me?" murmured Max. "What's to become of me?"

Without their bodies, there were no funerals for Ismaël and Jenny, only endless tears. Bittersweet memories and stories revisited and mornings where the unutterable loss hit them all over again like a ton of bricks.

Max asked Tina to make a promise, a small one, to which he could hold onto in the days and months that would follow.

Tina gently pressed her lips to his.

"No one before you waited for me. Nobody ever. Anywhere. No one has looked forward to seeing me. Your eyes on me make me burn brighter. Make me feel worthy. You know, I would have died there had it not been for the memory of what we had. Max, my Maxou, wait for me again. Wait for me a little while longer. Let me finish what I have to do, and I will come to you, free at last."

Max buried his face in her neck. Smelled her skin. Swept his hand over her smooth bald head.

I will wait because I have to, since you've asked me to.

Fear in my stomach, I will wait because I no longer believe in the promises of the future.

You have seen it for yourself. The time that goes by doesn't belong to us.

You hardly bat an eyelash, you hardly turn your back, And your family comes crashing down, your friends die.

The ground gives way beneath your feet,

Your life crumbles between your fingers and there's nothing you can do about it.

I will wait even though I never want to leave your sight, to keep you close to me.

I will wait even though I want to watch you sleep and be sure that every minute, every second your heart beats.

I will wait even though I want to keep us sheltered and protect us from the fury of the world.

I will wait because the eyes do not create beauty—beauty simply is! This is how it draws the eyes. You are the beauty and I am the mesmerized, the star-struck gaze. I will wait but I want to tell you,

That we will never be as free, as strong as in this fragile and distinct moment,

That what isn't right now might be lost forever because madness is on the lookout. Death prowls.

It is now, here, that we must love one another.

But I will wait because I have to, since you've asked me to.